The G[...]
Emily Wasnburn

Barry Dean

THE GARDEN OF EMILY WASHBURN

2nd Edition

This is a work of fiction. All the characters and events portrayed in this book are fictional, and any resemblance to real people or incidents is purely coincidental.

Copyright © 2017 by Barry Dean

Hague Publishing
PO Box 451
Bassendean Western Australia 6934
Email: contact@haguepublishing.com
Web: www.haguepublishing.com

ISBN 978-0-6480503-0-8

Cover Art by Justine Hamer

Typeset Garamond 12/14

Dedication

For Nick

Acknowledgement

To Morgana and Theresa —
whose encouragement is inestimable.

Preface

EMILY Washburn is one of those large and imposing women who cast a shadow over their surroundings and engulf the light like an old fig tree in a garden; the type of woman that no one wants to know but everyone wants around to organise things for them. To the unknowing she appears to be no more than an overweight frump, but she is much more than that.

Emily is a gardener and every year, at the same time, she purveys her collection of flowers to an admiring smattering of men. She doesn't sell to the glittering peacocks with reconstructed wives or the men with the jawlines of fate, but to those insipid souls who flounder for affability and want nothing more than to be seen in the presence of beauty.

Her collection does not consist of ordinary beauty, the kind that may turn heads for an instant, but embodies ethereal beauty that transcends the imagination and lasts for an aeon. Men would queue for days if they were allowed, but it is not possible for a man to choose to buy from the collection. It is far less egalitarian than anything that one can imagine.

To be eligible to purchase, one needs to be a member of the conscripted few who have been afforded the honour of being nominated for glory. To those, a gold embossed invitation is hand delivered to their place of residence two months before the event. This invitation is their opportunity to drink at the well of the exalted.

Many readers may not have heard of Emily Washburn. This is not surprising, as she, arguably, only exists in legend. For those who believe in the legend, it is said that she shuns publicity and only surfaces when it is time, once again, for the annual three-ring extravaganza of photo calls, publicity stunts, and otherwise serious promotion of film known as *le Festival international du film de Cannes* or, to English speakers, the Cannes Film Festival.

At all other times, it is impossible to find any knowledge of the whereabouts of Emily from any reasonably reliable, or even unreliable, source. There are those who whisper that she lives in a castle above a small village in Italy. Others expound that she resides in southeast England and still more say that she lives in a tiny village in southern Belgium. None can provide any detailed information and, when questioned, they all admit that their knowledge is speculation, at best. What they do know, however, is that for the two weeks leading up to the festival, Emily resides at a very exclusive hotel which overlooks Cannes' Boulevard de la Croisette and has its own private swimming pool. Not that Emily would ever use the pool, but it is widely rumoured that she likes to engage in naval gazing with the pool as a backdrop. You see, whilst she can cater for the number of positive replies to her invitations, her product is delivered on a first in best-dressed basis. The upshot of this is that sometimes she is required to make a decision concerning delivery and, at those times, indulges herself by looking at the faces of the applicants with the serenity of the pool as a backdrop. This is a necessity that is driven by the unfortunate fact that all of the applicants have faces that are at best unattractive and most have the personality of a dead mullet. If they were lacking these fine attributes, they would not be in need of her services.

You have seen the men of whom I speak. They appear at every self-congratulatory media event from every corner of the globe. The Oscars, Baftas, Emmys and Logies all have examples. You look at your television screens and see them on the red carpet. They are not the actors or directors or producers who share the limelight with a beautiful woman at their elbow. These men are the *other categories* who look lost in the glare of floodlights. You see the beautiful woman on their arm and wonder "how the hell …"

You may be wondering why I am telling you about a woman in whom you have no interest, and a festival that allows the French to overindulge their sense of worth, but the reason for this little story is to tell you of events, which plagued the life of this poor writer, following the strange demise of one Peter Mortimer.

Again, you might say that you do not know anyone named Peter Mortimer. This may be true, but the man in question is generally recognised as having the shortest lifespan, after receiving the award, of any recipient of a Cannes Film Festival leaf. After receiving his award, Mortimer lived for only one hour and fifteen minutes and it is for this reason, and the fact that his death thwarted his one and only shot at savouring fame, that I bring you this tale.

Prologue
The Unpublished Book Club

PETER Mortimer stood in the centre of the room looking at the moth eaten lounge and praying that seeing it move had been an aberration. Leaning forward, with arm extended, he shoved an empty pizza box sideways and stared at the accumulated spillage from lost weekends. He thought of microbes lurking within the never washed lounge covers and decided that the floor would be a much safer bet. He dropped to the floor, tucked his legs in and rested his chin on his knees before returning his attention to the face on the television screen that had mesmerised him since he walked into the room. The face looked as if someone had taken pale and mixed it with chalk until there was nothing left but bright red lips on a whitewashed background. He watched as the mouth movement reminded him of the pursed lips of gawping fish in his mother's fishpond. It seemed that the woman on screen was saying something but all he could hear was the sound of coffee beans being tortured in an adjacent room.

His moved his eyes from the screen as his friend Billy Squires entered the room carrying a wooden tray with two porcelain cups and a jar holding four coolies.

'Not listening, huh?' Billy said.

'Is this it?' Mortimer asked, pointing at the screen.

Squires leaned between two lounge cushions and extracted a remote control unit. He flicked crumbs from it as he aimed at the screen. 'Yeah, this is the show I was telling you about. That's Vera on screen now. She's Chicka's girlfriend.'

'Chicka?'

'You know him. The bloke from the pizza shop down the corner.' Squires pointed at the pizza box and read the logo '*Chicka's Rolls and Pizzas*.' Mortimer was sure that the box moved of its own accord.

Squires pressed the remote again, turning up the volume. 'It's about to start.'

'*And welcome to this month's edition of the Unpublished Book Club.*' The words emanated from the speakers with modulated tones that Mortimer placed somewhere between nasal congestion and a full-bodied head cold. '*And now our host…Vera Michelidis.*'

The canned applause of an audience of thousands made Mortimer laugh.

Vera smiled at her sole camera. 'Our first panellist today is Josephine Harridan. Josephine, as you are all aware, is the granddaughter of the famous author Vernon Harridan, who had two essays published between 1940 and 1970. Josephine works on the cosmetics counter at David Jones in the city but has taken the afternoon off to be with us again.'

Vera waited for more canned applause as the camera turned its lens toward a pasty looking woman with short cropped red hair and a spider's web tattooed on her right shoulder.

Josephine smiled and acknowledged the applause as the camera zoomed in on her left breast.

Vera continued, 'Our second guest is Bryce Forsyth. Bryce is a regular guest on the show and is the C.E.O. of Ponsie Publishing.'

The camera turned to Forsyth, whose coiffured silver hair reflected the light from the single umbrella floodlight that was slung from the light socket in the middle of the room. His roll necked jumper and suede jacket gave him the appearance of an eighties art critic. He acknowledged the applause.

'What is this crap?' Mortimer asked, as he wiped coffee froth from the side of his mouth.

'Just wait and see.' Squires lit two coolies and passed one to Mortimer, who sucked languorously on his smoke before relaxing and leaning against the lounge.

Vera waited for the applause to die and smiled at the camera. 'Our third guest couldn't make it today, so Joe Biggins from next door has agreed to stand in.'

A man wearing sunglasses bumped the table beside Forsyth and staggered before he sat down. Mortimer was about to comment on his clumsiness when he saw a guide dog enter from screen right and sit at the man's side. The man patted the dog's head.

'What's this all about, Billy?'

'Community television. This is the tenth episode of the show. Chicka told me that Vera only expected it to last for one.'

'Where are they?'

'At Vera's mother's place. She's got a Resitec unit in Balmain. The show's filmed in the lounge room.'

'Looks like it,' Mortimer said, as he studied the décor. He hadn't seen three flying ducks on flock wallpaper for years.

A balding man of around forty-five walked into shot and sat on a chair opposite Forsyth and Harridan. An elderly woman, resplendent in an auburn rinse and a blue floral dress, entered the scene and sat beside him. She straightened the man's collar as he wiped his spectacles lenses with a handkerchief. Obviously no one had bothered to tell them that they were on air.

Vera waited until the man perched the glasses on the end of a bulbous nose and pushed them into position with his forefinger before refocusing on the camera. 'Our author today is John J Johnson and he is presenting his first unpublished novel. Beside him is his harshest critic, his mother Joan.

Canned applause.

Vera continued, 'John wants to publish his novel, *My Life in Bexley*. It is an account of his life in the one suburb from birth until the present. The story tells of the exciting challenges that he encountered when being bullied by the girls at primary school and his memorable high school excursion to Jenolan Caves where the bus broke down twice.' Vera scanned her notes, 'John has never married and lives at home with his mother and father, John J Johnson Snr… Josephine, you have read the manuscript, tell us what you think.'

Josephine shuffled papers on the table, looked directly at the camera, discreetly coughed twice then returned her gaze to the lens. The camera operator went to a close up of her right breast before backing off and refocusing on her tattoo. 'Vera, I know that I have had the manuscript for a month but I'm afraid that I've only had time to read the first paragraph of the synopsis. From this first reading, however, I have concluded that if the synopsis reflects the rest of the novel, the manuscript may not be fully developed. Unfortunately, what I have read doesn't seem to have been spell checked. There are typing errors throughout the paragraph.'

Vera turned to Johnson. 'Did you check the work?'

Mortimer could sense the man's embarrassment as he watched him squirm into his seat. Johnson's face suffused a pinkish hue as if he had just realised that he was on a shark's menu. Mortimer sucked the cocaine from his coolie and drained the last of his coffee as he felt something crawling across his back. He slapped at it over his shoulder. Whatever it was died on impact.

'Another?' Squires pointed to the coolie jar.

Mortimer nodded as he waited for Johnson to answer Vera's question.

Johnson thrust his chest forward. 'I did check the spelling. It is correct.'

'No it isn't dear,' Mrs Johnson chimed in. 'I told you not use *add to dictionary*. I told you to use *change*.'

Johnson sighed and glared at his mother. 'Mum, I told you that I was happy with the story. If I hit *change* the computer would have changed what I wrote. I didn't want it to do that.'

'*Change* is how we correct spelling errors John. It doesn't rewrite the story,' Vera interjected.

'Ohhh!' Johnson's face flushed red.

Vera turned to Bryce Forsyth. 'What did you think Bryce?'

Mortimer could hear something happening off camera. Crashing crockery, childish wailing, a slap. '*I told you to behave while mummy's on television Sean. Look what you've done now you little bastard. You broke my best tray.*'

The television screen went blank.

Mortimer stood and reached over his shoulder. He removed a black mass with a red spot in its centre from inside his shirt. He counted the legs. He shuddered as he flung remnant spider across the room.

The screen returned to show Vera looking into the camera lens.

'You were saying, Bryce,' Vera said, as if nothing had happened.

Forsyth removed a sheaf of papers from a briefcase. As he spoke his top lip curled in a theatrical snarl. 'I think that Josephine is wrong, as usual. I have sent the manuscript to one of my best readers and we at Ponsie Publishing believe that the work has great merit. After all, this is Mr Johnson's first novel and it is incumbent on us to treat the novel with the respect due to a wannabe writer. With this novel under his belt, Mr Johnson can be assumed to have mastered his craft, and in our eyes, this novel stands out as his best work produced to date. I strongly believe that it will find its rightful place in the pantheon of unpublished novels and will become a leader in that market. We are impressed by the work. So much so, in fact, that we are prepared to offer Mr Johnson a self-publishing contract.' Forsyth paused for effect. Canned applause sprang forth. He nodded his head to acknowledge the faux audience. 'I have the contract here and Mr Johnson can sign as soon as the show concludes.' He waved papers at the camera and slipped a copy of the paperwork across the table to Johnson. Johnson smiled and scanned the pages. He showed part of a page to his mother.

'Come in sucker,' Squires said, as he re-entered the room.

Mortimer grabbed at another coolie and lit it from the butt end of the one he was smoking. The cocaine-laced cigarettes were taking the edge off the day. 'How so?'

'Vera showed me a typical contract. The amount at the bottom is how much the sucker has to pay to the publisher for the galleys. At first glance he will think that he's about to receive the money as an advance.'

'Surely that's taking advantage of the poor bloke's aspirations?'

'No, not at all. It's a legitimate contract.'

Mortimer noticed traces of powder around Squires' nostrils. 'You're cheating, you bastard. You've been snorting blow without me.'

'No…just a bit of left over from last night. Not enough for two.' Squires rubbed his right index finger across his nostrils then sucked on its side. He slumped onto his lounge and turned up the volume as Vera cleared her throat on screen.

'And now you Joe.' Vera looked at Joe Biggins.

'I wasn't supposed to be on today, Vera.'

Vera smiled at the camera as if taking the audience into her confidence and asking for tolerance. 'But mum said she gave you a copy when she asked you to stand in.'

'Oh…are we doing *that* book? I understand now. Yes, yes, yes. It is an excellent work. It's one of the best books that I have ever read. It's my favourite Tolstoy.'

Vera smiled, as if apologising to mall shoppers for a screaming child. 'Not War and Peace, the book that she gave you this morning.'

Biggins nodded. His guide dog emulated the action. 'I couldn't read that one. It wasn't in Braille. I've tried to tell your mother before that I wear sunglasses and have a guide dog because I'm blind. She thinks I'm trying to look cool and love pets. You need to remind her to give me a Braille copy, so I can read it.'

Vera looked at her watch then smiled at the camera. The camera operator zoomed in on her lips.

'Time to vote, people in television land. What should John do? Sign the contract with Ponsie Publishing or wake up to himself and leave home. The answer is in your hands.'

Telephone numbers flashed onto the screen as Vera talked in the background with her panellists.

Mortimer sat down on the lounge, atop the open pizza box. 'What next?'

'They grill the poor guy a bit more then ask for more votes on what he should do.'

'What's the point of it? Why did you get me over here to watch it? It looks to me to be purely exploitative entertainment…if you can call it that. I don't see how anyone can put themselves into the hands of such a gormless panel. I feel really sorry for Johnson.'

'Doco my friend. Doco. I talked to Chicka and he talked to Vera and she talked to her boss. They'll let us do a documentary on the show. It'll be great.'

Mortimer closed his eyes and watched his brain work. Its machinations made him smile. 'A documentary on a piss poor show on community television?'

'No…a documentary on the next big thing. Believe it or not, the show's going gangbusters. They pull in fifty grand every time it's on. The viewing audience is estimated at around a hundred thousand. All the aged care centres and hospitals get it live and it's a hit with the unemployed couch potatoes. Everyone wants to give the poor author advice on what to do and no one's ever reads any of the books. It's a winner.'

***

Mortimer went on to make his documentary and, to his surprise and the wonderment of all who knew him, his short epic was nominated for an award at *le Festival international du film de Cannes*. In fact, not only was the film nominated but it was awarded the gold leaf in its category.

Wet Baguettes

MELANCHOLY sat over the school like low hanging cloud. It was one of those days that starts off well enough but deteriorates as the minute hand on the school clock creaks from cog to cog on its ancient wheel. It should have been raining but it was early spring and the sun generated that aft winter warmth that invigorates the senses and makes one feel alive, despite some remnant chill. It was not the type of day that should bring tragedy and loss. I remember it well.

I was standing in the foyer of the school's Administration building staring at a buff envelope that had been delivered to my pigeonhole and attempting to predict its contents. There was time when I looked forward to receiving my list of upcoming work assignments, but that was before the enlightened owners of the European based assortment of boarding schools that I work for decided that the taking of sickies by their teaching staff should be more predictable and decreed that one cannot be sick without notice.

That single edict turned my world from one of exotic travel across the length and breadth of Europe to a monotonous pattern of knowing exactly where I would be at any given time. Where once I sensed the beauty of the unknown and unpredictable I now tend to notice the stucco peeling from the walls of the ancient buildings, when I stare at them from the same window as the year before. But that is the way of life of an itinerate part time teacher with an international boarding school corporation. Some say I'm lucky to have a job at all. Maybe they are right.

I closed my eyes and read the letter's contents across the rear of my eyeballs.

From June end: Florence to replace Signor Luigi Vespucci, who suffers from a heart condition that will flare up on 1st June and render him incapable of carrying out his duties as language master at L'institut Arnaque Firenze until 16th June.

I ripped the seal from the envelope and opened my eyes to read the contents. Clairvoyant at least.

I was reading the part that advised that they would, as usual, be prepared to pay me a small sum to live in my own apartment in the Val d'Arno when I noticed Pierre Lacoste, school caretaker and wearer of green monogrammed tee shirts, calling from the window of the school minibus. 'Did you hear what just happened?'

Unless it was the grinding of teeth at the thought of another hot month in Florence, the answer was in the negative. 'What?'

'Monsieur Knight, Taro's father … there's been an incident at the river.'

An image of a fourteen-year-old snivelling weasel entered my mind's eye. I shuddered. It had no right being there. I had been trying to rid myself of any image of the brat ever since he scalped tickets to the free screening of his father's latest film in the school gymnasium. Not that he was selling tickets to the screening per se. It was more the fact that the buyers received a free photo of his scantily clad stepmother with each purchase.

'Where?' I called to Lacoste, as he pulled the bus into a parking bay.

'The punt crossing at Duclair,' he said, jumping from the driver's seat and sliding back the side door to allow access to the trays of meat, fruit and vegetables that he would flog to the staff to supplement his meagre income.

'What happened?'

'I assume it's still happening. I saw Knight open the driver's side door of his car into the path of some old geezer on a bike. Granddad hit the car door, flew over the handlebars and hit the ground like a poleaxed boxer.'

'Was he hurt?'

'I saw him getting up in my rear view mirror. Looked fairly pissed off.'

'You think they might have got into it?'

Lacoste shrugged, handed me a tray of mandarins, and then stacked another two on top. 'Give me a hand will you. Just across to the staff room. I need to get everything sorted before the lunch break.'

'What's my cut?'

Lacoste thought for a moment. 'My cousin in Hondaribbia may not be feeling well in June.'

I imagined a breeze billowing sails in northern Spain. 'I'm booked for Florence.'

Lacoste shrugged again. 'Bunch of grapes?'

'Done.'

I was making the final crossing from the bus to the staff room when I noticed a local gendarme and an obviously distraught woman heading for the Principal's office. I recognised the woman as Jeanette Culver, an Englishwoman who was the personal assistant to the British film director Sir Lucian Knight. I had known her for some time as she often visited the school to play nanny to Taro Knight.

I headed for the office to find out what was going on and I found our revered Principal standing stiff legged with knotted fists pushed into the laminate of his desktop, berating the gendarme.

'What's happening?' I asked

The Principal glared at the gendarme. 'Sir Lucian Knight has drowned in The Seine. This is a fucking disaster.'

'I can imagine,' I said, struggling for something to say.

'A fucking disaster,' the Principal repeated. 'He hasn't paid for Taro's next semester yet. And this clot of a policeman has brought a burbling woman onto school premises. If I could speak French I'd give this oaf a piece of my mind.'

'Un petit morceau,' the gendarme said.

The Principal glared at the gendarme. 'What did he just say?'

'He said that he would be pleased to have a small piece of your mind...but he is concerned that his intelligence may lessen.'

'He said all that?'

'Rough translation.'

'He's right though. He would gain more intelligence if he took English lessons.'

The gendarme smiled. The principal's brow furrowed.

'He agrees,' I said. 'I'll see him out, if you like.'

'What happened to Knight?' I asked the gendarme, once we had reached his car.

'The matter is under investigation. Too early to tell.'

'Rough translation.'

'I'm afraid I don't know. I was called to escort Mademoiselle Culver to the school and explain to your head that Monsieur Knight had died. That's all I know.'

I found Jeanette Culver and young Taro in one of the small anterooms just along from the Principal's office. She seemed to be trying to explain the horrific news to her charge, by telling him that his father would not be available to buy him the latest iPad on the day of its international release. Obviously she knew the boy well enough to have discerned his priorities. He began to join her in sobbing but I was sure that the cause of the distress differed. However, seeing them shedding tears piqued my interest. I remembered that I had the afternoon as a student free period and decided to take advantage of the fine weather and drive the few kilometres into Duclair to perform the role of sticky beak.

***

I arrived to find chaos. There were cars on both sides of the riverside road, parked like shirts in a specials bin. Shopkeepers had set up stalls on the pavement and the patisserie and ice cream vendors displayed inflated prices. There was even a riot police van. I noticed that the car ferry was moored on the southern riverbank and, on the northern side, old men in berets stared blankly into the water.

I parked with the other shirts, locked the car and made my way along Avenue President du Coty to the ferry crossing. As I approached, I saw the reason for the traffic jam. The police had closed off the entry road to the ferry. This meant that both ferry and through traffic had to use a very narrow road section. It didn't explain the presence of the riot police, but then I saw their van was in line to catch the ferry. I made my way to where the police had cordoned off a small area and joined the other men staring at the water and listening. It soon became evident that this was the spot at which the incident had occurred.

A young gendarme was taking measurements with a laser device and transcribing into an electronic notebook. I leaned across the cordoning tape and asked him what had happened.

His initial reaction was a Gallic shrug, accompanied by the sneer of his best *fuck off* expression. I explained to him that I was a teacher of the son of the dead man. He told me that I could have explained with half the words and returned to his measuring. I told him that the boy might have to survive without a new iPad and he seemed to understand that I might have an interest in what happened, on counselling grounds alone.

He took time to explain that the initial investigations indicated that there had been a minor altercation between a French bicyclist named Jean Claude Ronin and Knight. During the altercation, Monsieur Ronin dismounted his bicycle and hit Knight across the side of the head with his luncheon baguette. Knight had toppled backwards into the river and was swept downstream, to the cheers of the old men who fished from the landing. While the men stood around, a young woman was seen to dive into the river in order to assist Knight. She was able to drag him to the riverbank but unable to revive him.

I asked if Ronin had been charged with anything and was told that he would be charged with either wasting food or common assault, pending the result of the autopsy on

Knight and the official report. It sounded more like a vaudeville sketch than a real incident. Maybe it was just too French for me to understand

I noticed that there was a black Mercedes S400 within the cordoned off area. The gendarme told me that it was Knight's car. I asked what was happening with the car and offered to drive it to the school for Ms Culver. He said that he didn't really care what happened to the car, but it would have to be moved soon, to allow traffic flow for the mid-afternoon peak. I thought for a moment and realised that I, too, had no interest in the Knight car, so returned to mine and drove back to the school.

***

During the journey I envisioned of a man being hit with a baguette and then toppling backwards. It seemed impossible, even with a *flute*. A full blow to the side of the head with a flute might render the opportunity for a bad pun but it would be unlikely to make you topple anywhere. There had to be more to it.

On returning to the school, I decided to have a chat with Jeanette Culver. I found her still in the anteroom, weeping noisily and smudging her makeup with tissues but, other than that, she seemed to have her emotions under control. I sat opposite and asked if she needed anything. A cup of tea, perhaps?

She thanked me and nodded.

'Is Taro coping?' I asked as I returned with tea and biscuits from the secretarial stash.

'Yes, I think so. The Head told him that he had to be a man and stop crying. He told Taro that when he was at school, during World War II, boys were told every day that their fathers were dead. They took it like men and got on with life. He said that he expected Taro to do the same and sent him back to class.'

Very sympathetic; especially from a man who wasn't born until the nineteen seventies. 'I've been down to the river. I noticed your car is still there. Could I give you a lift to pick it up?'

Jeanette nodded as she blew her nose with a small handkerchief.

***

During the short drive, she consumed a box of my tissues but managed to relate the events as she saw them unfold. She explained how she and Knight had arrived at the dock and pulled off into the lay-by to wait for the ferry to cross from the other side. Knight wanted to stretch his legs and opened the driver's side door. As he did so, the car door came in contact with the front wheel of a bicycle that was passing. The rider tumbled over the wheel and landed on the road with the grace of a dead bird.

When the man regained his feet he began to yell at Knight in a foreign language that she couldn't understand, and shook his fist in Knight's face. Knight said something back to the man, which she understood but wasn't prepared to repeat, and a scuffle broke out when the man removed his beret and hit Knight across the shoulder with it. Knight laughed at the man and called him a *stupid frog*, or something like that. Then the man leaned over and picked up a baguette from the handlebar basket of his shattered bike. He swung the baguette at Knight and hit him. Knight staggered backwards, tripped over a low wall and fell into the river.

No way, I thought. 'I'm sorry to ask but did Sir Lucian stagger or was he driven backwards by the force of the blow?'

'I really don't know. All I remember is that when he was hit, Lucian was standing with his hands on his hips telling the man that Waterloo wasn't a French victory and neither would there be one at Duclair.'

'He was off balance then?'

'I couldn't tell. I was in the car and could only see him from his knees to his elbows.'

'You didn't see the impact of the baguette then?'

'No. I just saw the man swing it.'

'What happened next?'

'The man threw the bread roll into the water and yelled at Lucian that he hoped he drowned.'

I was puzzled. Moments before, Jeanette had said that the man spoke in a foreign language. 'Did he say that in English?' I asked.

'No. In his own language, but I'm sure that's what he said. I could tell by the look in his eyes.'

After dropping Jeanette at her car, I returned to the school to find that Taro Knight had been sent to his dormitory for upsetting the tenor of his afternoon class by listening to the teacher. I was a little surprised that he could be so stupid but I accepted the teacher's decision and looked in on Taro in his dorm room. He was sitting on his bed shaving his head. I decided not to disturb him.

I felt that I had to do something. There was a question without an answer; a physics conundrum that defied logic. After some thought, an idea made its way to the head of the line. I went to the school canteen and ordered three flute baguettes. They were fresh and their aroma sent a note of solicitation to my stomach. I walked them to my small apartment, placed two on the table and took the other on a visit to my old landlord and neighbour, Gerard Duplus. I chose Gerard because he is a crotchety old bastard of seventy and built like an anorexic pigeon. He has a bad heart and holds himself upright with the aid of a walking stick. I figured that if he could survive the impact of a baguette then anyone could.

Half an hour later he was ready. He stood before me with a wide grin displaying his half mouthful of wine stained teeth and a crumb guard he had fashioned from a piece of cardboard and attached to the side of his head.

I leaned back and let fly. The baguette pounded into the crumb guard and fell apart. Gerard didn't move. He just laughed at me and told me I would have to do better. I laughed with him and handed over the half case of wine that had been the basis of his agreeing to the stunt. Phase one was complete.

Two days later I picked up my second baguette. It had attained the consistency of granite. I thumped it into the palm of my left hand. It hurt. My idea could work. Gerard crossed my mind but I couldn't afford more wine. I tried to think of someone who was both daring and cheap. No one came to mind so I decided to use an inanimate object and film the experiment.

Fifteen minutes later, I was ready. I set my digital camera to movie mode and pressed the go button. I stood back and drove the baguette into the side of a fence post. The baguette shattered like glass and crumbs flew helter-skelter.

I downloaded the film and examined it, pausing in appropriate places. The baguette had shattered on impact. Once the surface tension was broken it had acted as expected; it was just a stale bread roll. It wasn't a weapon.

I slept on the problem that night. Something had made Knight stagger and that thing was a baguette.

The answer dawned at sunrise. I could turn a baguette into a weapon. I could also, very easily, dispose of the evidence.

At eight thirty I was in my local boulangerie. At nine I was in the manual arts department of the school. At nine fifteen I had a weapon in my hand. It was a very fresh flute with a fifteen-millimetre pipe inserted along its length. At ten, I was talking to the young gendarme that I had met at the scene. I had seen the look on his face before; when we had first met. He tried to explain that there was no motive and no planning. He reminded me that one does not purchase baguettes complete with iron pipes. This was, at worst, a case for assault: a small fracas gone wrong, with incalculable results.

If I was right, there had been premeditation. How could that be? Knight was a tourist who was about to visit his son at school. The gendarme was right, of course. There could be no premeditation. I had espoused some scatterbrain scheme that had no basis in logic. My problem was that I believed that it did have logic. In fact, logic was the only virtue my idea possessed. The nagging question was *why*.

I returned to the ferry dock and stared into the middle distance across the river. If I was right, there would be a pipe of some sort lying at the bottom of the river, resting on the silt. I considered diving in to find out but remembered how the ferry needs to turn into the current to prevent their heading downstream. Diving in would be both futile and dangerous.

'You have done well. Mr Mawson.'

I hadn't heard anyone approach. I turned toward the French accented voice. A woman stood beside my car, face hidden in the shadow of a cowl. The image was tall and thin and stood motionless. I imagined a panther, toned to perfection, as leather pants and jacket moved seductively toward me. She pushed the cowl back to reveal long wavy hair and lipstick that matched the colour of her clothing. I had never seen anything so attractive in black in my life. Her face was narrow with a small, pointed nose, high cheekbones and wide expressive eyes with a hint of allure that belied her solemn expression. I realised that I knew the face. No, not the face, the eyes. I recognised the eyes. But larger…much larger than life and on a screen at the school in Lucian Knight's latest epic. The test screening for a captive audience that gave Taro cred. Queen of the Night. This woman was Quenna Knight, Taro's step mother and Lucian's wife.

'I'm sorry,' I said, indicating that I hadn't heard her correctly.

'You have solved the mystery concerning what happened.'

'An accident,' I said, lamely.

'Destiny, Mr Mawson.'

'Destiny?'

'You had no reason to do anything, but you did. I thank you.'

A black Mercedes S400 pulled into the ferry by-pass. Jeanette Culver sat primly in the driver's seat. A motor hummed and Taro Knight poked his newly bald head through the resultant opening of the rear window. 'Good-bye, Mr Mawson, see you next term,' Taro called, with the wide grin of someone granted an early holiday. '

'That head needs a hat,' I said, imagining a sunburnt scalp.

'That head need a father.'

'Yeah.' I wrenched my foot from my mouth. 'Lucky he has you and Jeanette Culver.'

'I must be going,' the woman said, leaning forward and kissing me on both cheeks. 'Thank you again.'

I stood mesmerised as I watched her walk toward the car. 'For what?'

She stopped and turned. 'For being interested in what happened to my husband.'

A futile thought on a faulty premise, I thought.

'Not at all. You will be vindicated.'

A futile thought on a faulty premise. I hadn't said it out loud but she commented anyway. I looked at her eyes.

She blinked twice then smiled. 'Just keep wondering. You will encounter much more on your journey. When you meet my mother tell her that I will be fine.'

'What journey? What mother?'

'You will know when the time comes. Au revoir et prendre soin, Scott.'

The car pulled away before I could say anything. I was left staring at Taro pulling faces at me through the rear window.

As the Mercedes pulled out onto the main road, a police van pull into the lay-by. I watched closely as two men donned scuba gear and another prepared some ropes. I couldn't believe it. They were going to look; they would find the pipe. I stood to one side and watched them work. A short time later, another vehicle arrived and the young gendarme jumped out. He began to talk to the third man of the scuba team. He smiled, when he looked across at me, but said nothing. They both looked down into the murky waters of the river and waited.

After a few minutes a hooded head breached the surface, followed closely by another. They waved some sort of prearranged signal to the man on shore. He, in turn, began hauling on ropes. A box like container, which had been lowered into the water earlier, started to half float in the current. I waited to see what it contained and strained forward for a better view. I saw a rusty rod sticking out of the top of the box. My heart started to race. I had achieved something. I looked again. There were two rusty rods...no... three...no...six at least. My heart pounded but there was no elation. I shook my head in disbelief.

I watched as the divers unloaded more than a dozen rods and pipes from the box. Each one was marked, wrapped and placed into individual plastic bags.

The young gendarme approached me as soon as the divers finished loading. He was smiling and nodding his head. 'Congratulations my friend. You were right. Ronin walked into the station this morning and confessed. He could not live with his guilt. He did it exactly as you said was possible.'

My breath expelled like a busted balloon. My shoulders slumped. It was more like defeat than victory. 'Did he have a motive?'

'Yes. That is why he confessed. He was preparing for a man in a black Mercedes whom he had seen leave his house and put his car on the ferry. His wife would not tell him who the man was. Monsieur Knight has such a car. He thought that the man opening the car door was to start a fight with him.'

'He had the baguette prepared?'

'Every day.'

'Why are so many pipes?'

'This ferry was sunk twice during the war. There are many more pipes down there to bring up. If we don't get the needed DNA from these we will take more.'

The Police freely acknowledged my part in solving the case and the Media beat me up as a hero. The case became known as the *Duclair Baguette Murder*. That's not its official name, of course but that name was the one coined by the media.

Val D'Arno

JULY in Val d'Arno is hot: too hot. The sun moves slowly and burns its way across the Tuscan sky like a slow laser in a sci-fi movie. The grass and weeds strangle the olive groves and green snakes and adders lie in wait for unsuspecting tourists. The romantic times of the Tuscan spring have deserted the landscape for another year and the land lies in the precursor to the season of summer holidays. In Florence, tourists already swarm like plague locusts sucking oxygen from the city, yet they continue to come in droves and clog the street and thoroughfares until everyone walks as though their ankles are shackled by unseen chains. July is not my time. I hate Florence in July but the regular teachers concoct regular illnesses prior to the summer break and I am left to stay in my apartment and endure the stagnant dryness of the heat. I would prefer to be there in Spring, when love abounds amongst the olive groves and wildflowers stain the fields with red and yellow hues. Then it is cooler and people gather in the piazzas and village streets and friendship abounds on the hills.

I guess that it was because it was July that I found myself taking a more than casual interest in a letter that appeared in my e-mail folder. It was from someone signing themselves K.J. Mortimer and concerned a desire to have me investigate the events leading to death of one Peter

Mortimer, an Australian film director, in Cannes, in May. The first attachment to the e-mail was a short snippet from French television showing two men, on stage, delivering acceptance speeches. One of them reminded me of a hippie penguin in someone else's tux. The other was tall, with a shock of unruly hair, a narrow face and beady eyes perched either side of an eagle beak. The second attachment was a minuscule article from page 26 of a minor French tabloid indicating that there were no suspicious circumstances surrounding the death. That generally meant suicide and I wondered why a person would commit suicide on a night of triumph. Surely, even the most highly prepped person would wait until the omens had turned sour. To extinguish oneself whilst on a high seemed ludicrous. I opened the third attachment. It was the front page of the Sydney Telegraph with the banner headline NATION MOURNS: *Aussie Icon in Cannes Tragedy*. An underlying photo showed that eagle beak was Peter Mortimer. I knew nothing of Mortimer so I read the article. I expected to read references to great works but his entire life's output seemed to be limited to one documentary film. I guessed he was lucky to have won. If he had lost, his death would have been a New Zealand tragedy nestled amongst the classifieds. I looked closely at the photo and smiled as I decided that I had already solved the case. It was obvious that Mortimer had seen his reflection in a mirror and decided to end it all.

I read the rest of the e-mail and found that K.J. stood for Kendra John and that she was Peter Mortimer's half-sister. The final lines advised that Kendra was prepared to travel to Italy to meet me and discuss the case. I replied with my address and a local phone number.

Four weeks later, I was amongst the noise and bustle Pisa's Galileo Galilei airport, sipping black coffee and waiting for someone whom I had no idea how to recognise. Most people would have made some arrangements for a recognition method but I hadn't thought of anything until I arrived at the airport. I sat in a cafe and watched the passing parade, ticking off and discounting until I saw two women dragging suitcases on rollers through the arrivals gate. One was tall and elegant, with wavy brunette hair and deep green eyes. She wore a lightweight cotton knee-length dress with matching high-heeled shoes. The other was a mouse; short and thin with hair tightly pulled back in a ponytail. She looked like she had been dressed by a blind friend and wore a green blouse and pink cardigan with a plaid skirt and yellow sneakers. She squinted at the world through thick-rimmed glasses and seemed to have straight whiskers pointing horizontally from under her nose. I knew in an instant which one would be Mortimer's sister. I started to move toward the mouse but, just as I was within speaking range, she waved to someone behind me and walked straight past. I turned to search again for the other woman but she now strolled arm in arm with a brunette woman with the mien of a middle-aged mother.

'Scott Mawson?'

I spun on my heels to see a woman, whom I had discounted earlier. She looked to be around thirty-five and confident. She wore a blue cotton dress and her long dark hair resided in an unkempt twirl atop her head. Blue shoes matched the dress and her brown eyes sparkled, despite twenty-five hours of travelling. She was pulling a soft bag that appeared suitable only for hand luggage. I had given her an initial glance then discounted the possibility.

'Yes,' I said. 'Kendra Mortimer?'

'Lucky I knew what you looked like. You would have been wandering around for hours. I expected you to be better organised.' Her smile was broad and sensuous.

'Lucky me,' I said lamely, as I scanned her body from head to foot, noticing that her face possessed the languid sexiness of experience and everything else was there in pleasant proportion. 'I'm pleased to meet you. Welcome to Italy.'

***

I loaded her case into the boot of my BMW and headed along the Fi-Pi-Li toward Florence, only to be caught in the late afternoon traffic and forced to assume the forward momentum of a snail.

'It's always like this at this time of year. Only the Italians would organise to do major roadwork during the summer holidays,' I explained.

Kendra sat back, closed her eyes and leaned back into the seat. 'Where are we going?'

'I live near Cellai; about twenty k's south west of Florence. I have an apartment there. There's a spare apartment at the moment and I've organised for you to stay there.' She didn't respond.

I turned my head to find that she was asleep. The expression on her face had a dreamlike quality and was fixed with a smile that indicated satisfaction with something. I wondered what it was.

Half an hour later she opened her eyes. We had travelled only a few kilometres. I handed her a tic tac and she closed her eyes again.

'Is it a long way?' She asked.

'No, just traffic. They're doing road works near Empoli and it always jams. We'll be off soon. Long trip, huh?'

She looked across at me with a lazy smile. 'Far too far and far too long.' She sucked on the tiny sweet and resettled into her seat. 'You look different. Took me a moment to recognise you.'

I didn't understand. 'Look different from what?'

'Your poster.'

'Poster?'

Kendra smiled. 'I'll tell you when I wake up properly.' She proceeded to unclip her hair and let it fall around her shoulders.

She was still asleep when I pulled into the car park of the renaissance castello that houses my apartment. I moved her bag into the spare apartment and went back to the car to wake her up. She was missing.

***

I found her standing in the garden, staring at the row of villages along the ridgeline on the far side of the Arno valley. She smiled as she watched me approach.

'Nice spot here. But it's very hot.'

'Too hot really, unless there's a stiff breeze. We don't have air conditioning here and there are a million carnivorous bugs that consider humans an eminently edible meal.'

'Are we?'

'If you don't protect yourself you might find out. There's a mosquito net around your bed. Hungry?'

'No. Too much plane food. I think I'll get some sleep and get into the right time zone. That okay with you?'

'Sure. I'll show you the apartment.'

The sky was burnt orange when I heard a knock on my apartment door. I answered to find Kendra standing, case in hand, on my doorstep. Her hair was tied back in a bun and frameless glasses perched on her nose. She wore a blue peasant blouse and crushed linen skirt. There was no sign of makeup and she looked ready for business. I ushered her in and she made herself comfortable on my sofa while I mixed her a gin and tonic. 'You've missed a full day.'

She said nothing but stared into the distance, toward the lights along the ridgeline. 'It looks like one long strip of lights.'

'There are quite a few villages up there. Nice view isn't it?' I called from the kitchen. 'You hungry this time?'

'Famished. What have you got?'

I thought for a moment. Half-eaten pizza might not suit; everything else would take preparation time. 'Nothing that you could stomach. I thought we might go down to Burchio...to the restaurant there.'

She walked into the kitchen and opened the fridge door. I heard the gulp. 'Does this have a label?'

'What?'

'Does this fridge have a biohazard label? This place is toxic.'

I was embarrassed. 'It's not that bad.'

'Carrots should be an orange colour,' she said, her nose crinkling. 'Look, I don't feel like going out, so you amuse yourself for an hour and I'll sort something out here. You may have something edible.'

I considered arguing that it was my kitchen, but then it dawned that I would get fed without any input. I decided to take the advice. 'See you in an hour.'

***

An hour and a half and three beers at a local bar later I returned. There was no sign of Kendra. Then I heard voices coming from the garden. I looked over the balcony to see Kendra leaning against the parapet wall and chatting with one of my neighbours. There was a table laid out and covered with food and bottles of wine. I joined them.

'Wine?' Kendra asked, as she held out a glass for me.

'You move quickly.'

'I had to. The only things that you had that weren't past their use by dates were a jar of olives, some biscuits and a few cheeses…and, of course, a warehouse full of wine. I introduced myself to your neighbours and suggested an impromptu party. They provided the food, I brought the wine. Loaves and fishes stuff really.'

I was instantly impressed. All of the neighbours were tourists who had taken the apartments for various lengths of time. I had nodded pleasantries to all of them but hadn't thought to introduce myself. 'I'm impressed. They're all new. I don't know them.'

'I'll introduce you then.' Kendra laughed.

I was finishing a conversation with a female American neighbour when I noticed that Kendra had managed to get herself surgically removed from a dour Englishman whose hobby was stating the bleeding obvious. She made her way across to where I leant against the parapet of the ancient outer wall of the castello.

I turned toward her and leaned against the wall. 'What poster?' I asked, continuing an earlier conversation.

'The one in the library, of course. The hero of the Duclair Baguette Murder. Great photo of you.'

I took a sip of a Chianti that I had expected to be able to cellar for a week or so. 'I'm no less confused.'

'How do you think I contacted you? You're not well known and not easy to find.'

It was an excellent question. I hadn't even thought about it. 'You tell me.'

'You probably don't know it but your exploits are monitored by my library. You see, I work in a high school library in Sydney and a colleague and I read an article on the net that an Australian teacher had helped police in France to solve a murder. We were impressed so we decided to stalk you.'

'Stalk me?'

'That's right. The photo in the article that we came across had you looking a bit delish so we contacted your school to find out what you were like. We gained a contact there and she sends us stuff on you.'

Stalked by proxy? I had never heard of such a thing. 'Sounds a bit boring to me.'

'No more boring than a school library. We decided to follow your career for something to do.'

'Now it's sounding bizarre.'

'It's perspective. My colleague and I are mid-thirties women. We're neither attached nor gay. Anyone who seems to have a life, other than going to work at the same place every day, seems like they're having fun to us.'

I shook my head. 'You are in *dire* need of a life.'

'Exactly...that's why I'm here. I wanted to leave the humdrum of my existence for a while. Naturally, I would have preferred to do it without losing a brother but I *am* in Italy and that's about as exotic as anything that has ever happened to me.'

She finished her wine then walked across the small lawn
to get another bottle from the table. She returned with a
rare vintage from my supposedly hidden stash. 'You
should eat. It's almost all gone.'

'I've got a pizza in the fridge.' I said, staring at one of
my prize possessions being poured into a cheap tumbler.

'No you haven't.'

'Ohh. Eaten or thrown?'

'It was never edible.'

I grabbed the bottle of wine from her hand and poured
a full measure into my glass. 'When do you want to start
talking about your brother?'

'As soon as we can break up the party, I guess'

***

Two hours, and the best part of my wine stash, later, I
was sitting on my sofa listening to a lilting voice and trying
to comprehend what I was being told. At best it was an
unusual tale. At worst it reeked of conspiracy and artifice.
It seemed that every barrier imaginable had been put in the
way of making the death of Peter Mortimer a simple tale.
The woman who had escorted him to the awards ceremony had disappeared. She didn't appear in any of the
television footage of the event – in the fleeting seconds
allocated to a minor award recipient – despite Mortimer's
business partner, one Billy Squires of the penguin resemblance set, saying that she had been by Peter's side
throughout the evening. There was nothing to be seen in
the television footage or magazine articles on the presenta-
tions that lined up with what Squires had told her by
phone or Peter had written in his diary.

Peter's diary was full of details about him meeting a woman by the name of Jacqueline du Pre. Squires confirmed that this woman had been Peter's escort to the awards ceremony and yet there was no indication of her existence. This included the red carpet walk, where available footage showed Peter Mortimer to be alone, despite Billy Squires asserting that he had Jacqueline du Pre at his arm for the entire journey. Kendra said that Squires' story lined up with the phone call that Peter had made to her just minutes after the award but Squires was having trouble getting anyone to believe what he recalled.

I became more and more intrigued as the tale unfolded. I listened intently until Kendra was finished. 'Do you have a photo of the woman?'

'No. Peter was mad on taking photos but there was nothing in his belongings that the police gave to me. There's a word picture in his diary that gives a description, but it's abstract and doesn't really make sense. No one is as perfect as the word picture he painted.'

'Maybe he was in love. That always clouds impressions.'

'This was poetic. Peter was never poetic. This was something that was having a deleterious effect on him. It was more than love.'

'You're saying that it was bad for him. Why?'

'You've seen Peter's photo. Peter's looks and personality would have stopped him from ever having a woman who was any more than homely. I loved him dearly but he was plain at best, ugly at worst. When you add his charisma bypass and shyness, you have someone who can only be hurt by a beautiful woman'

'Maybe you're being a bit harsh. What did Squires think of her?'

Kendra stood from my sofa and walked to the open window. 'That's one of my problems. Billy says that she fitted the description in Peter's diary. He says that his heart melted when he saw them together. He just couldn't believe that Peter could be with such a woman.'

I took another mouthful of wine and slid into its lethargy. 'There is an obvious explanation...money. Money buys or attracts beauty every day.'

'I know he was paying for her services. He says that in his diary. He even says why he was doing it. It's just that this woman was well beyond anything that he considered he was paying for and she was treating him like some kind of hero. She doted on him ... and sex wasn't part of the deal.'

'I assume that it's possible that you can pay for an escort, without sex. You know, someone to be seen with.'

'That's what he was doing. He had an escort to allow him to feel good at the awards ceremony. The mystery isn't that he did it. The mystery is that the woman doesn't exist.'

'You must be mistaken.'

Kendra suddenly slapped herself on the side of the neck and jumped. 'Shit, what was that?'

'Your welcoming party, probably a mosquito. You get nice little itchy welts.'

Kendra shut the window and returned to the sofa. 'I'm not mistaken. Upstairs I have the film from the award ceremony and Peter's diary. I also have a photocopy of a strange invitation that he received...after he was nominated for the award. I want you to look through it all and then we can talk again.'

'What do you have to play it on?'

'My laptop of course.'

'Now or tomorrow?'

'I always say that there's no time like the present. You can do your research while I have a bath.'

The sound of the showerhead played as background music as I rifled through Kendra's computer files. I had thoughts of her sitting in the bath with the showerhead spraying water over her breasts. Pleasant thoughts that were being offset by the recording of the awards ceremony. The television footage ran for an hour but Peter Mortimer and Billy Squires were on screen for a mere seven seconds in several shots taken prior to the award winner being announced. I noticed a single white rose on the vacant seat beside Mortimer, but that was the only odd thing that I saw. With a full house, I was surprised that it hadn't been crushed or, at least, pushed to the floor. I picked up the Mortimer diary and carefully read the hand written pages for Cannes festival period. He was definitely in love with someone special.

The next item I studied was an account from a panel shop in Cannes for the damage done to the vehicle that hit Peter. An explanation attached to the account stated that he was not in a pedestrian crossing when he jumped out onto the road. I considered that the repairer's position was untenable but found that the account had already been paid.

Next was a photocopy of an invitation advising Mortimer that he had become eligible to avail himself of the services of someone named Emily Washburn.

I was still reading the invitation when the water stopped running. I stood and switched on the electric kettle. I searched for cups while I waited. Stocks were low. I finally selected a bright green and white football cup and a chipped porcelain cat mug from a selection of four possibilities. I spooned cheap coffee and looked into the fridge for milk. We would drink it black, irrespective of preference. I was stirring sugar into one cup when the bathroom door opened.

Kendra appeared, surrounded in mist like a distant memory. She wore a huge bath towel and a smaller one wrapped around her head. "What do you think?' she asked.

'What am I looking for?'

She sighed with despair. Her eyes clouded in disappointment. 'The film. She isn't there.'

I felt as thick as two planks. 'I don't understand.'

'Peter wrote in his diary that he was taking his woman to the ceremony. Billy told me that she sat beside Peter. Where the rose is.'

'And?'

'There was no rose.'

I was missing something important. 'There is a rose. I can see it. It's on the seat.'

Kendra ruffled the towel through her hair and then threw it aside like a used thought. She sat on the sofa beside me, played with the video image and paused on the rose. 'Look at it.'

I looked at the rose.

'Describe it.'

I decided that she was the perfect schoolteacher. 'It's white with a magenta seed stalk. Beautiful really.'

'What type is it?'

I was suddenly enlightened by the thought that I actually knew the answer. I had never had an interest in botany or the realm of the garden lover but, somehow, I knew the name of the rose.

'Jacqueline du Pre,' I said.

'Are you beginning to understand?'

'Now there are three.'

Kendra sipped her coffee and sputtered. 'This is horrid…yours?'

'No, it was in the cupboard.'

She tipped the coffee down the sink. 'I noticed some at your place. We can have one down there as soon as Q&A time is finished. You're doing pretty poorly so far. There aren't three there are only two.'

'Being?'

'A wonderful cellist and the rose that was named after her.'

'And Peter's Jacqueline?'

Kendra shrugged. 'Let's get some coffee. Grab the case. Leave the laptop here'

I felt an imaginary tug, as if I was being led by a cow ring through my nose, and followed her down the stairs to my apartment. She made coffee while I looked through the credit card receipts and bills that were in Kendra's case. 'I'm glad that I didn't have to pay these.'

'He must have gone mad. Peter didn't have that sort of money either. I had to inject funds into his account to cover the bills.'

I read one invoice. 'Lucky he had a good limit on his card.'

'He needed that for his business. Otherwise….' She let the sentence drift as she sat down with a new coffee in her hand.

I read the bills and invoices again. A credit card bill for $16,050 for a dress and $1,800 for underwear at one shop. A credit card bill and receipt for $11,170 for a dress at another shop. The purchases had been made in Euros and then converted by Mortimer's bank. I placed the paperwork on my tuneable wooden coffee table.

'He bought all that for someone special. I want you to find Jacqueline du Pre.'

I looked across at Kendra and shrugged. 'But you think that she doesn't exist.'

Kendra didn't answer but a come-hither expression bathed her face in a wondrous glow. 'Your bed looks more comfortable than mine. Mind if I use it?'

'My sofa isn't comfortable at all. I've tried it.'

She smiled with the same relaxed affectation that I had noticed in my car. 'You don't have to sleep on the sofa. I don't mind sharing.'

I remembered something that she had said earlier. 'I'm still being stalked, huh?'

She ignored my comment. 'You look like your poster. I like that. You have nice brown eyes and I like the way your hair brushes back over your ears. Mind you, the poster doesn't show grey flecked highlights but then I didn't expect that you would dye it. And, of course, there's your name. Anyone with a name that sounds like an Antarctica fetish has to be good value. Besides, we're about the same age and I know you aren't married.'

'I *am* being stalked.'

'Only until you tell me that you'll find Jacqueline du Pre for me.'

'And if I say no?'

'My contact at your school says that you won't. I'm on her side.'

I figured that it was decision time. I decided that I would, at least, begin the journey. As I did I wondered if this was the journey Quenna Knight had referred to. Then something popped into my head. It was a poor segue but if I was going to become a horizontal dancer then I had to ask. 'Where did you get your name?'

She walked to the bed and dropped her towel before sliding in under the sheets. There was no disputing what my eyes could see. 'You mean Kendra or the name that ruins my sex life?'

'It's a *Boy Named Sue* in reverse.'

'It's a mother who's quite deranged and has been since before I was born. She's postmenopausal but still suffers from pre-menstrual tension. I'm lucky that my father talked her into Kendra. She wanted Kenneth. She wanted a boy. He compromised on the rest.'

'What about Peter?'

'We share a father only but my mother thinks of Peter as being her child. She even told me about her difficult labour with him. His mother died when he was two.

'Why don't you change?'

'My mother or my name?'

'The name, of course.'

'I'd rather change my mother. You know, she thinks that Peter was an idiot. But then, she thinks that anyone who would have Billy Squires as a business partner had to be off his head. She even convinced the insurance company that handles Peter's life policy that he committed suicide. They have jumped onto the matter and are now espousing the line that he did commit suicide, thus leaving them in the clear with no payout.' She threw back the sheets on one side of the bed. 'With a mother like mine, I guess that I got used to it all. The ribbing about my name stopped when I grew up. Since then it's been a joke. It hasn't really ruined my sex life but I do seem to meet a lot of men with homosexual tendencies. If you're not one of those, join me in bed. I need mosquito protection.'

The Family

FORTY hours later, I couldn't stop looking at the woman who stood at the other end of the corridor of her Glebe semi-detached, talking animatedly into a phone. She looked as if someone had drawn a straight line from head to toe and then painted one half of her body white and the other half black. Even her face and hair were imbued with the colouring. At a distance, she looked like an albino mime artist standing in deep shadow. 'Does she always look like that?' I asked.

'No, of course not,' Kendra said. 'When she was in full mourning, she was totally black. You can see that her mourning period is lessening. She is now half white. Soon the period will be at an end and she will be all white.'

'Most people just wear black,' I said.

'Obviously they don't know how to mourn.'

'Why didn't she start at the top?' I asked. "By now she would have a white blouse and black skirt. Surely that would look better.'

'Like I said, most people don't know how to mourn. Everyone knows that mourning is a vertical space observance. If mum did as you suggest, she would have to lie down all day.'

I should have known. Kendra throwing open the windows of my apartment, allowing the Italian version of a mosquito squadron to dive bomb my naked body, causing great consternation and libido withering, should have given me a minor inkling that all would not be well with her mother. But I didn't think clearly enough and, while scratching at the most inopportune times, I had travelled with Kendra to Australia where I was now walking along the corridor of a Sydney suburban terrace toward an extra from a Hammer horror film. I couldn't wait to start interviewing the woman.

'Mum, this is the man that I was telling you about,' Kendra said, as her mother placed the phone in its cradle.

The woman turned toward me and sneered. 'He doesn't look like an insurance salesman. They all wear loud ties and speak to you as if you're their closest friend and they're doing you a favour. This one isn't even wearing a suit.'

'Mum, he's not an insurance salesman. He's helping us find out what happened to Peter.'

'Peter who?'

'Peter your son,' Kendra said.

Tears welled in the woman's eyes and she began to wail. 'My son is dead. He reached nirvana and committed suicide. The glory was too much for him. Can't you see the depth of my loss? Look at me I'm in mourning,' she said, waving her arms about like a fluttering butterfly, to emphasise her attire.

I turned toward the front door, as the woman started dabbing at her tears with a huge handkerchief. 'I'm out of here,' I whispered to Kendra.

Kendra held me by the arm to stop me fleeing. 'You're embarrassing me, mum. Scott wants to ask you a few questions. Now sit down and answer him.'

The woman stared at me. 'He's looking at me as if I'm some kind of freak,' she said.

I was surprised as to how quickly she had grasped the truth.

'He's not mum. He just wants to ask you a few questions. That's all.'

'Tell him not to look at me.'

Kendra let forth a deep sigh of resignation. 'Could you talk to mum without looking at her?'

'It would be preferable.'

'Good,' she said, turning back to her mother. 'He'll look away from you, okay.'

The woman opened the door at the end of the corridor and disappeared through it. Kendra held it slightly ajar but stopped me from proceeding. 'You have to understand, she isn't of our normal world. She's a pantheistic magus.'

I scoured the dictionary of my mind for a reply. 'She's a godlike ancient magician then, huh? I would have thought that loony was closer to an apt description.'

Kendra spun me a look that would freeze sand, but said nothing. She opened the door and I found myself striding into what appeared to be a different house. Whereas the front steps, stained glass front door and entry corridor were the embodiment of fifties poverty, I was now confronted with the stainless steel, whitewash and honeyed timber of modern chic. The back yard of the property had been replaced with a postage stamp sized Japanese garden and the extension to the original structure was a two storey concrete and glass edifice with vaulted glass panelling from floor to ceiling, topped by a pyramid shaped glass ceiling. It seemed odd that such a setting could belong to the monochrome harlequin who was now sitting at the kitchen table, a broadsheet newspaper acting as a deterrent to any wayward gaze.

I sat opposite and switched on my mini-tape recorder. The sooner I accomplished this task, the better I would like it. 'Now, Mrs Mortimer, Kendra has told me that you think that Peter committed suicide. Why is that?'

There was shuffling on the other side of the paper barrier. A page turned. 'The bill for the car. They would not have sent it, if it had been an accident.'

'What bill?' I asked, knowing the answer, but wanting to get Mrs Mortimer talking.

'Tell him, Ken,' she replied.

'No...I want your answers. I already have Kendra's version,' I said.

There was a pause with the gestation period of an elephant's pregnancy but, finally, she said something. 'I knew it was happening. I was with Peter...helping him cross over. I could see the car coming, but Peter just wanted to step out in front of it.'

'You were there?' I asked

'Of course. My astral projection has always been linked with Peter's ever since he was born. I saw the car and knew that he wanted to cross over...so I pushed him out onto the road.'

I switched off the tape. The interview was going downhill with the speed of a jet-propelled billycart. I changed tack 'When you were there, did you see the girl that Peter was with?'

'Yes...but she did nothing. She just stood there...gawking. She didn't even try to stop me.'

I began to read the headlines on the front of the dated newspaper. *Hicks Guilty*. The hicks are too easy a target. I thought. 'And at what time of the evening did you push Peter in front of the van?'

The paper folded and a pinched head appeared. For the first time, I noticed that the black and white hair was a wig. Mismatched eyes gave me a malevolent stare. 'You're trying to trick me aren't you? You know that I would have looked at my watch. You know that it was eleven o'clock in the evening, when he died.'

I looked around for a broadaxe. It would be a mercy killing. 'Yes, I'm sorry. I tried one on, just to see if we were on the same page. Tell me about Peter's insurance. Why did you tell the company that Peter committed suicide, when *you* pushed him?'

She looked indignant, and then smiled softly with the black half of her lips tilting slightly upward. 'No-one is to know. It's between me and Peter. I had to tell them something.'

'But he didn't commit suicide. What you did has cost you his insurance pay-out,' I said. I was surprised at how annoyed I was becoming with the situation.

She looked at me with ferret's eyes. 'You don't understand. He wanted to commit suicide. He took the opportunity when it arose.'

'Why?' I asked.

The pinched look on her face seemed to be fighting demons. It was as if a dim light was trying to make its way out of her head. When the sound came, the voice was reed thin. 'Billy Squires, his business partner. Billy forced him into it. Peter was a good boy until Billy Squires came along.'

'I don't understand. I thought they were friends and colleagues.'

'They were friends. That was the trouble. If they hadn't been friends then none of this would have happened. If they hadn't met, Billy Squires would not have been in Cannes and Peter would have been able to get the award alone. Do you have any idea what it is like to have to share everything? Do you imagine how hard it was for me to congratulate Billy Squires after what he did to Peter?'

I was lost. For a moment I had thought that something might be said that made sense. 'Just what did he do to Peter?' I asked, almost spitting.

The malevolent stare hit me again. 'He halved him. Once they became partners, they had to share everything. It was Peter's movie, but he had to share with that demon.'

'But Kendra told me that Squires raised the finance and did the second unit direction. Surely that is sharing the load?' I asked. I looked to find Kendra, for confirmation.

I saw that she was standing in the Japanese garden staring down into a small pond. The expression on her face was serene, as if she was standing in her place of stone walled tranquillity. I gazed around the space in which I was sitting. Kendra seemed to fit in this place; she looked part of it. I wondered if she had designed it and had created a special place for herself to avoid her mother's eccentricities. I heard a voice from the other side of the newsprint but found that I wasn't listening to what was being said. I watched as Kendra bent down and cupped a handful of water. She stood and let it drip from her hand, back into the pool. She seemed to be pondering one of the mysteries of life. She gazed toward me and gave a wan smile. She raised her hand to her mouth and appeared to suck at something. I saw a fish tail disappear between her lips. My stomach turned.

Kendra wiped her mouth with the back of her hand and the smile returned. I envisioned the space adorned with gargoyles and set around a cauldron; broomsticks near the doorway. I realised that I didn't fit. I didn't exist on the same stratum as Kendra and her mother. I noticed that the voice from the other side of the newspaper was still talking. I listened in but heard no ramblings of consequence. I watched Kendra as she opened the back door and disappeared from view. Time to leave. Time to return to Italy and forget the foibles of the Mortimer family. I stood and walked toward the doorway that led back to the street.

As I opened the door at one end of the entry corridor, the front door opened and I could see a figure haloed by a sunlit aura. At the end of the figure's arm was suspended a small rectangle. The front door closed and the vision turned into a woman carrying a suitcase. She looked to be in her early sixties and conservatively dressed in a grey skirt suit. She smiled as she walked toward me, proffering a hand and setting the suitcase on the floor, as she approached. 'You must be Scott Mawson,' she said

I blinked my eyes to focus and remove the last vestiges of sunlight. Then I closed them again and opened them slowly. It didn't work. I saw the same thing. I closed and reopened again. Nothing changed. Kendra stood before me with the etching of age carved lightly into her face. Her hair was lustrous grey and she appeared to be a hundred centimetres shorter and twenty kilograms heavier. Impossible. Kendra could not have exited the back door, run around the front, changed appearance and entered the front door. But she had. I could feel microscopic needles dancing along my spine and perspiration beading on my brow. I was in a world that I couldn't comprehend. I held out my hand and felt a soft pudginess when our hands met. Soft pudginess was not a sensory perception when touching Kendra's hand. I leapt in. 'And you are?'

'Oh, sorry. Madeleine Mortimer. Kendra's mother. I'm pleased to meet you.'

'But...' I turned my head toward the door from whence I had just come.

Madeleine smiled and released my hand. 'By the look on your face, I can see that he's dressed up again. He promised Kendra he wouldn't do that when you visited. It always scares her boyfriends off.' She strode past me and threw the door open. '*Felix!*'

I followed her through the door, just in time to see a wig being pulled from a head and a black and white countenance suffusing to deep crimson.

'You silly man. Felix, you should know better. Get upstairs...shower and change. You look like a sideshow freak in that getup. You know black doesn't suit you.

Felix flew past me, wearing the hue of deep embarrassment. He slammed the corridor door as he went.

Madeleine stared after him and sighed deeply. 'He'll be okay soon. Then I can introduce you to my husband. Is Kendra around?'

'She just went out the back door.'

'Did she eat a fish?'

I winced at the thought. 'Yes.'

'Good. She'll be settling it in the inside pond then,' Madeleine said

The back door opened and Kendra appeared. She waved at her mother as she walked to the indoor fishpond. She spat a fish into the water. 'You met Scott then,' she said as she walked into the kitchen and flicked a switch on the electric kettle.

'Yes.'

'Did you yell at dad?'

'You need to stop encouraging him. I think that Scott was leaving when I came in. Felix probably scared him away.'

'It's okay. I told Scott what he was like. He understands.'

I felt like an eavesdropper at a bedroom wall. I was being mentioned in a conversation as if I wasn't in the room. I decided to interject. 'You know, Kendra, I don't understand. I thought that your father was your mother. Everything you told me led to that conclusion.'

'It's a bit like you don't understand mourning. You just don't listen,' Kendra retorted, pouting.

I became peeved. 'I listen…obviously to rubbish.'

'Men!' Kendra screamed. 'You're all the same. A woman lets you into her bed and you just take liberties and lose respect for her. None of you ever understand.'

I found myself agreeing with her. I certainly didn't understand what was going on. Not for the first time, I considered dropping the case. I was beginning to believe that Peter Mortimer had committed suicide and that would mean that there was nothing to investigate. Maybe he had lived with his family for too long and decided to end it.

'Coffee?' Madeleine asked, as the kettle boiled.

Kendra nodded. I followed.

We drank in silence until Felix Mortimer re-entered the room. I was surprised at the transformation. The drag queen was replaced by an ageing Peter Pan, complete with green tights and a feathered hat. I waited for comment from Madeleine, but none came. Felix joined us as we all contemplated the beginning of the universe. 'Look,

Kendra,' I said, breaking the drought. 'I'm not sure that I can help you with your quest, after all.'

'You can't pull out,' Felix Mortimer said, a look of consternation smudging his ancient boyish features. 'We need to find out what happened to Peter. Not knowing is driving us all mad.'

A short journey, I thought. 'What am I supposed to do? I thought you had something tangible that I could follow. All I've heard this morning is demented rambling. Besides I don't have the money to go traipsing all over the countryside. We haven't even discussed a fee for my services.'

'You're being tested and, so far, you're not doing very well,' Madeleine said.

'Tested?

'Of course,' Madeleine said. 'The search for the truth is not going to be easy. There will be obstructions and red herrings everywhere. We need someone who can think laterally and not be restricted by narrow-mindedness. Kendra told us that you were suited for the task. That's why she looked you up. So far, you're not meeting expectations.'

I was swamped by indignant fervour. I was sitting in the midst of a bizarre family, being lectured on my narrow-mindedness. What did they expect? Was this entire scene an act for my benefit? Were they right? Was I up to the task? What bloody task? There were three sets of eyes looking at me. Each face emitted the expectation of a football crowd, the moment before a goal. Would I score, or shoot over the crossbar and into the crowd. I wasn't sure, myself. 'You're all fucking mad,' I said.

'That's an A for observation, young Scott,' Felix uttered. 'Keep to that thought when the going gets tough.'

I looked at the tea leaves at the bottom of my coffee cup and started to read them. Maybe I did require more lateral thought and open-mindedness. If it was all an introductory sojourn into the wacky, I had been far too intolerant. 'Okay. Just let me know what you have… give me a place to start.'

'Ahhh…we're getting somewhere,' Madeleine said.

'Maybe!' I shrugged. 'Let's see what you have.'

Madeleine leaned forward in her chair and rested her elbows on the table. She placed her thumbs under her chin and interwove her fingers. Her eyes bored into my psyche. 'We believe that you will get a long way by starting with those who want to get at the truth of what happened. First there is Billy Squires. He is interested in the truth because, at the moment, there are people in the world who believe that his memories of events are at best unreliable and at worst affected by chemical stimulants. The French police don't believe his version of events. I don't believe his version of events and Squires himself is very sceptical. He's also having problems on another front. The morning after Peter's death, allowing for an appropriate mourning period, Squires contacted the company lawyers and attempted to have the contract with Mario Pitelli, the distribution agent for Peter's film, declared null and void. He was on a winner and believed that he could get a better distribution deal from one of the majors. Second, there is Mario Pitelli. At present, Pitelli wants to distribute but there is a court injunction against it. His deal to distribute the film wasn't ratified and now the rights are in limbo. Now that the film can boast a gong from Cannes its sales potential has increased on an exponential scale. He still wants to distribute, but each passing week puts the film closer to the discount bin. Very soon, people will be thinking about the next Cannes and Peter's film will only ever be seen by the pimply popcorn set who think that every badly made film has cult status. A film with an instantly dead director is a prime candidate for such an honour. Then, of course, there are us three. We need to know what happened…and how Peter died. You see…there are a few who want the truth and we want you to find it for us. As I said, start with interested parties and see what happens from there. I'd start with Billy Squires. He's in Australia at the moment and we know where to find him.'

I was impressed. 'Okay…Squires it is then. Just a few questions, though. Some things aren't clear to me. First, why pay for the van repairs?'

'Logical,' Kendra said. 'The cops won't tell us who the driver was. By paying the bill, it allows you to investigate the car repairs. That should lead to the driver.'

'One to you,' I said, impressed. 'Second, why tell the insurance company that Peter committed suicide?'

'We didn't…directly.' Felix replied. 'We just started the story to see where it would lead. '

'I understand that that led to them refusing to pay out on the policy. That's one all. Are you sorting out the Squires/Pitelli dealings?'

'We tried…but Squires won't talk to us,' Madeleine said, as she reached into her handbag and took out a pill bottle containing fluoxetine. She slipped one into her mouth. 'He knows that we hate him and that makes him very sceptical of anything that we propose to him,' she said, as she wrapped her tongue around the pill and swallowed. 'You think that he would see common sense and realise that his holding out doesn't help our bank balance.'

I was amazed by Madeleine's oral dexterity as she spoke fluently while juggling a pill but it made no difference to how I viewed the family. After due consideration, I decided that, despite some logic in the collective Mortimer approach, there was only a mild trace of sanity in the prevailing winds. 'You say that you know where Billy Squires is. Let me know and I'll be away.'

'You don't want to discuss your fee then.'

Some sanity at last. 'Frankly I don't know how to set one. I have no idea where this folly will lead.'

Kendra kissed me on the cheek, then stood back and evaluated at me like a newly purchased car. 'Then we will organise for you to have access to Peter's account. He isn't using it and it will give you as much freedom as you need.'

The Land of Purple Sunsets

BILLY Squires is an enigma of the Australian film industry. He is the only man in the country to have ever won a film award without a soul in the industry knowing that he existed. It had once crossed his mind that if he and Mortimer had been homosexual lovers they would have been well known as a couple but, in his experience, the insiders tend to ignore those who fly around the perimeter of the circle. Everyone knew Peter Mortimer, of course, but none seemed to know that his now famous documentary was partially financed and co-directed by a man who believed that filling your head with chemical wonderment was as important as eating a hearty breakfast. Some insiders knew him by sight but even they thought that he and Mortimer were just mates. But then, he wore insignificance like a badge. A first generation immigrant, Billy's parents had brought him from Albania when he was a child. Abject poverty and only a smattering of strine ensured that the other students did not accept him at school. He always put it down to the Australian's love of hating anything that they don't understand but, in reality, it was more aligned to his habit of bathing once a week in his mother's used bath water. This made any potential school chums a little standoffish. As he grew into young adulthood he changed his habits and showered in clean water once a week, but the summers always let him down.

Maybe it was because of his lack of friends, or perhaps because his father owned a theatre in Albania before migrating to Australia to become a school cleaner, that Billy grew up with a passion for cinema. Peter Mortimer knew this, because Billy told him, and when Mortimer had the opportunity to direct his first film, he upgraded his squash partner to a full partnership in his fledgling company and they rode the wave of success together.

***

Madeleine Mortimer knew exactly what Squires was doing so I found myself waiting in the small roadside café for Billy Squires to join me for lunch. It was early September and spring sunshine heated the corrugated tin awning of the Roadkill Roadhouse and baked everything inside. This wasn't an authentic roadhouse but part of the set of Squires' latest attempt at gaining an entree to Venice or Cannes and beyond. However, it appeared that the roadhouse was used as the set canteen and populated by anyone who needed a feed in the desert, halfway between Broken Hill and Silverton.

The menu offered such delicacies as fricassee of Mack emu, left shank of Ford kangaroo and bulldozed wombat with a delicate mint sauce. It sounded trite until I found out that it was real. I ordered a stale bottle of piss and waited for Squires to arrive.

As I watched a black Hummer negotiating an almost vertical slope on its way from the main film site, I hoped that Squires hadn't let money or position change his real self. I needed to talk to the friend of Peter Mortimer, not Mr William Squires, film director.

After ten minutes of discussion I could see that the friend still existed somewhere under the table. 'I guess that I need the whole story, from your perspective,' I said to Squires as soon as we had both ordered the dynamited crayfish bisque with melon dressing and I ordered a glass of Chablis.

'I can tell you what I know, but I'm afraid that the available evidence doesn't back my story. That's the problem. Nothing in my story gels with the official film from the Cannes' people. I've already told the French cops but they acted as if I was loony.'

'I want to hear *your* story. I'll check the rest later.'

'Where do you want me to start?'

'Wherever it suits you, I guess.'

Billy tugged at his beer and thought for a minute. 'I guess that you only need to know about what happened in Cannes. So I won't go into the stuff before that.'

'I may need something, see how we go.'

Billy shrugged and wiped beer froth from his top lip. 'I arrived in Cannes the day before the ceremony and went to the hotel that Pete had booked. Just after I get there, Pete shows up with the chick. She's a knockout so I ask him what gives. He tells me that there's this sheila who provides beautiful women for the film festival. I ask if I can get one and he says that I needed an invitation. I thought that he meant their business card, like a high class brothel or something, but he says that it's not like that and that the chicks are for show only.'

Billy stopped for another swig at his bottle. 'Next thing we're at this meeting with this distributor bloke called Pitelli and Pete's taking a hammering about the deal. We need the deal but what this bloke is offering will send us broke. Then Pitelli makes us a final offer and wants to shake on the deal. Pete's about to agree when this chick of Pete's pipes up and tells Pitelli that she's the financial controller and there's no deal. Well, I coulda killed the bitch. Then she looked across at me and I froze. It was as if her stare was coming from a demon.' Billy stopped again as the waiter dropped the bisque onto the table. The plate bounced and sauce spilled on the plastic chequered tablecloth.

I cleaned it up with a serviette. 'Go on Billy, I'm listening.'

'Well, she tells us to walk out of the meeting and we do. Next thing this Pitelli's bit comes out and invites us back inside for more talks. Then Pete's chick says that it's to be one on one and she sends Pete in alone. Next thing, Pete's coming out smilin' from ear to ear and when he tells me how much we've got I feel like kissin' 'im. He says this Jacque has done it for us. Then I left 'em to it. I figured they'd want to go out and celebrate so I heads downtown to see what I can pick up.'

I could tell that Billy was in his stride but I needed to eat. I suggested that we continue after we had eaten. Then I looked at the dead eyes of a crayfish on my plate and caught its delicate tang. I wasn't that hungry.

'I thought that film set food was always good,' I said, loudly enough to be heard by the cook.

'It is. The canteen's down over the hill. I thought you wanted to eat here.'

'This isn't your canteen?'

'Yeah, it's mine. I love this rough food but none of my crew will eat what Luigi cooks so there's another canteen down the road.'

I was totally confused. 'This is your canteen, but not your canteen?'

'Yeah, that's right. This is the set for the film. Luigi cooks the roadkill and crays that he gets from the dam and that's the food that's seen in the film. I don't like waste so he and I eat what he cooks.'

I had visions of a night spent cuddling a toilet bowl. 'I trust that you're not going to tell me that the stale bottle of piss is really...'

Billy laughed out loud. 'No, of course not...but it's English beer, so it might as well be.'

I now understood the set up. I wished that my knowledge had remained lacking. "Go on with the story, if you will.'

'Sure,' Billy said. 'So when I get into *centre ville* Cannes, I go to this bar and see this chick sitting on a bar stool...'

I cut in with a hand gesture. 'I only need to know about what went on when you, Peter Mortimer and this Jacque were together. I don't need the rest.'

'But this is a good story. The chick was a really good fuck. My mates love the story'

'I'm sure that she was and they do, but I don't need that detail. Jump forward to the awards night.'

Billy seemed a bit miffed, but carried on. This time there was a solemn tone in his voice. 'I guess that it doesn't matter until after the awards.' He said then, after a long pause, continued. 'We went up to the stage to collect the award and were then guided backstage. I was sipping on real champagne and feeling good when this woman approached and started talking to me. She was really pretty but she hardly spoke English at all. I think she was Swedish. Anyway, she takes my hand and gives me this great smile. Then she says *you take me to party?* I guessed that she would have gone with anyone, but she was too good looking to let slip. I told her that I would take her and she guided me to a corner of the room and started sticking her tongue down my throat and feeling me up. I was in love. Anyway, we got hold of Pete and Jacque and told them about a party that I'd heard about. It was supposed to be at the Carlton. Chantelle, that was my girl, wanted to walk along the beachfront so we all walked down that side. The four of us were laughing and giggling and Chantelle was letting me put my hand up her dress. We were having a great time.' Billy stopped and took a swig of beer. 'When we were as close to the Carlton as we could get, Chantelle made a run for the median strip and I followed. Pete and Jacque followed us. They were being daring too. Chantelle and I took off again but this time Pete and Jacque stopped. I looked back but there were a lot of cars passing. I couldn't see them clearly but it looked like they had stopped for a kiss. Then a car went past and the next thing I know Pete's on the road...all smashed up dead.'

Gone was the strine and idioms. This part of the story sounded studied and mindful of events. There was concern in the tone and creasing around Squires' eyes as he rambled. I waited until I was sure that he wasn't going to continue before I spoke. 'So I can fill in some gaps. What happened to the woman after Peter was killed.'

'That's one of the weird things. She just disappeared...literally disappeared. I looked after Peter for a while but there was no sign of Jacque when the ambulance arrived.'

'Do you know where she was staying?'

'I don't know. Peter didn't tell me.'

'I know she's important to resolving this for everyone concerned. Do you have a photo of her? I know that you take a lot of photos.'

'No…nothing. I've been looking as well. That's where the weirdness starts.'

I was intrigued. 'What weirdness?'

Squires looked around at the empty canteen as if someone would overhear. 'It's why the cops think I'm mad.'

Squires paused. I assumed that the director in him wanted dramatic effect. 'They think you're mad, why?'

Squires gulped another draught from his beer. 'I told the cops about Jacque and they got hold of the official Cannes television recordings so that they could identify her. They said she had left the scene of the accident and shouldn't have. She's not on any of the film.' Squires' face was suddenly grey, as if someone had sprayed him with a fine mist of ashes. He started wringing his hands as if he was having trouble coping.

'She's not on film. She's not. She's not there.' He stopped and looked at me. His eyes were alive and terror ridden. 'She's not there.' He repeated.

I had no idea how to help him, but I had to understand what he meant. 'Do you have the broadcast?'

Squires nodded. 'Back at the Hill. I watch it every night.'

'Would you mind if I had a look?' I asked.

'Come round tonight after the pub. You can watch it then.'

In the distance I could hear the faint sound of a horn blaring. Squires' colour returned and he stood from his chair. 'Back to work.' He said, softly. 'If you've nothing else to do, hang around. One of the girls will look after you.'

He pointed toward the Hummer. There were two women standing beside the open door. One was resplendent from head to toe in black leather. Her hair was black and cut into a pageboy and, as I neared the vehicle, I saw that her eye makeup and lipstick were also black. The other woman was at the other end of the spectrum. She wore a short white cotton dress and held a white parasol above long blond hair. Her legs were albino and her face seemed to be dusted in white blush. They held the door open and I climbed into the back of the most fundamentally useless street vehicle that I had ever seen. I looked into the rear view mirror and caught the eyes of the driver. There was danger and malevolence etched into the stare and I felt like the unwelcome stranger in an English village novel. I looked at the blue singlet and the tattoo on the left shoulder.

'This is Jessica and Jessica.' Squires said, as he settled into his seat. 'The driver is Blossom.'

'Afternoon ladies.' I said. There seemed no point in asking which Jessica was which, but it was good to see that Squires had avoided the pitfall of letting minuscule fame go to his head.

The Hummer roared and we climbed over the steep hill. I wondered how far we would have to travel but then we stopped, just over the crest. I could have walked there faster than the time it had taken to get into the monster and drive.

***

Half an hour later I was reclining in a cane chaise longue under a huge umbrella, with the letters BHC scrawled across its sky blue surface in bright yellow lettering. What I had initially thought to be a film turned out to be an advertisement for a Japanese chicken shop. I was mesmerised by the process but had no idea what the ad was about. All I could see was a small Japanese man, resplendent in a stark white singlet and white shirt cooking a chicken over a small round gas fired barbecue plate. He would cook the chicken and be splattered with chicken fat and scream something at the camera. Then he would change into another set of brilliant whites and repeat the process. Apparently this was the second part of the ad.

'Mind if I join you?'

I shaded my eyes to see Blossom standing with the sun at her back. 'No, not at all. Take a seat.' I pointed to another chaise that was covered by the same enormous umbrella.

Blossom settled onto the lounge and reclined against its back support. I saw that she had breasts that would make a melon envious and was surprised to see they didn't appear to need support and yet didn't look enhanced. I also noticed that her auburn hair shone like gold and bounced loosely. Her nose was small with a slight tilt and her lips were full but, again, not enhanced. She wore the blue singlet of a truckie and tight denim cut-offs. She had hiking boots on her feet. I noticed that it was a knife through a heart tattooed on her shoulder. She said nothing but looked at the film making process with a look of slight disdain curling her top lip.

After having asked to join me, I waited for her to speak but she just looked ahead as if she found the process as boring as bat shit. I felt a little uncomfortable in her company and was still unnerved by the look that she had given me in the meat wagon.

'Been with Billy long? I asked, out of desperation for something to say.

'No.'

'You like working with him?'

'No.'

This would be a long afternoon. I leaned over and took a beer from the esky that Squires had laid on for me. 'Want a beer?' I asked.

'No.'

It was a bit like baseball. I had three strikes and struck out. I called it a day and pulled the top from the can.

Blossom put her hand over mine and stopped me getting the can to my lips. Shit! I thought. She doesn't want to talk and now she doesn't want me to have a drink. I threw her my best quizzical stare.

'I wouldn't mind a bourbon and coke.' Blossom said. I noticed an American twang.

I looked toward the canteen. Did she expect me to run and get her one?

'They don't have my brand here. They have it at the Silverton pub though…and the beer's on tap. Billy never finishes until seven in the evening. You'll be fried and drunk by then if you stay here.'

I could see the logic. 'Would you like a bourbon and coke, ma'am? We have a fine selection at the hotel down the road. My car is just over the hill.'

'I can take the SUV.' She said.

'Nah, it's a woman's car. Last one I saw had a woman driver.'

She smiled at my inane comment. For some reason I expected her teeth to match the tatts but they were white and straight.

'How'd you get involved with Billy? I asked as I drove along the narrow bitumen road toward Silverton.

'Mr Squires hired the SUV. I came with it. It's a promotion thing that my boss wanted to do. You hire the Hummer for a week or more and get a driver. I'm it.'

'Can't be cheap.'

'I'm told that the Japs have a good budget for the advert. Mr Squires is helping them spend it.'

'How long are you here for?'

'Five days. That's the length for this shoot. Then there is the editing, but he only has the SUV for five days. Apparently the first part of the ad is already in the can. I'm told that was done in Japan.'

'That would have been stuffing chickens with whale meat then?'

'No, lead balloons. Bit like that attempt at a joke.'

'My hit ratio's a bit low at the moment,' I quipped.

'It's okay. Actually the whole thing is a bit of a joke really. Do you know what BHC stands for?'

'No.' It was my turn for the short answer.

'How about Battery House Chickens,' Blossom said.

'Ohhh… a little bizarre for my taste.'

'The ad's worse. Apparently the road kill and the guy barbecuing show that you don't know what you're getting from free range or farmed chickens. The other part of the ad is showing the cleanliness, orderliness and consistency of the chicken from a BHC shop.'

I smiled and shook my head as I manoeuvred through the dry creek bed on the eastern side of Silverton, trying to avoid an oncoming motorhome. I succeeded but not without my seeing the first chink in Blossom's armour. She was frightened of dying in a car crash. I took the turn to the left past four tourist mounted camels and an angry kelpie cross, and pulled up to the Silverton Hotel, which stood in the blazing sun, in its red soil basin, shaded by a single tree.

'We're here,' I said as I left the car.

'Did you even see that trailer?' Blossom screamed, acid following the spit from her mouth.

I took the Blossom approach. 'No.'

We entered the small bar just as the last word was spoken. It was crowded with locals and tourists and there wasn't an eye in the place that didn't notice Blossom's singlet as she strode to the bar. I found that she didn't even need to order. There were four glasses of her favourite tipple already lined up at the bar's edge. She had obviously been in before. I made my way to the end of the bar and stood like a stale piece of toast waiting for service. The barman smiled my way and nodded to the beer taps. I yelled my preference over the sound that had sprung up again, after everyone copped an eyeful, and waited patiently for service.

'Nice set,' the barman quipped.

'She's been here before then.'

'Third day this week. Always around the same time. Usually drives that horrible yank thing. Don't know you though. You new on the site?'

'Just passing through really. I have some business with Billy Squires. Scott Mawson's the name.'

'Like me. I'm doing the same thing. Bond...James Bond.'

We shook hands as I noticed that Blossom's breasts were, literally, leaning on the bar. This was no shrinking violet. Her actions had to be good for at least a few more rounds. No wonder she accepted a lift. 'Blossom usually get carried out at night?'

'Not at all. She just likes to flirt and have a good time. The drinks only have cola. The blokes think that I'm giving her bourbon cheap so that she'll come back, but they're only paying for the cola. Even the cola's hers. She brought me in a case of it for her use. Unsweetened apparently.'

I was watching a young girl trying to mount a camel, whilst staying at great distance from it, when Blossom appeared in the doorway. She carried a glass of cola in her hand. I held it to my nose. The barman had lied.

'I always finish with the real thing.' Blossom said. She looked at her watch. It was just past six thirty. 'We better go back. Mr Squires will be finishing soon.'

I noticed the hangdog expressions on the men's faces as Blossom followed me through the side gate of the hotel. I felt as if I had just stolen their toy.

I jumped in the driver's seat of the car and waited. Blossom walked to the passenger's door and opened it. She seemed to hesitate. From my sitting position I could only see her from waist to shoulder. I noticed that the twins were riding high and I couldn't see her arms. In the rear view mirror I could see three battered Akubras waving to her from the veranda. Other heads appeared through windows. Suddenly there was a flash of blue and a singlet hit me in the face.

'What the heck,' Blossom said as she finally entered the car.

I handed the singlet across to her.

'It doesn't matter. I won't be back. It gets a bit boring after a couple of days. They're always the same guys.'

I could hardly wipe the smirk from my face. A legend had just been created. If she went back it would be spoilt. 'They'll be up for a week.'

'Two minutes, maybe. Why are you here?'

'What?' I needed time to think. The tone of Blossom's voice threw me.

'I was wondering what you're doing here. You don't fit.'

I glanced across at her breasts, which she had made no attempt to hide. 'Neither do they.'

'Word is that you're on a flight of fantasy.'

'Whose word would that be?' I asked.

Blossom ignored the question. She slipped the singlet back on and fastened her seat belt. 'I don't eat with the others at night. Would you care to join me?'

I looked across at her. 'I have work to do.'

'He won't let you see the broadcast until after he has his dinner and plays for a while with his toys. If you recall he said, "come round tonight after the pub. You can watch it then." That's what he meant. He eats, fucks and drinks…in that order. You won't see what you want until around eleven.'

I dodged a ute that was travelling west with the sun in the driver's eyes and taking up the centre of the road. Blossom was holding on. 'How do you know that?'

'What he does every night, you mean?'

'Yes.'

'He watches the broadcast every night. He remembers something that didn't happen. He's trying to work it out. It'll drive him mad eventually. He never goes to sleep until after he watches the replay.'

'What do you care?' I asked, as I pulled into the Road-kill Roadhouse.

'I don't. I just want company for dinner and you will be by yourself as well.'

'Where do you eat?'

'There's a decent restaurant on the hill in the middle of town. I'll be there at eight thirty.'

'We'll see,' I said, as Blossom opened the car door and got out. She waved as she started to walk over the hill.

***

I was both piqued and perplexed when Billy Squires confirmed what Blossom had said he would do. Reluctantly I agreed to meet him at his motel at eleven. At around eight thirty-five, I found myself walking through the door of a restaurant feeling like a boy who had taken on a task and failed. I could have avoided the embarrassment but figured that my abashment would only be avoided until the following morning when Blossom picked up Squires in the Hummer and asked him a few questions. Besides, a quick discussion with my friendly motel owner indicated that Blossom ate at the best place in town. The restaurant was busy so I looked around for the brassiest tart in the place but found that no one present fit the description that ran through my mind. In fact, the only spare place in the restaurant was a single seat opposite a woman who was, at that moment, reading the menu. The woman's hair was a similar colour to Blossoms but the style was more refined. She wore a red and white patterned sleeveless dress, which looked to be below knee length. I continued the journey to see red shoes with conservative three-inch heels.

'May help you sir?' came a voice from behind me.

I turned to see a man in a plaid shirt and yellow bow tie hovering just inside the door. 'No, thanks, I was looking for someone who I understood would be here. I was mistaken. I'm sorry.'

'May I have the person's name sir? Maybe there is a later booking.'

'It's okay. I'll catch 'em later.' I could never have said that someone named Blossom should be here.

I was returning to my car when I heard the restaurant door open behind me. I turned to see the woman with the menu standing at the door.

'I told you he'd do the minstrels first.'

I closed my eye and tried to scan the manuals of my mind. She was standing in front but the image wouldn't come. I needed my laptop like a junkie needs a fix. I was in Quenna Knight land again. I was lost with too little information. I opened my eyes, smiled and shook my head in minute horizontal movements. 'Amazing. Truly amazing.' I looked at Blossom's dress. It was perfect. A red pattern appeared to ride from the bottom of the dress like flames and peak just above the waist. It flared at the hips in perfect proportion. A picture was coming to mind. Slowly developing like an image through fog. 'You look lovely. If you don't mind me saying.'

'I don't mind. Are you going to join me?'

I felt like a puppy again. 'That's why I'm here.' I followed her inside and watched her sway. Still brassy but far more refined. 'The tattoo?' I asked as I sat on a chair near the window.

'Transfer. Just part of the image. He rejected your advance, huh?'

'I was surprised... because I think what he wants to show me is important to the both of us, but I guess he has other priorities.'

'I guess for what it's costing him he wants to make sure that nothing goes to waste.'

'You mean the Jessica's?'

'Of course. They're lesbian hookers from Darlinghurst. They've been doing a double act for a couple of years. It's costing him four grand a night to feel that someone likes him.'

'I thought that a little fame was helping him.'

'Maybe...but not out here. Here you pack your own lunch.'

I decided to change tack. 'What about you. What did you do before last week?'

Blossom's eyes blinked. I had an image of her changing internal hard drives. She picked up her menu and began to read it again. She was playing for time. Maybe her imagination was faltering.

She set the menu down as the yellow bow tie approached. 'You ready to order?' She asked.

I hadn't looked at the menu. 'I'll have whatever you're having. Red or white.'

'Red.'

I picked up the wine list and read from the top. I settled on a good Shiraz from the Barossa.

I waited until yellow tie had the food order then added the wine. I noticed that Blossom had a gin and tonic so I requested a beer for starters. I was still waiting for the answer to my question.

'I'm still wondering what you did before last week,' I said.

I felt two knees touch mine and noticed an adjustment at the top of a dress. 'Maybe I was waiting for you to come along.'

'Then maybe you weren't,' I said, pulling my knees in.

The waiter delivered my beer to the table, breaking the moment.

'You first,' Blossom said, now leaning forward and resting her elbows on the table. She moved her chin to sit on her intertwined fingers. 'You tell me why you're here visiting Billy Squires.' The words were spoken in a whisper that sounded like a shouted command.

'Who wants to know?' I asked.

Blossom spired her fingers and rested her chin on her thumbs. 'Let's just say an interested party…with more than a modicum of authority.' The last phrase sounded like the precursor to a threat.

I sipped my beer then looked into the glass as if examining the colour. I needed time to think. I was on the back foot at the moment with no forward momentum. 'It's no big deal. I want to find out what happened to Peter Mortimer. I'm working for his family. Squires was there when Peter died.' Maybe the truth would out.

'You sure that's all.'

'As sure as your name isn't Blossom.'

'Counters the image. I like it. You have no other interest in Squires?'

The waiter smiled as he placed two plates of smoked salmon rolls with caper dressing on the table. He left with a *bon appétit*.

I was ravenous so I dived straight into the food without savouring the delicacy of its flavours. Blossom looked aghast as she delicately cut the food and stabbed a small morsel with her fork. 'You should stick with pizzas,' she said. 'You eat like a pig.'

'You should see me at home.'

Blossom scowled.

That was all that was said until both entrée plates were left with only a small smudge of sauce attesting that they had been used. We remained sitting in silence until we were half way through the seasoned rack of lamb with tomato coulis, steamed asparagus and potato. This time I was only keeping pace with Blossom and utilising my cutlery in a civilised manner. The waiter had poured the wine and I was applauding myself for my choice.

'What did you do before last week? I repeated to break the silence.

'Same as this week and next week.'

'That's no answer.'

'It's all you're going to get tonight. Maybe in the morning.'

'A woman of mystery, huh. But I guess that we've established that you aren't a truck driver.'

'It's an SUV actually.'

'It's another thing that tells the world that the States are out of step.'

'You guys are right up our ass. You don't like us huh?'

'As a people, I think you're wonderful. But you have a government with a foreign policy that's shitful.'

'I really don't care.'

I stopped talking and returned to my food. If Blossom was what I thought, she would have no interest in politics. I'd flown the flag looking for a nil reaction. What I received in return was a definite reaction. *I really don't care* was a means to terminate the conversation, not a statement of fact. I was beginning to feel that I was letting fantasy and reality percolate in my head to become indistinct. I remembered what she had said earlier. *Word is that you're on a flight of fantasy.* I had wondered what she meant. Maybe I was wasting my time and other people's money but I had to take the train to the end of the line. I looked across the table and noticed that Blossom was likewise somewhere in space. 'Did you order dessert?' I asked.

'Of course. Poached pears with cinnamon cream. I've had it here before. Very nice.'

I poured the last of the wine into Blossom's glass and tilted it toward her. 'Another?'

She shook her head. 'Coffee will be fine.'

I've always found that, in the desert, the stars seem more distant. It's probably because they are better defined. On this September night they appeared as a million distant lights. I noticed that one was blinking as it moved slowly toward the horizon.

There was a stiff breeze as we left the restaurant and a slight chill in the air. It stung my senses as I walked with Blossom toward her monster. I looked at my watch. 'Billy should have unloaded by now.'

Blossom smiled. 'The minstrels will be as fresh as daisies. He has no stamina.'

'You seem to know a lot.'

'They're bored. They talk about anything to fill in time.'

'That why you're here?'

'I'll see you in the morning.' With that, she kissed my cheek and clambered into her cabin. I noticed that the high heels were kicked off. 'Have a good night.'

***

Billy Squires opened the door to his motel room seconds after the knock. He ushered me inside and directed me to one of two chairs set up in front of a laptop. Jessica squared sat at the head of the bed, both naked and smiling. The laptop was fired up and waiting.

'There's only a few shots of us. One is in our seats just before the announcement. There is another of Peter walking along the red carpet. Just watch them.' He left me near the laptop and went to the bed. One Jessica was on his left and the other on his right. He put his arms around both of them and they snuggled into his sides. I felt like a spare prick at a wedding. I clicked the mouse and watched the screen.

In the first sequence, Peter Mortimer and Billy Squires sat talking to each other in their seats in the theatre. I noted the time line on the screen. There was a vacant seat beside them. In the second shot, five minutes on, they were sitting with a look of childish anticipation on their faces. On the seat beside Mortimer was the white rose that Kendra had pointed out. The scene changed and Mortimer was walking along the red carpet. He seemed to be walking a little strangely, as if he was about to flick a flat stone across a still pond. I noticed that he wore a small white rose in his lapel. It seemed to set off the hired tux. There was another shot of Mortimer on the carpet from behind. Nothing of interest. The scene finished. There was nothing of interest: no mystery woman and nothing to fill in any of the puzzle.

I turned around to ask Billy what was going on. He had the look of a man whose world had collapsed. He was foetal and shaking like a leaf in a gale and the Jessica's were hugging him. I didn't understand.

'What is it Billy?' I asked.

He began to cry. 'She's not there. She's not there.' He stuck his thumb in his mouth.

I saw that black Jessica was looking at me. 'What gives?' I asked.

'He says that there was a woman on the seat beside them and that his mate walked a woman down the red carpet.'

I turned back to the screen and ran the scene again. Mortimer seemed to be mincing down the red carpet but nothing else struck me. I turned around again. White Jessica was masturbating Squires furiously with her hand.

'We have to relax him. This is the best way. It's like this every night. He watches that video and then breaks down.'

An idea struck. 'I'll be back in a minute. Keep him calm.'

I rushed from the room and across the gravelled garden bed to my room. I picked up my flash drive and ran back to Squires' room. White Jessica had finished her task. Squires looked to be on the verge of sleep. I sat down at the laptop and inserted my drive. A minute later I had the information copied across.

'He going to be okay?' I asked of no one in particular.

'We'll get him to sleep. You get out of here and we'll look after him.'

I nodded and left.

An hour and what seemed like a thousand replays later I was still confused. What was it about the film that shook Squires to his foundations? I understood what he was saying but I was like the French cops, I didn't believe him. There was no evidence. Had the shots been doctored? Not possible for an organisation like Cannes. Locally retouched maybe? Possible, but Squires would have access to any number of tapes. If it were done locally, there would have to be another source somewhere. I was convinced that Squires saw something, but where was the missing woman?

I decide to look at the detail. I went to the first sequence of Mortimer and Squires on their seats, talking. Nothing. I went to the next. I decided to look at the rose on the seat. I paused the shot and zoomed in. A beautiful rose, but a rose none the less. I noticed a black spot on one of the petals. I went to the shots of Mortimer on the runway. This was where I expected to find something. The way that Mortimer walked, with his elbow against his hip and his arm out, just seemed odd. I looked at the front view and examined the rose in his lapel. Close inspection showed a black spot on a petal, but the view was blurred by too close an image. I looked at the rear view. Nothing. I paused the frame and blinked. I wound back and tried the run through again. I looked at the edge of the frame instead of the central character. It was there, I was sure that I saw it. I ran it through again. *Billy you aren't mad*, I whispered to myself. I ran it through again. There on a wall behind the crowd, when the shadow of Mortimer's head flashed past, a split second later it repeated.

I ran outside to go to Squires room but found that it was in darkness. Who to tell? Suddenly it dawned. Who really cared? It was now obvious that someone did.

***

I woke the next morning to my breakfast being manipulated through a slot in the wall of my motel room. My stomach rumbled a little at the thought of bacon and eggs but that's the joy of ordering twelve hours in advance. The bacon was fine but the egg was a waste of a life. I showered and dressed. Today it would be a run out to BHC heaven and then a flight to Sydney.

When I opened the door to take the luggage to the car, I was not surprised to find the motel yard almost deserted. I was surprised, however, to see the two men walking in and out of Squires room carrying boxes. Boxes I hadn't noticed when I was in there last night. Something was wrong with the scene. The men were wearing jeans and tee shirts under vests with POLICE emblazoned across the back. This wasn't an unpaid parking fine.

I jumped into the car and headed for the film set. I didn't know why, except to tell Squires that I had found something. I headed out of town and past a local cop car, which was parked beside the road. I looked over my shoulder to see if he was following me. He didn't. I arrived at the Roadkill Roadhouse to find four cars that I didn't recognise. The Hummer was atop the incline. I stepped from my car and headed up the hill.

'Where you going mate?' asked a voice from behind.

I stopped and turned around. It was another cop in a blue vest. 'I'm looking for Billy Squires.'

'You are a friend of his?'

'Business acquaintance.'

The man stepped from behind one of the cars and walked toward me. He held a gun in his hand. I blinked and looked again. He still had a gun in his hand. 'Being a business acquaintance of Squires may not be a healthy thing to be. Come with me.'

I had survived for more than thirty years without someone finding the need to point a gun at me. I was glad of the fact. The man walking up the hill behind me wasn't exactly pointing a gun at me but a feeling of immense tension pierced my soul like a sword swallower needing to cough during his act. I reached the top of the hill to see buzzards picking at the set. All of the cast and crew were being held to one side whilst a dozen or more police rifled through everything that stood still. I looked around to see whether Blossom had been caught up in the dragnet. There was no sign of her.

I found out why when the cop behind me half pushed me through the canteen door. Blossom was inside. For some reason, I wasn't surprised that she had taken on yet another mode of dress. Now she wore faded denim jeans and a loose blue shirt over her singlet and bra. She also wore a vest. A mid blue one with POLICE inscribed across the back.

'Agent Aliput, I found this guy wondering about. Says he's a business acquaintance of Squires.'

'Thanks Joe,' Blossom said. 'That'll be all. I know Mr Mawson. I can vouch for him.'

'Okay,' the cop said as he disappeared through the doorway.

'Like a coffee?' Blossom asked, as she poured herself a mug of coffee from a dripolator.'

'No thanks. Bit early to start my heart yet.'

She walked to a table and sat on its edge. 'Did you get what you wanted last night?'

I leaned on the table beside her. 'Bit of good, bit of bad. Pretty run of the mill really. What's going on here?'

'Police matter I'm afraid. Seems Mr Squires has two professions. One of them is illegal.'

'Oh.'

'Yes … oh … did you know?'

'You going to tell me what it's about.'

'You're not involved and you don't need to know. Let's leave it at that.'

I could see that she was all business and I had no reason to be there. 'I guess that it's okay with you if I go then.'

'I would prefer it in fact. Look after yourself Scott.'

'I'll try Marilyn but I can't guarantee anything.' I stood upright and walked to the door. I counted as I went. If I was right, I wouldn't make it to the door. I was still counting when I traversed the hill. The distance was a bit further but it was an easier walk along the road between the two film sets. I stopped counting when I made it to my car. My assumption was another flight of fantasy.

The Dealer of Kent

TODAY there are other terms used, but to many of the old school Mario Pitelli is the epitome of an old style spiv. Officially he makes his money by distributing films to the cinema and television markets. He is seen to have a good track record in this field, having gained the European distribution rights for more than a dozen award winning films. This is more commendable when it is considered that the end of the market in which he deals is the "arty" end where profits are minimal unless the marketing is brilliant. It is said that Pitelli's marketing team is up to the task and he now attracts offers from most of the small independent filmmakers involved in film in the western world. This would be good for his business except for the fact that the time involved in this pursuit detracts from his time available to pursue his real interest. That being the buying and selling of goods of dubious provenance. For this purpose, Pitelli owns three art galleries in England, two vehicle sales yards in the Czech Republic and a brocante in France. It is also associated with this purpose that Pitelli surrounds himself with a human shield. Not in the way that you would imagine but with a series of individuals who stand between the person desirous of meeting Pitelli and the man himself. Their function is to ensure that Pitelli speaks to no one who can harm him in any way.

My first encounter with the shield came when I arrived for my appointment so see Pitelli in his suite of offices in an abandoned farmhouse outside of Ashford, Kent. I had arrived fifteen minutes before the appointed time, but stood at the gate like an uncomprehending moron reading and rereading the instructions. The place looked deserted. The surrounding hedge looked as if it hadn't been shaped in years and the locked gate rode on rusty hinges. I had taken the left turn at the Tudor gates, which look as if they once fed Eastwell Manor, and found my way into the maze of small lanes and hedgerows and had finally found the gate with the hand painted sign. Until then everything seemed okay. Now I was lost. I looked back along the lane to see that my car was almost out of sight within its small lay-by. I was beginning to panic. It had taken three weeks to get an appointment and I wanted no reason, like my non-arrival, for Pitelli to postpone.

I climbed over the gate and trudged through ankle deep grass until I reached the farmhouse. Once there, I looked through a translucent window. I stood back then looked again. I shook my head in disbelief. The outer walls and roof of the farmhouse were a façade. Inside was a square, rendered brick building with a flat roof. It was modern and functional and had been fitted into the old farmhouse framework. I noticed someone sitting at a desk, typing. I knocked on the window to get her attention. She looked up and smiled before nodding toward a door.

'Mr Mawson?' The woman asked, in what foreigners believe is an English upper crust accent.

'Yes.'

'Please come in. I'm Tuesday, did you have any trouble finding us?'

'Not really, but I stood at the gate for ages, trying to convince myself that I'm in the right place. What gives?'

'Mr Pitelli likes the abandoned look.'

'He's been very successful,' I quipped. 'Are you the only one here?'

Tuesday pointed toward another door. 'No, they're all here except Mr McWhirter. He's delivering a new Rolls Royce to Lord Wankdorf of Sleasby.

I couldn't understand the connection between film distribution and vehicle delivery. 'Delivering a car?'

'Yes. He wanted a silver grey. We took a month to find it for him. Did you want to see Mr McWhirter?'

'No. Just Mr Pitelli.'

'Good. I'll get Julian Jones for you then.'

'Who's he?'

'He's our financial controller. Have a seat.'

Five minutes later, I was ushered into Jones' office. The first thing I noticed was that it had no window. Instead, half of one wall was covered by a huge flat screen complete with moving images of cattle in a field. Jones smiled as I entered the room. I smiled back but that was because I was trying to hold back a smirk. Jones was a caricature. He was too thin to exist. Sitting, he was as tall as me standing. He wore a bright red cotton shirt with a yellow tie. His black and blond streaked hair was slicked straight back to emphasise his long thin nose and wisps of blond hair curled around the edges of his mouth in an unformed moustache. His most prominent feature, however, was the fact that he had no depth. I had never seen a man so painfully thin. He looked to be around thirty, with the body of an emaciated man of seventy. He stood and bowed formally, as I entered his office.

'Mr Mawson, I believe. I understand that you want us to finance your next film. Is that right?'

There was no invitation to sit, so I stood looking Jones directly in the eyes. 'No. I want to talk to Mario Pitelli about his deal with Peter Mortimer.'

'You're representing Mr Mortimer. I understood that the financial matters concerning that film have already been expedited. Why do you wish to raise them again?'

I looked around. There was no seat in the office other than the one Jones occupied. I leaned stiff armed on Jones' desk before answering.

'I don't as such, I'm researching the events leading to Peter Mortimer's untimely death.'

Jones seemed to think for a moment. 'I think that I have it now. You don't need finance but you're looking for us to distribute a film that you're doing about the death of Peter Mortimer.'

My head was starting to ache. I realised where this was heading but needed to stay in the game. If I faltered I would miss seeing Pitelli. 'It has nothing to do with any film, other than Mortimer's. I just have a few questions for Mr Pitelli.'

'Oh, I see. Just some general questions to make sure that you get the ground rules sorted out. Okay fire away?'

The opening was too good to miss. 'When you were negotiating your contract with Peter Mortimer was there a woman present?'

Jones thought for a moment. 'Yes, there was. bethany sat in. I'm sure of it.'

The name Bethany meant nothing to me. 'Any other woman?'

'You will need to ask bethany. I'll see if she's available.'

'Where does she fit in?' I asked. I was becoming annoyed but tried not to show it.

'She's the company lawyer,' Jones said, as he picked up the phone.

I waited while he carried on a lengthy conversation with someone on the phone. I assumed that it was Bethany but the call seemed to delve into matters other than checking if she was free to see me. He hung up and stared at me. 'bethany says that we have no contract documents for you to sign. But she is free, if you want to walk down to the next office.'

I walked to the next office and knocked. There was a mumbled cry from within that seemed to say *come in*. I entered the office but there was no one there. Like Jones' office, it had no windows and her screen was showing water filtering along a babbling brook, complete with sound. It was somehow soothing. I noticed a door half open at the opposite end of the room. I heard a muffled cry coming from behind the door. It sounded like someone in pain. I took two steps toward the door, then stopped dead in my tracks, realising that it wasn't the sound of pain that I had heard. I knocked softly on the door. A woman opened the door, smiled and told me that she would be finished in a minute. She then closed the door, returned to her task and seemed to lose interest in the fact that I was there.

I looked around for a chair but, like Jones' office, there wasn't one available. I returned to the corridor outside and grabbed a cane and chrome office chair. I sat it opposite Bethany's desk and waited.

Bethany re-entered her office about ninety seconds after her guttural growl had turned to a high pitched squeal. She walked to her desk and sat down on her chair. 'You're Mr...?

'Mawson, Scott Mawson.'

'You're from...?'

'SE and B. I'm an investigator looking into the death of Peter Mortimer.'

'Oh, I see. I understood that you wanted to see the proforma of our standard contract for film distribution rights. What you really want seems quite different.'

'Maybe. Look...I made an appointment to see Mario Pitelli. I just need to ask him some questions.' This had the potential to head down the Jones path.

'I'm sorry. Mr Pitelli doesn't see anyone unless all legal ramifications have been analysed. I should have introduced myself. I'm bethany, Mr Pitelli's legal advisor.'

'I'm pleased to meet you Bethany, but I don't see any legal implications,' I said, as I offered her my hand.

She stood up and leaned forward to shake my hand. I noticed that she was not wearing anything to support breasts that were screaming out for assistance. She sat down again and I noticed that she seemed to want to say something but wasn't sure of her ground. Her face was becoming flushed and she was avoiding eye contact.

'What legal matters are there for us to discuss?' I asked.

'None I don't think. It's just that...' She left the sentence hanging.

'What is it?' I asked.

'Look, I know it's trivial and of no importance to anyone except me, but I have a problem with the way you pronounced my name.'

This was absurd. Unless one has a *th* issue, it isn't easy to mispronounce Bethany. 'How's that?'

'I'm afraid that you pronounced it with a capital B. My name has a small b. I'm sure that Julian Jones would have pronounced it for you. He always gets it right.'

Fuck. 'Yes I'm sure that he does. I'm afraid that I failed to pick up the nuance. Could you just pronounce it for me, so that I don't make the same mistake again?' I asked. I could not believe that I was pandering to the situation.

'It's easy. The b is almost silent. bethany. bethany.'

'Yes, I understand now,' I said, determined never to utter the word again, in her presence. 'It sounds lovely. Preferable, really. Did it ever have a capital?'

'Yes, my parents spelled it with a capital but when I joined the lifestyle my master insisted that I change it…to show my subservience.'

'Lifestyle?'

'Yes…I'm in the BDSM lifestyle. I'm a sub.'

'Oh, I see,' I said. This conversation was heading to places where I had no intention of going. 'I was wondering if you had any questions that might allow us to move on. I've come a long way to see Mario Pitelli and I would like to get the vetting over with.'

Bethany sat back on her chair and activated her computer monitor. 'You're employed by Kendra John Mortimer.'

How could she know that? I hadn't told anyone. 'Yes. She just wants to know what happened.'

'That's understandable. I felt the same way when my master died.'

I purposefully failed to comment. 'I think that Mr Pittelli can help me solve one riddle. You see, Peter was with a woman during his negotiations with your boss. I just want to find her.'

Bethany looked back to her screen. 'A woman called Jacqueline du Pre, is that right?'

'Yes, that's the name I was given.' I had no inkling as to her source.

'I was with Mario on that night. I don't recall any woman. But then, we were all pretty high. Jerome Balltacks had just had a replacement eye fitted and we were celebrating.'

I felt that I had to keep pushing. 'I'm sure Mr Pitelli would remember.'

'Yes, I'm sure that he would. Would you like me to see if he's in?'

Finally. I must have passed the screening test. 'Yes, thank you.'

Bethany picked up her phone and dialled. After a few seconds, the phone answered. She hung up and looked across at me. 'Mr Pitelli is out at the moment. He will be back on Thursday.'

'Today is Tuesday. Our appointment is for today,' I spat. I was losing it. I was prepared to play while I thought that I would eventually get to Pitelli, but now I was at the end of my tether.

'I will see what I can do,' Bethany said. She left the office and shut the door.

I watched the water burble over the rocks. The sound was, now, annoying. I had a vision of someone else being primed to annoy me. Maybe it would be tomorrow's secretary. What would her name be? Wednesday. I decided to call it quits. Kendra would be disappointed in me but this was a cul de sac. I opened the door and walked along the short corridor to the reception desk. Tuesday was elsewhere. I stepped outside the shell to the outer frame of the building. Once outside I noticed that there was a

pathway of small stones leading to a disused shed at the
edge of the property. I hadn't noticed it when I arrived.
The stones were polished with wear. I followed the path to
the shed and smiled. It was similar to the farmhouse, in
that it was the dilapidated outer shell for a modern vehicle
garage. I noticed that there were four cars inside. One for
Tuesday, Jones, Bethany whatever, and another. I thought
that *another* probably drove the green Aston Martin DB9. I
opened the door to the garage and walked inside. The
Aston Martin was unlocked. I settled into the maroon
leather of the passenger's seat and waited.

***

I heard the garage door open and then watched as the
main doors started tilting. Half of the front face of the old
shed seemed to be rising. I spotted Bethany, and a man I
hadn't met, in the side mirror. The man fitted the description that I had. He would have reached Jones' waist. He
was handsome, in an oiled up way, with slicked black hair
and long sideburns. He wore a black silk shirt and matching tie under a grey knee length coat. I watched as he
chatted with small b. His teeth were straight and clean and
he had a smile that would have been cute on a woman but
seemed a little feminine on him. I would have liked to get a
glimpse at his eyes but they were shaded by wraparound
sunglasses. He possessed the aura of a theatrical pimp.

He opened the car door and was two thirds of the way
to his seat when he first glimpsed me. He jumped back in
fright and slammed the door. I felt like a snake at a kids'
birthday party.

I waited.

The door opened again. this time a head popped into view. The cute smile was replaced by a snarl.

'Who the fuck are you, sport?' reverberated around the car's cabin. It sounded like bad cockney in a rainy weekend restaurant.

I deliberately looked at my watch. 'I'm your eleven o'clock. It's now twelve thirty. But I'm a patient man.'

'Who let you in?' he demanded.

'The door was open.'

'Look, whoever you are, I ain't got time for this. I've got a lunch date in Faversham.'

'Good,' I said. 'You can drop me off. We'll talk on the way.'

He dropped into his seat and started the car. 'Okay Mawson, what d'you want?'

'Simple really. I'm trying to track down the woman who was with Peter Mortimer on the night he died. I believe that she was also at his meeting with you, the previous evening. I just want a description and anything you know about her.'

'That all? I heard you wanted me to finance your next picture for ya.'

'I think that I've had enough of that for one day. Can you help me?'

Pitelli smiled as we drove from the garage and past my car. How would I get back to it? I notice a shrewd intelligence in his eyes, which seemed to dance with the sunlight. 'I felt sorry for Mortimer. Just when he hit the spotlight. What a way to go. But I don't know if I can help. I don't remember seeing him with a woman.'

'Mr Pitelli. That's the wrong answer. Billy Squires, his business partner, swears that Mortimer was with a woman at your meeting. I suppose that you'll tell me that you don't know Squires either.'

Pitelli accelerated toward the rear of a pantechnicon. I braced and waited. 'Of course I know bloody Squires. He tried to rip me off after Morty died. Said he hadn't signed the agreement for fuck's sake. He probably doesn't remember the facts. Both him and Morty were so high at the meeting that I had to back off. He would have given me the picture for free if I'd wanted it. Squires was just a pain.'

I ignored the comments. 'I understand that you wouldn't forget this woman. Supposedly beautiful and intelligent.'

'Not ringin' a bell,' Pitelli answered. 'And I'm a man who notices these things.'

Stonewalling or lying, it didn't matter. Pitelli was as useful as a singlet in a snowstorm. I had wasted a day. I looked across at him. 'Thanks. That's all I need. Just drop me off ...anywhere.'

Pitelli pulled to a kerb and unlocked the door. I climbed from the car and closed the door. The passenger's side window opened. I looked in.

'What do you do now?' Pitelli asked.

'I don't know. I keep searching I guess. There are other avenues to try, but I'm getting a bit jaded.'

'I wouldn't give up just yet. It's never over till the fat lady sings,' Pitelli said. He wound the window up and sped into the traffic.

I silently thanked Pitelli for his help. I was three miles from my car.

Cobra Lilies in Cannes

THE roof of the small portico was encrusted with the guano of a million pigeons. Light filtered through gaps in the plaster walls and the reception area reeked of curried dog merde. *A hotel for the rich and famous* I thought, as I signed the register and handed my plastic to an unshaven miscreant in a dirty white singlet and bull dyke armpits. No wonder reception was on the second floor of the four-storey building. From the outside, it looked like the two star establishment that it purported to be: standing on a street corner, seven blocks from the ocean and five metres from a contaminated water drain. It was arte deco tawdry, with just a touch of drab and a hint of blue-grey in its white painted wrought iron balconies. There was a small park on the opposite corner where old men played pétanque boules in the lazy afternoon sunshine. It was only after you have walked through the glass and encrusted grime entry door that you hit the hotel industry's equivalent of a dog pound that was three stars short of its goal. I couldn't believe that Mortimer and Squires had booked into the place. Surely an award nominee deserved better.

I retrieved my plastic and walked to the lift, room key in hand. I closed the scissored mesh of the inner lift door. The open steel cage made me feel like a zoo animal as the lift screeched out a discordant tune. The lift descended, reached a point halfway between floors, stopped, shuddered and changed direction. A lift with independent thought – very French.

It finally reached my floor and stopped. I manually opened the doors to a world where the sun filtering through the cobwebs and dust of the hotel's skylight gave the corridor of the fourth floor the soft glow of suffused decay. I half expected to see Peter Mortimer as I opened the door into the room that he had occupied on the night before his death.

Surprisingly, the room was clean and airy, with a clean window facing an internal courtyard and another facing the park. The bed was unwrinkled; sheets crisp. A small television set swung from the ceiling on a Pivotelli. A minibar fridge rested in the corner, filled with a variety of libations. I sat on the bed and momentarily closed my eyes, trying to imagine Mortimer in the room. Nothing. I hit the remote for the telly. A woman was opening a blue box as another woman frowned. A man in a crew neck skivvy smiled and looked soulful. Some quiz show. I hit the remote again and the screen went blank.

I was opening the front door, to leave the hotel, when a cigarette feted voice drifted from the shadows behind me. 'You want girl, monsieur tourist?'

Not with a voice like that. I turned to see an old wizened figure lurking beneath the stairwell. He wore his great grandfather's valet uniform and his long beard rested on his chest like a bib. 'No thanks,' I said.

'Beautiful girl. Good for you.'

'No thank you,' I emphasised.

'Okay, monsieur tourist, very beautiful girl. Virgin, in high heels and short dress.'

He looked older then the building. Maybe? I extracted photos of Mortimer and Squires and walked over to him. 'You ever seen these two?'

'Pardon, monsieur, my eyesight is very poor.'

'Maybe I can show you the photos outside?'

'It would not help, monsieur.'

I twigged. I added a ten Euro note to the photos. 'Maybe you can check this one as well?'

'I can only half see them, monsieur, pardon moi.'

I complied with the request. He examined the photos carefully and smiled as he handed them back. 'Monsieur Squires. He holds the record. Four jeune filles in four nights. He is very good customer.'

'I thought he and Mortimer were only here for two nights?'

'Non, monsieur. Monsieur Squires is here for a week. The other man joined him later. I not like the other man.'

'Why?'

'He not use my services.'

'Do you remember the girls that Squires was with? I would like to talk to one of them.'

The old man went into another blindness phase, but this time I held out. 'There's plenty. When I speak to the woman.' I reached into my pocket and retrieved a small calendar from my wallet. 'The fourteenth of May and possibly the fifteenth.'

The man looked forlorn. He rubbed sinewy fingers through his beard, in deep thought. After a moment, he nodded. 'I will bring her to you at night. You must pay her.'

'Till tonight then,' I said, as I left him and strode from the hotel. Maybe a stroke of luck on my first day? I fished

a city map from my pocket and headed for the first circled
street intersection. *La Mode* beckoned.

***

Six blocks to another world. There was no stench and
marble replaced patchy stucco; street gardens were mani-
cured; chrome and brass gleamed in window frames.
Paradise for the platinum set. La Mode was in the centre of
the block; exclusive and unique. I entered the door to the
discreet tones of a warning buzzer.

A willowy advertisement for Chanel turned her face
from a gilt framed wall mirror, peered over bright pink
frames and dismissed me with a flash of painted eyelashes.
I waited beside the reception desk. A woman, in lingerie
and high heels, walked from a dressing room and picked
up a dress that was draped over a lounge. She glanced at
me, but then joined Chanel. I realised that I had joined the
invisible; neither handsome nor rich looking enough to be
of interest. A string quartet rendered soft music through
ceiling mounted speakers. I wondered where the worker
bees were. The front door opened and a mid-forties
extravaganza with more curves than a mountain road and a
melange of bright colours strolled through. Chanel smiled
and almost made a move from her narcissistic mirror. She
stopped as the lingerie model reappeared in the dress that
she'd taken those few minutes earlier.

'May I help you, Madame?' she asked the woman.

'I'll let you know,' came the reply, in a Carolina drawl
that nobody really believes.

I waited beside the reception desk, feeling ignored. I
looked across at Chanel, who had returned to her mirror.

Maybe she had an eyelash out of place; it was too hard to tell. I watched the new customer as she rifled through the few dresses on show, ignoring the fact that the largest would be many sizes too small. I coughed, in the hope of getting some attention. Chanel looked past me, again — definitely a misplaced eyelash.

I heard a sound from somewhere in the depths of the boutique. Chanel moved like a cheetah and was by my side in an instant. 'May I aid you, monsieur?' she asked.

I gave her the best thrawn gaze that I could muster. Scots would be proud. 'I wish to speak with the manager, if that's possible.'

'Madame Darlington is not here at this time, pardon.'

'I'll wait,' I said, as Chanel returned to her mirror.

A rear door opened and I was visually assailed by an exemplar in a full lycra bodysuit; *The Phantom* in maroon and green. She nonchalantly removed headphones, unzipped the bodysuit to between her breasts, slid the hood back and ruffled her burgundy hair. Rollerblades dropped into a bin. 'A towel please Celia,' she called to Chanel.

'Oui, madame. Immédiatement,' Celia said, as she blurred from the room.

I overtly watched the woman as she dabbed a towel to her face. She had beautiful features: big black eyes, small finely chiselled nose, high cheekbones and the most voluptuous, full lipped mouth. She gave me the slight hiss of a sibilant smile from the small gap between her front teeth. 'Are you being taken care of?' she asked. When she opened her mouth, to speak, I saw that one tooth on either side of the mouth seemed to be slightly elongated.

'I'd like to speak with the manager, if I may.'

She crossed the few paces. 'That would be me, Cali Darlington. How may I help you?'

Quenna Knight entered my thoughts again. I shook my head and replayed the voice in my head. I had expected a French accent. This was California gold. 'I just need some information,' I said, as I watched perspiration bead between her breasts.

'If you can give me five. I'll be with you,' she said, dabbing the towel at her cleavage.

Five became ten before drifting to twenty.

Women entered the boutique, walked past me and through an inner door. The mountain pass walked out carrying a green and maroon bag and broad grin. Maybe they sold tents. I walked to the inner door and opened it. Worker bees and clients; lounges and dressing rooms; coffee and champagne.

I closed the door and returned to the reception desk. Celia brought coffee.

A panel slid sideways and Cali Darlington stepped through the wall. Gone was the sweaty rollerblader, replaced by a businesswoman in a green skirt and maroon and green blouse. The hairstyle was pageboy, the makeup dark and sensual.

'Sorry to keep you Mr...?'

'Mawson.'

'And what may I do for you?'

I removed papers and photos from my briefcase. I handed her invoices and a photo of Peter Mortimer. 'I'm trying to trace what happened to this man. He purchased a dress and some lingerie from here. I'm trying to find who he bought it for.'

'Umm...under what authority?' Darlington asked.

I had no answer. It matched the weight of my legal influence. 'I'm just a friend of the man's sister. Doing her a favour really.'

'I see. Follow me,' she said as she slid back through the wall.

I followed her into an office from the mindset of modern vogue. She sat behind a chrome and glass desk with mahogany inserts and starting punching computer keys. Her hair dropped across her face, shading her eyes; fingers flashed. She shook her head. 'Something odd,' she said 'My records show the purchase as being for Madame Worthington-Peters. The amount is the same. There's no purchase for your Mr Mortimer...you may look.'

I did, for fifteen minutes. I was given unfettered access to the files. Everything was detailed and appeared to be normal. There was nothing to indicate that the invoice and associated credit card paperwork for Madame Worthington-Peters was not in order. At the end I had a bank statement and a computer full of information that didn't match. I was lost. If this was to be the first rung on the ladder of success, I had tripped before leaving the ground. I mentally noted the Worthington-Peters address in Nice. 'Not what I expected.' I commented.

'As you can see, we have no record of a purchase by monsieur Mortimer.'

I changed direction.' Do you know a woman named Washburn...Emily Washburn?'

There was a flash in her eyes, like the reflection from a distant lighthouse. Something had stirred. I looked closely at her eyes. There was something strange about them, something unworldly.

'I don't think so. But we have so many customers.'

I thanked the woman and left. I glanced at my watch; time for my next visit. This time I had a receipt.

La Bouton Noir Boutique was less than five minutes from La Mode. Slightly down market but still with platinum melting power. This time, I was made welcome by a saleswoman, as soon as I entered. I asked for Janelle, the name on the invoice, and was told that she had left to work at La Mode. Coincidence? Maybe. I checked the name tag and told Lauren what I wanted. She was less forthcoming than Darlington but the information was far superior. Within minutes, I had the paperwork showing the description of the dress and the exact time of purchase. This one existed.

I returned to the afternoon sun, deflated and weary. What had been achieved? A crap hotel room, no record of one purchase, information that I already possessed confirmed for another and tired feet from beating the pavement. There had to be more to life. I looked at the briefcase dangling from my hand like an unwanted appendage and realised that I would have to drop it back at the hotel. Six blocks. I began the journey.

I was three blocks in when I noticed something in a mirrored shopfront. I was being followed. I recognised the walk. It had travelled from mirror to window and back for more than twenty minutes. There was precision in its cadence, even on the uneven pavement of the footpath. I stopped and looked into a shop window. My pursuer stopped. I moved on and crossed a street. I was followed across. I walked faster; the sound of high heels on concrete increased pace. I reached my hotel and stood on the pavement opposite. I turned around. She was still there, looking into a shop window. Too obvious. Why? I walked into the hotel and waited in the dingy foyer. No one followed. I dropped the briefcase in my room and returned to the street to find no sign of Celia.

***

The vehicle chop shop was hidden under an expressway overpass. From outside, it resembled a medieval remnant, covered with the scars of some ancient battle. Inside, it resembled the same medieval remnant. I rifled through my pockets for the receipts for the van repairs but was suddenly assailed by the thought that the receipt was one of the reasons that I was carrying my briefcase. I would have to wing it. I entered the dingy building and coughed to get attention. Three panel beaters and a waxen model of a receptionist coughed along. An overused ploy.

'Do you speak English?' I asked the receptionist.

She laughed and started typing on a blank invoice form. This was going to be difficult.

'Excuse moi, mademoiselle, parlez-vous anglaise?' I tried.

'Anglais?'

'Non, australie.'

'Oui, monsieur. I speak English…a little.'

The advantage of not being a pommie. 'I have a small problem, which you may be able to assist with. You see, a friend received an invoice from this company and I need to know who was driving the car.'

The reply was succinct but unhelpful. No receipt, no advice. I had visions of the journey back to my hotel and thence a return to the panel-beating shop. It seemed too tiresome an outing for my already aching feet.

I was in the throes of beginning the journey when a vertically challenged man in blue overalls and a cloth cap walked from a small office. He waved me over. 'I overheard, monsieur. I know of the invoice. It is very famous. We did not expect to be paid,' he said. He pointed to an un-presented cheque pinned to a noticeboard. 'They were very prompt.'

'Good,' I said. 'I work for the daughter of the woman who wrote the cheque. She wants to know who was driving the van.'

'So that she can sue, monsieur. Is that not what you do in australie?'

'Yes, but no. We're really trying to find the woman who was with the man who was run over by the van.'

'You do not want to sue the driver. I am pleased. He already aches with the guilt of causing an unwanted death,' the man said.

'I'm sure. I have no interest in the man…just trying to find the woman.'

I stood with my head slightly bowed as the man climbed onto his chair and pulled down a box of files from a shelf adjacent to his desk. He rifled through the files for a few minutes and then wrote a name and address on a slip of paper. The man's name was Emelio Pim. The address was in Nice.

***

Midnight and eerie darkness settled on my hotel's foyer like a magician's cloak. Gargoyle shadows littered the walls in the dim light. I trundled down the stairs looking for the concierge, who I had expected much earlier. He was nowhere in sight. I noticed that the lift had broken down some time during the evening. A sign on the door said *Walk*. No wonder it had not responded to my pneumatic pressing of the call button. I looked around and opened the front door. The street was dark and shadows danced in the small park across the street. The smell of the evening. A dog howled. I closed the door and waited in the darkness. The front door opened. A drunk weaved through; a girl under his arm like a rolled newspaper. Three steps and a stumble. The girl ran; the man cursed, then continued his upward journey. I waited in the darkness. The door opened again. A long grey beard over a tatty uniform. I stepped into the half-light. He was alone.

His eyes flashed. He tried to remember something. 'She not coming. Gone to Paris. More work there.'

'Did you look?' I asked, annoyed

'No. None of my business,' he garbled

Something was wrong. His attitude couldn't change so markedly from afternoon to evening. I moved into the low light. I wanted to ask him about the change. A weak shaft of light smudged his cheek as he turned away. I spun him around. Blood in his mouth. His teeth red. 'What happened?' I half screamed at the old man.

He shook his head. 'Leave me alone. The lift. Upstairs.'

The lift. Upstairs. Why would he say that. The old man stumbled for the door. He didn't make it. He bent over and vomited at the base of a sculpture. I looked at the lift. Who placed the sign? Shit! I raced up the stairs two at a time. Two drunks sat drinking on the stairs. I had to separate them. One grabbed at my ankle. I shook the hand off. Fourth level. I reached my room and inserted the key into the door and swung it open. The room was dark but filtered light oozed from behind a closed shutter. I hit the light switch and my fingers slipped. I hit the switch again. The light fired. I looked around at my scant belongings. There was an air of disturbance; a desecration of space. The briefcase was on the floor; I had left it on the bed. I heard something outside. The window was open. There was someone on the fire escape ladder, going up. I raced into the corridor and took the stairs to the roof. I pushed at the roof door. It was jammed. I pushed again but it wouldn't give. I ran back down the stairs, along the corridor and onto the fire escape. I climbed the ladder to the roof. Once there, I stopped and listened. Wind in the trees and the wail of a distant siren. Light from the stairwell. The roof door was open. Shit! I should have waited. I stopped. What was I doing? Who was I chasing? What would I do if I caught anyone? I was breathless and low on adrenaline; fantasy and reality jumbled in a blancmange. I glanced down. Someone was running down the stairs at a lower level. I glimpsed a green and maroon bodysuit three floors below. No, the green was emanating from the ground floor. Pale green light drifting up the stairwell. What was its source? I ran down the stairs to the bottom level. There was something reflected on the wall. I stopped and sweat beaded on my forehead. It couldn't be. A cobra's shadow on the wall, ready to strike. I stopped dead in my tracks. I couldn't move. I heard the front door crash shut, the green light waver and the cobra's head distort. I took a deep breath and ran into the foyer. I peered in on the inimical features of the ancient concierge. In his hand he held a torch with a green filtered beam. The light played over a single cobra lily in the garden at the base of the sculpture.

Nice Daffodils

IN France, there are some who prefer to live in small villages or in houses on hectares of land. Others prefer the solitude of walled enclaves with security systems that keep the contamination of the world at bay. Most people, however, live in cities in interminable rows of apartment blocks. Some of these blocks have a golden address and concierge; others have dingy corridors and broken faucets. Madame Marabou Worthington-Peters had a golden address, concierge, dingy corridors *and* a broken faucet. The faucet, normally in pristine working condition, was in a state of abject disrepair when I leaned on the bell press of her penthouse apartment on the sixth floor of La Palais d'Or apartments midway along Promenade des Anglais on the Nice seafront.

A slim young woman opened the door. She was wearing a slight black outfit with a deviant's idea of a French maid's apron and a lacework tiara in her lustrous black hair. I looked down at long willowy legs to see them tucked into a pair of high-heeled yellow galoshes. She stood in a pool of water that seemed to be part of a carpeted lake.

'Not a good time, huh?' I asked

'A minor mishap, monsieur. I received a phone call while I was running a bath for Madame. It is nothing. You are Monsieur Mawson?'

'Yes.'

'Walk this way,' the maid said.

I knew that it would be impossible, but I tried. She led the way past two men in yellow overalls, who were nattering in some guttural dialect as they contemplated the workings of a mechanical supersopper, and through a set of ornate double doors that led into a photo shoot from a belle époque edition of Vogue. A Louis XV1 settee reposed under a painting of a young girl by Adolphe Etienne Piot. A Charles X mahogany pedestal table was counterpoint to a pair of patinated Louis XV1 style benches. A painting of a Bretagne market by Montassier hung beside a wooded landscape by Henry Grosjean and Richebe's "Portrait of a Girl in Pink" took pride of place above an ornate faux fireplace. All of the walls were a vibrant blue.

I was pleased to see that the carpet was drying and that small sandbag walls had been installed in the doorway between the sitting room and the bathroom that was the root cause of the miniflood.

'A very minor tsunami.' A throaty whisper drifted by on an aircushion.

'I hope that it hasn't ruined the carpet,' I said, lamely, recognising that the voice had floated in from the balcony. I stepped through French doors and onto a small roof garden overlooking the eight lanes of traffic and pebbled beach that reached to the horizon in both directions. 'Madame Worthington-Peters?' I asked the soft curve of a white pantalon covered bottom that was tending to an assortment of potted daffodil bulbs with a watering can.

'Mr Mawson, I presume,' came another throaty whisper. 'To what do I owe the pleasure?' the woman asked, as she stood and turned toward me.

The pleasure is all mine, I thought, as I immediately surrendered to the woman's intangible beauty. She looked to be around forty, with wavy blond hair surrounding slightly slanting blue eyes and high cheekbones. Her nose was small and lips slight. She wore no makeup but her lightly tanned skin shone with wondrous lustre. 'Call me Scott,' I said, 'You have quite a garden…here on the roof.'

'Thank you. My husband's pride and joy. He loves daffodils. He used to show them,' she said, as she placed the watering can beside a roof drain and led me back into the sitting room. She appeared to check herself in a wall mirror as she continued through another door. I followed her into what looked like a music room. Half of the space was taken up by a glossy white grand piano, its stool gold lacquered with soft cushioning. Across the room was a curved mahogany desk with a coat of arms inlaid into its surface, its modern leather chair incongruent in the surroundings.

She walked to the chair, swivelled into place behind the desk and sat down. She beckoned me to sit on the piano stool. 'You said on the phone that you wanted to talk to me about some underwear that I purchased. Is that not an odd request, Mr Mawson?'

I smiled. 'Put like that, I guess it is. But it isn't the purchases that I'm interested in. I just want to check that what you purchased lines up with a receipt that I have, showing that someone else made the same purchases.'

'A coincidence surely,' she said with a broad smile that melted my soul.

'Unfortunately not.'

'And this information is important to you, Mr Mawson?' she asked.

I spent the next few minutes reiterating the Peter Mortimer story. Madame Worthington-Peters inspired me with her best *why are you telling me this rubbish* look but said nothing to interrupt. Occasionally she would gaze through me, as if looking for divine intervention, but mostly she looked at me with a slightly patronising smile that showed the depth of her indulgence. When I finished, I smiled and waited.

Madame Worthington-Peters stood from her chair and walked over to the other side of the room. She pressed a button on the wall. 'Coffee?'

'Love one,' I said. At least I wasn't about to be thrown out.

The button was pressed again. 'So you seek this woman who, you say, was with this Peter Mortimer. Have you tried the phone book?'

'My client tried every phone book in France, but to no avail.'

'Aaah. I see. And just what can I do for you?'

I had no idea. 'I don't know really. I guess that I just need confirmation that you made the purchases described on the invoice.'

'If possible, I will show you. May I see the paper?'

'Of course,' I said.

I was opening my briefcase when the maid appeared through the connecting door. This time the galoshes were missing. They had been replaced by slim black shoes with six inch, silver spiked, heels and silver pointed toecaps. In the heels, the maids legs appeared elongated and the skirt shorter. She was carrying a silver tray supporting two fine bone china coffee cups matching milk jug and sugar bowl. She moved to a low coffee table and bent at the waist. Her legs remained straight and the skirt moved higher. My eyes followed stocking seams to visual heaven. I heard a small laugh and realised that I was being watched.

'Try not to stand for a moment,' Madame Worthington-Peters said.

I felt a crimson flush of embarrassment and felt foolish. I handed her the paperwork, head bowed.

She read the paper. 'I have not seen a receipt for what I purchased. La Mode sends my account monthly. But I will see what I can do.' She hesitated for a moment, as if trying to make a decision. 'Come with me,' she said.

I followed her into a bedroom. She opened a closet and removed a dress. It was a turquoise silk sheath with the spilt down the left side. 'Voila,' she said.

I nodded. I had no idea what to say

She looked at the paper again. She moved across to a dressing table and rummaged through an assortment of flimsy lingerie. She lifted a silver grey set from the drawer and smiled at me. She removed a blue set and smiled again. She continued her search but seemed to be unable to find what she was looking for. Then, she stuck her finger up into the air as if an idea had finalised its formation. She stood and undid the top three buttons of her pink blouse. She pulled the blouse aside to show the half cup of a pink bra. 'My underwear matches. Do you desire to see more?' she asked.

More desire than she could imagine. 'No...I believe that I have put you to too much trouble already.'

'Je suis désolée,' She said, as she rebuttoned her blouse and walked from the bedroom.

I caught a glimpse of myself in a bedroom mirror as I followed like a prosaic lapdog, being led by an unseen leash, from room to room. Then another view, as I entered the music room. I had not realised it previously, but everywhere I looked, there were mirrors. None stood out, but one could catch a glimpse at oneself from anywhere in the room. It was an odd sensation. Once I started, I just kept looking for other viewing angles, wondering why someone would set up such a system. I looked across at Madame Worthington-Peters, who was pouring coffee into two cups.

'Milk and sugar?' she asked.

'Unsugared black will be fine,' I replied.

'The way I like it,' she said.

I sat on the piano stool as she handed me the coffee. I sipped slowly, wondering what to say next before seeing something that I hadn't noticed when I had been in the room, previously. On the mantle, behind the desk stood two, thirteen and a half-inch, gold plated statues of Oscar and Moore's Athene in the form of a BAFTA statuette. I pointed to the Oscars. 'Yours?'

Madame Worthington-Peters smiled as if she had grabbed an affectionate thought. 'No, they belong to my husband.'

'An actor?'

The smile turned to a laugh, which was whispered and throaty like her voice. It seemed to have a seductive quality that I found enticing. 'Nothing so glamorous. One Oscar is for sound mixing, the other for sound editing. Athene is for sound editing, as well...I think. He won that before he met me.'

'Your husband is away working?'

'No, not at all. He's in the next room.'

'Ohhh,' I pondered. 'May I be introduced?'

'But of course,' she said, laughing again. 'But, we should finish our coffee first.'

I heard a knock on the door. I looked to see a pair of yellow overall enter the room.

'We are complete, Madame,' the man said.

'Would you please excuse me for a moment, Monsieur Mawson.'

My eyes followed her through the door. I looked at the Oscars but then saw myself looking at them from an oblique angle. The mirrors were beginning to annoy me. I lifted one Oscar from its shelf and weighed it in my hand; heavier than I imagined. I thought of standing at a lectern, giving a much rehearsed speech and thanking everyone in the universe. I replayed Peter Mortimer's short Cannes speech in my head. It had been succinct and pleasant. I replaced the statuette and picked up Athene. I noticed that the stem between the head and base had been repaired. I looked for an identification phrase; to see in what category the award had been presented, but found nothing. I returned to the piano stool and waited. And waited.

I was beginning to feel as neglected as an unused condom when the mistress of the house returned. 'Shall we meet my husband?' she said

I felt the leash pull, as I followed her into another room. I expected an office or some such but, instead, found myself in a small chapel. The room was encased in black marble; empty, except for a white marble alter. One light fitting doused the space in subtle white light whilst another played on a life-size portrait of a man, which was hanging on the wall behind the altar. The man, whom I assumed to be the husband, looked as if he had been painted in caricature. Below narrow beady eyes, shaded by

overhanging eyebrows, was a proboscis fit for a hippopot-
amus. One ear was an elongated shell, whilst the other was
cauliflowered and appeared to have been gnawed by rats.
The chin was dimpled, as was one cheek. I was surprised
that such a painting would be hung in such an austere
setting. One would think a photograph more fitting. I tore
my eyes from the portrait and noticed a miniature coffin
atop the altar. It was in green marble surrounded by white
daffodils with orange-pink ruffles.

'My husband's ashes,' Madame Worthington-Peters
said.

I nodded my head then looked again at the painting.
'Do you remember your husband like this?' I asked.

'Of course. It is a perfect likeness. He was proud of it.'

I gulped, then pulled my foot from my mouth. 'What
type are the daffodils? They are lovely.'

She shrugged and smiled. 'With your quixotic quest, you
need to know things. You should study your genus at
length; otherwise you will continue to let opportunities slip
by. Opportunities will be very rare where you are going.
Do not let them pass unattended.'

I had no idea what she meant. Then something seeped
into my brain. 'Was you husband ever nominated for
Cannes?'

She smiled again, as if I had understood some sublimi-
nal instruction and was reacting accordingly. 'Claude was
nominated twice, but didn't win.'

Adrenalin began to run. 'Did you meet your husband in
Cannes?'

'You should have asked to see my panties. I would have
been far more forthcoming,' she replied.

***

It was hard to believe that I had moved only two blocks and ten minutes on foot from the Worthington-Peters opulence to a single bedroom apartment on the narrow Rue de la Buffa, where sunlight is no more than a shadow on a high wall and apartments are the size of dog kennels. When I knocked on the door, it was answered by a slight man with sparse hair who wore anorexia like an enlightened promise. He smiled through gapped teeth as he dabbed reddened eyes with a tissue. He looked at me as if his world had just crumbled and I was the cause.

'I'm sorry,' he said, in a tweedy English chirp, as he wiped the last vestiges of self-respect from his face.

I had no idea what he was talking about. Sorry for what? I thought of the phone call that I had made to him. I had played the cards close to my chest and given him no more information than was absolutely necessary. I looked at the man named Emelio Pim and realised that I had never seen a man with such deep grooves etched into his face. It was as if he had been crying all of his life and tears had carved elongated tracks from his eyes to his chin. 'Sorry for what?' I asked, waiting for an invitation into his apartment.

'This whole business. I feel like crying all the time. It's all too much for me.'

'You mean the accident?' I asked, wondering if we would conduct the entire interview in his doorway.

Anger flashed through his eyes as he peered at me as if I was a moron. 'Don't be silly. That was long ago. No one understands. I have lost my Juliette and there is so much pressure from my agent. It is just too much to bear.'

I muddled through the words. There was something about an agent and bereavement. 'I'm sorry for your loss,' I said, wondering what I was talking about. I stepped across the threshold into an overused landfill site.

He began to cry again. 'Yes, it is terrible,' he said between sobs. 'Three months and the police have found nothing. I don't even think that they are looking any more.'

Someone had gone missing. My timing was way off. 'Someone has gone missing?'

'Yes…of course…my beloved Juliette Binoche.'

'Juliette Binoche, the actress?' I had no idea that she was missing.

'No, Juliette Binoche my Japanese bobtail. She has gone. The police told me not to worry, that they would find her…but they never have any information for me. I think they know something and don't want to tell me.'

I tried to be positive. 'Cats always come back. I'm sure it will show up soon.'

Pim smiled for the first time. 'Do you really think so?'

I had given him a glimmer of hope. I decided to pursue the line. 'Yes, of course.' I lied. 'I once had a cat that was missing for six months. Then, one day, it shows up on my doorstep.'

'What breed?'

Shit! I had no time to hesitate but had no knowledge of cat breeds. 'A Ragdoll,' I said, remembering a friend's cat.

'Seal Lynx or Flame Point?' Pim asked.

Trust me to pick a cat with more than one type. 'I don't know. It was a friend's cat that I was looking after.'

'Strange,' Pim said. 'You would expect a runaway cat to return to its home…not to where it was being looked after.'

'Funny, that's what my friend said,' I said. I tried to change the subject. 'How long has Juliette been missing?'

'Three months on Sunday. I am so distraught.'

I looked at his furrowed cheeks. 'Yes, I can see that. Mr Pim, I know it's a bad time for you, but there is something else that I would like to discuss with you.'

A mournful looked crossed his face. I thought he would cry again. I waited for an aeon before he spoke. 'Okay…but can you wait here until I get some cat food. Just in case Juliette returns.'

'No….not at all. That's fine by me.'

'Good, good,' he said. He removed an old army great-coat from behind his door and slipped it on. It was far too warm for such apparel but he didn't seem to notice. 'I'll only be ten minutes or so.'

Then he was gone. I looked around the residence, shaking my head. For some reason, I was making constant comparisons with the Worthington-Peters apartment. It was such a short distance that I was sure that you could see one from the other. Here there was no antique furniture, gilt trinkets or silver baubles. In this living room, there was a sagging fabric settee with a visible spring. A small television set sat atop a case of empty wine bottles. In the kitchen, dirty dishes were stacked on a sink that hadn't been cleaned since the Roman invasion. Empty wine bottles lined the sink like targets in a shooting gallery. I opened a refrigerator and reeled at the stench; mine was pristine by comparison. I opened a door leading from the kitchen and found the toilet. I was surprised to find it sparkling. On the toilet floor was a copy of a novel. It was dog-eared and had umpteen slips of paper and post-it notes marking pages. I picked it up and found that it to be a script copy for Shakespeare's Merchant of Venice. On closer inspection I found that the marked pages followed the role of Shylock. Surely not! I dropped the script to the floor and returned to the kitchen. I needed a drink so I looked into an overbench cupboard for a glass. There were two; neither clean. I was rinsing one in the swamp when I noticed that there was something on the floor behind the half open door that led to the living room. There was an unwelcome growth on the floor: mutant pond scum. It was either a science lab experiment or Emelio Pim had not cleaned behind the door for some time. I looked around the room, at the evidence of an impotent life, and knew the answer.

I moved to the door and pushed it toward closed. *Morning Juliette,* I said to the skeletal remains of a well-hung moggy. *He left you suspended a little then.* I shook my head as I observed the remains of the cat, still in its studded leather collar and hanging from a suspended leash. I wondered if Pim had ever seen it. Obviously not.

I found myself needing longer arms as I scooped the furry lime jelly from the floor. Inert, it was odourless but, as soon as I moved it, the manifestation of a biblical plague descended on the room like a planeload of unwashed feet. I shovelled the mess into the only plastic bag that I could find and then added the skeletal remains of the cat and its leash.

Fifteen minutes later, I sat on Pim's settee, avoiding the sharp edges of the spring, and waited for his return.

On Pim's return, he rushed through the door; looking backwards and panting like an overwalked dog. He stared me as if unsuspecting of my presence. Then he smiled with recognition. 'I hope that I didn't keep you too long,' he said as he let tins of cat food drop onto the table from the sleeves of his greatcoat. 'I'm sure that when Juliette returns, I'll now have plenty of food for her.'

I thought of the remains in the plastic bag that I had pushed to the bottom of the pile in an alleyway bin. 'More than enough.'

He removed his coat then raked his fingers through the remnants of his hair. 'I'm so sorry...but I've forgotten why you're here,' he said.

'Like I said on the phone, Mr Pim, I just need some information. I'm looking for a missing person. I understand that you were involved in a vehicle accident some months ago and the person I'm looking for was with the man who was hit.'

I watched tear well in his eyes as he began to cry again. 'You don't understand. None of you understand. I killed a man with my van.'

I realised that my opening gambit had been a touch insensitive, but I needed to move on quickly. I couldn't stand another bout of burbling, so I forged ahead. 'I'm not here to either persecute or prosecute you. I just need an answer. Look, I do understand...but it was just a set of circumstances. You could have done nothing else.'

He wailed. 'But you see...I could have. I shouldn't have been looking at the woman. I should have been looking at the road.'

I thanked the god of small mercies. Maybe I was onto something. I feigned ignorance. 'There was a woman ... where?'

Pim wiped his eyes again. He looked around his apartment as if searching for some hidden bugging device. 'You're not from the gendarmerie?'

I was annoyed. 'Do I sound French?'

'No, your accent is terrible.'

I was piqued. 'Well!'

'I was looking at the woman, when the man stepped onto the road.'

'Can you describe the woman? I just need to know if it was the woman who I'm looking for,' I asked.

'It was night time.'

'I know that. Just tell me what you can. I really need to know.' I had an idea. 'Just tell me what happened. Start as you approached the man that jumped out onto the road-way.'

Pim sniffed away demons. 'I was heading west along the Boulevard de la Croisette, at around twenty three hundred, when I saw two men and two women on the median strip about a hundred metres ahead. Then one man and one woman ran across the road between two moving cars. I noticed right away that they must have been drunk, because they just stepped out onto the road against a green light. They made it across, but they were lucky. The other man and woman stayed. This made me think that they must have realised that they couldn't cross. I got closer and saw that the man was kissing the woman.'

He stopped talking. There was a pained expression on his face, as if he was trying to relive the scene. I waited for him to continue. He didn't.

'Go on,' I said.

'Well, the woman mustn't have wanted to be kissed because she pulled away and stepped back.'

'Onto the road?'

'No…just back.'

'Then what happened?'

The river returned to full flood and Pim turned his head from me. I could feel the anguish of a thousand lost souls.

'I wish I knew. But I was looking at the woman. She was so beautiful. I couldn't take my eyes from her face. She was the perfect Portia.'

'To your Shylock?'

Pim's face brightened. A light had been switched on somewhere in his mind. 'You know, don't you?'

'Know what?' I asked.

'You're just being coy. You know that I'm about to play Shylock at the Globe in London.'

'I knew that. I was just wondering when,' I said.

'I guess it's really up to me. My agent has it set as soon as I learn all my lines. I work on it all the time in my rehearsal room.'

'I can't wait to see you in it.' I looked at my watch. 'Look at the time. I have to run.'

'Good. I'll see you out,' Pim said.

As I reached the sunlight of Rue de la Buffa, I realised that Shakespeare was wrong. The quality of mercy is strained. In some cases, very strained.

***

I stood at a set of traffic lights on Boulevard Gambetta wondering why the woman who was beside me was wheeling something strangely furry in a stroller. She was either a fervent dog lover or had given birth to the ugliest kid ever born. She seemed inured to my quizzical gaze but then spat on my trouser leg. I was still wiping it off when I heard a familiar throaty laugh. I looked up to see a shimmering vision in pink and white Chanel.

'You do not love dogs?' Madame Worthington-Peters asked, continuing to chuckle at my attempt to remove spittle from my trousers.

'More than cats,' I said.

'You do yourself a disservice. I heard that you have just performed a very noble deed for a devoted feline lover.'

'Devoted! I think not.'

'You're wrong. Mr Pim loves his cat. He didn't even drink until that terrible accident in Cannes. He has never forgiven himself.'

'How do you know that I was with Pim. Did you follow me?' I asked.

Traffic lights changed green and Madame Worthington-Peters crossed the road, heading toward the Promenade des Anglais. I followed her across, intrigued with how she knew about Pim. She stopped and looked me straight in the eyes. 'Is there a reason why I would follow you? There is no need. You are on a quest and Emelio Pim formed part of that quest. He drove the van that killed your Mr Mortimer. It is obvious that you would want to talk to him. I would, in your position.'

'How do you know about the cat?' I asked.

She smiled again, but I began to feel that the ethereal beauty belied a subterranean demon. 'I'm on my way to my favourite brasserie. Would you care to join me for lunch?'

'If you promise to tell me how you know about the cat,' I replied.

She walked on. I walked beside her for a few minutes, saying nothing. There was no common ground other than a duplicated invoice and her knowledge of Pim's cat. I wondered how she knew. She wouldn't have followed me but her maid may have been sent on a mission. Yes, that was it. Her maid followed me. Probably saw me put the plastic bag into the bin and then checked the contents when I went back upstairs. Yes. It made sense.

'My maid didn't follow you,' Madame Worthington-Peters said, as she opened the door of a small hideaway brasserie for me. 'Your scent is dead feline. It's simply a matter of guessing what may have occurred.'

I wanted to know more of the woman. I wanted to know less of the woman. I was caught between curiosity and the beginning of a deep and abiding fear. She could smell the dead cat on me. No one has a nose that good. My olfactory senses worked overtime sniffing the air. I could smell nothing. I remembered the fettered air of the kitchen and hoped that I wasn't wearing it like some form of unseen veil. Maybe she was a nose. After all, we weren't that far from Grasse. 'You work in cosmetics?' I asked.

A waiter ushered us to a table by a window and took Madame Worthington-Peters' jacket. He offered her a menu but she refused it. 'My usual,' she said to the waiter. 'My friend isn't staying. He has decided that he must be elsewhere.' She turned from the waiter to me and continued. 'No, I don't work in cosmetics. I just sense things that float in the air. I am sensitive to a lot of things, people included. I sometimes sense what is happening before the event. It's a matter of perception. Some have the sense, others don't. I am one of the lucky ones....Scott...and I have decided to help you.'

At last, a glimmer of hope stuck its head above the horizon. 'How are you going to help me?'

'I will guide you to people whom you need to meet. Only then will you understand why you may not complete your journey.'

'Am I in danger?' I asked

The smile was warm and affectionate. 'Only from your own lack of imagination. You don't see things clearly enough. If you keep blundering along, you may do harm without realising what you have done. That is why I have decided to help.'

'Thank you,' I said. 'How will we communicate? By thought?'

'E-mail is much easier. Just give me your address.'

I laughed. The answer was so obvious. I handed her one of my business cards. She looked unimpressed with its quality. SE&B. What does that mean?

'Seldom employed and broke. May I call you Marabou?' I asked.

'That is why we need to keep an eye on you. Some of your guesses are profound. I will stay in touch,' she said. She then reached into her handbag and pulled out a small white paper bag. 'A gift for you.'

I looked into the bag. 'I guess that I should leave no stone unturned. I should always see the evidence.'

'Pink is my favourite colour,' she said.

Dahlias at the Chateau de Trouffe

MARABOU did stay in touch. It was an e-mail with no more than a name and address but when I looked up the name on the Internet my interest was more than piqued. There was always the same person in the background when candid photos were taken. That person seemed more interesting that the person whose name had me leaving home at around six, while the morning fog enveloped my Tuscan valley and tyres crunched on icy roads.

Hours later, as I drove through southern France, it was a day for believing that the same man who had once spilled dustbins on my doorstep was now responsible for putting the sun up in the mornings. Its oblique angle, several degrees above the horizon, showed the same lack of appreciation for the feelings of others as a slack garbo with a hangover. It was as if he had put it half way up the sky and then gone on with other matters. But then, the wintry mantle of December was upon us and the golden orb of the summer sun was now just a washed out copper medallion, so I couldn't expect much more. I drove for six hours with glare in my eyes and the squinting left me with a headache. From Florence to Beziers I was on motorways and wound the kilometres off in rapid succession. Then speed gave way to the slow monotony of windy mountain road surrounded by the gnarled brown stumps of winter's grapevines between Beziers and Mazamet. From there my

satnav roadmap was useless and small roadway signposts
became de rigueur for the journey until I finally reached an
eighteenth century chateau in the rolling hills north-east of
Lautrec. It was just off the Castres to Lautrec road but was
hidden within its own primordial forest. From the roadway
there appeared to be only rusted iron gates and peeling
concrete pillars with the name Chateau de Trouffe on a
hand painted sign leaning against one pillar. I stopped the
car when I noticed a metre high bollard between the
pillars. No way through. I eased myself from the car and
stretched my legs and back before taking a look. The gate
and pillars may have been a couple of hundred years old
but the bollard was new and hydraulic. There had to be a
control mechanism. I checked the left pillar. Nothing. I
checked the right. There was a small call box fitted into the
rear of the pillar. I pressed a button and waited. Nothing. I
pressed again. The same lack of response. *Shit!* I exclaimed
to the trees.

I decided to leave the car outside the gates and walk and
trudged along a narrow, once cobbled, path that now acted
as a rainwater sluice. It was muddy and moss threatened to
engulf the entire route. I turned a corner and could see the
chateau amongst the trees. It reminded me of a castle from
the classics with four corner turrets. A square impregnable
fortress with narrow slit windows and satellite dishes
adorning one slope of its slate roof. A huge bay window
with a Juliet balcony, faced south and there was a glassed
in stairwell that fitted to the side of the building like an
afterthought. I noticed a gate and arch in the centre of one
wall. I pushed at the gate and it opened onto an inner
courtyard with sail structures and an inground swimming
pool set within a potted garden.

I looked for a door. There were eight set within the four walls of the courtyard. Which one did I want? I walked to the first and struck paydirt. The name Joshua Arbour was inscribed in a brass plaque beside the door. I pulled on a ball in hand doorknocker and let it fall against its pad.

The door was opened by a tall weedy man, skeletal and bald with slanted beady eyes and a mouth that looked as though it spent all its time sucking on a lemon. I figured him to be, at least, eighty but the step was sprightly and he had the gaze of a true observer.

'Joshua Arbour?' I asked.

He stared at me for a few seconds, opened his door and ushered me into his elaborate apartment. As soon as I entered, I felt off balance. Everything within the apartment was curved: walls, ceiling, doors, windows. Ancient red dominated the spaces and gold leaf edging surrounded the doors and ran along the skirting and cornices. The furniture was Rococo revival. Four Picasso's hung on a wall of the living room. Two Dali bronzes rested on an ivory tusked coffee table. A pre-fame Lautrec adorned the dining room wall. A human skull, on a marble mantel, smoked an unlit cigar A stuffed black cat curled around a lampshade.

Arbour smiled at me by curving his thin lips and handed me a half-empty glass of clear liquid, then grabbed another from a tray on a sideboard. 'Vodka,' he said. 'Clears your mind.'

And addles the brain. 'Thanks.'

'You have travelled great distance, Mr Mawson. To what do I owe the pleasure?' he asked, as he sat on an under-filled maroon fabric lounge.

Straight to the point.

'I need information and I was told that you might be able to help me.' I sat beside him on the lounge and commenced the story that now had a slight whiff of déjà vu. I ran through the Mortimer incident, and my search for his escort. I told him of the Billy Squires revelations about not being able to see Jacqueline du Pre and the lack of information from the Cannes boutiques. I held back on my visit to Nice. The story flowed like treacle from a tin and he developed the lean forward with mouth slightly open look of the interested.

About two thirds in, I was surprised when he stopped me in my tracks. He just held up his hand and shook his head, his eyes narrowing under a continuous eyebrow. 'You said that you are looking for Emily Washburn.'

'Not directly, but yes. Do you know her?'

Arbour peered into my eyes, his gaze cogent. 'Look around you. What do you see, young man?'

I looked at the artwork and furniture. Surely he didn't mean that. 'I don't understand the context of the question.'

'Do you see the ordinary within this room. Is this of a style that appears in every house that you visit?'

I looked around and smirked. 'No, I don't.'

'That is your answer,' Arbour said.

'I'm no clearer.'

'This room came from my imagination. It's a little like Emily Washburn. She appears only in the dictionary of dreams within one's mind. Every man dreams of meeting Emily Washburn or someone like her. Some never awaken from their dream and many have tried to find her…me included…but I concluded that she doesn't exist. That is the conclusion that we all reach, eventually. She may have existed once, but not any more.'

I had heard it before. I sipped at my vodka. The skull sucked on the unlit cigar. The stuffed cat moved on the lampshade. I walked to the bay window and looked across the pink garlic fields toward the old windmill on the edge of Lautrec. I hadn't travelled for nine hours to be put off easily. I decided to try a ploy that I had worked and reworked during my long journey. 'Would you mind answering a question for me?' I asked.

Arbour finished his vodka and poured himself another, before he spoke. 'The question is?'

I removed a notebook from my shirt pocket. I wanted to get the dates right. I began to feel like a tabloid journalist in search of an exposé. 'My research indicates that, in 1986, you were nominated for best new director at the Cannes film festival. You didn't win. In 1996, you were nominated for best screenplay at the same awards. Again, you didn't win. In 2003, you were nominated for directing but you didn't win. Are those dates correct?'

Arbour blinked rapidly and frowned. I felt that he was perplexed. 'I'm exceedingly pleased that you have sought to investigate my failures,' he said. 'But to what point?'

I took a deep breath. 'The point is that at each of the ceremonies, you were accompanied by an elegantly dressed and beautiful woman.'

Arbour smirked 'I hope so, I like beautiful women. They keep me young.'

'I'm sure they do,' I quipped. 'My question is simply to ask you how it is that you aged between 1986 and 2003 but your escort didn't.'

Arbour sipped his vodka and levelled his Lautrec. 'It's quite simple. They are different women. A different woman for each occasion.'

'What if I told you that it was the same woman, and she didn't age in seventeen years.'

Arbour walked across to the bay window and looked into the middle distance. I expected a comment on my revelation, but he just shook his head from side to side. 'I'm afraid that you are mistaken.'

Time for my first lie. 'How so? I checked articles and photographs from the years mentioned and I have had the photos of the woman checked by experts. It is the same woman.'

Arbour smile benignly, then started as if mentoring a retarded child. 'I have always liked a particular look in my women. The agency, from which I procure them, takes great pains to ensure that the women supplied comply fully with my requirements. You say they look the same. It is entirely possible. They look similar because I want it that way.'

My head was beginning to pound like a teenage drummer with no sense of rhythm. Obviously, long drives and vodka didn't blend. I tried to focus and reset my equilibrium but there was nothing straight to focus on. The pounding increased its intensity. I began to feel dizzy and disorientation became severe. I felt myself falling into an abyss.

'Are you alright?' came a voice through a descending fog.

'Headache. Must be the drive. There was low sun all the way.' I felt myself stagger and then an attempt, by weak arms, to halt my descent. I landed on the carpeted floor with an unheard thud.

***

I awoke in darkness, my head pounding like a reciprocating air hammer. Desiccated cuttlefish filled my mouth and my eyes beheld the inside of the world. I tried to sit, but found that my head simply lowered its pain threshold. I held still; wondering where I was and letting my eyes become used to the low light.

Slowly a picture dawned like slow processed film. Light filtered through closed slats over a window. A soft orange glow seeped under a door. I was on a four-poster bed, complete with mirrored canopy. I closed my eyes, keeping rhythm with the pounding headache. More light entered the room. The door opened to a haloed apparition in the doorway. The curved silhouette approached and sat beside me on the bed. It wasn't Joshua Arbour; the shape was of a young woman. I felt a lukewarm cloth being placed on my forehead. Then delicate fingers stroked my temples.

'Feeling better?' the apparition asked.

The words gave me a feeling of unease. They were spoken in the dialect from a part of the world where people eat iggs for brickfast or f'sh and ch'ps or add muwk to tea. Just across the ditch from Australia but far too far to be hearing the accent in this place.

I waited for more words for confirmation, but none came. It was, obviously, my turn. 'Long way from home,' I said.

'Bit further than you...but not much,' the voice replied with a rhythmic lilt.

'Where am I?' I asked around a swollen tongue.

'Where you think you are...in Joshua's bed.'

'What happened?'

'I'm afraid that Joshua is getting old. He didn't control the dose properly and you collapsed.'

I thought that I had misheard. I thought that she said something about *control the dose properly*. Surely not! Was she saying something about my being drugged? I tried to rise but the movement compounded the thunder in my head. I closed my eyes again. 'Did you say control the dose?' I whispered, in disbelief.

'Yes. Joshua drugged you. He just overdid it a bit. You'll be okay though. Just rest for a while. The pain will ease soon. When you're awake, just join us downstairs.'

'Why?' I muttered.

'Why do we want you to join us or why were you drugged?'

I pushed my fists into my temples to ease the pain. 'The latter.'

'We needed to check you out. You'll be pleased to know that you passed scrutiny'

'If I hadn't?'

The woman smiled. 'What do you think?'

I shrugged, unknowingly. 'Disappearance in a deep forest?'

She laughed. 'You'd have to be a character in a crime thriller for that to happen. You had no chance here. Joshua and I would have disappeared and you wouldn't have found us again.'

I tried to move, as soon as the woman left the room, but was stopped by the constant thumping. I remained motionless until I drifted off.

***

I awoke to a feeling of weightlessness; floating on the bed. I could move freely; nothing held me down. I realised that the pain in my head was gone. I sat up, half expecting the ache to return, but found freedom. I walked over to where I saw light filtering under a door and felt the wall for a light switch. I pressed the switch and the room was bathed in subdued light. I looked around to see that the woman had not lied. I was in a man's bedroom. It was stark and unkempt. There was a shirt hanging on the back of a chair and a pair of black dress shoes sticking out from under the bed. I walked to a shuttered window and pulled the lever to open the shutters. For some reason I had expected bars but all that was there was a window, looking out to the sails and the swimming pool that I had noticed on the way in. The pool was lit and looked serene but incongruous in a darkened landscape that was now covered with a fine smattering of snow. From the window I could see the wall that surrounded the chateau. I saw that there were now three cars in the car park. One of them was mine. I recalled leaving it at the external perimeter of the property. I felt in my trousers pocket for the keys. They were missing. I touched the window and felt ice on my fingertips. Chimes rang and I looked at my watch. Twenty three hundred. I felt the door handle and twisted it. There was no resistance and the door opened smoothly. I had expected that I would be prevented from free movement. Why would I be sedated otherwise? There was a corridor outside the room; wide with brightly painted walls and stylish cornices. Painting and photographs suspended from a picture rail and the entire ceiling was awash with light from hidden sources.

I noticed a staircase ahead and moved toward it. I had almost reached it when something caught my eye. My shoulders became tight and perspiration began to bead on the back of my neck. I blinked to refocus and then looked again. On the wall, at the top of the stairs was a mono-chrome photograph of three people. On the left was Joshua Arbour. In the centre was a huge woman who wore obesity like a fashion statement and on the right, in the half shadow of the woman, was a face that I, instantly, recognised. I took a closer look to make sure. There was no mistake.

'You m'st be hungry.' Came a rhythmic voice from the bottom of the staircase.

'Famished,' I said, over my shoulder.

'Good. I'll get you something. Come down…Joshua's in the living room.'

I turned from the photo, but the woman was gone.

***

Arbour reposed on a slingback chair, reading a newspa-per and looking ancient. He looked up as I entered the room and smiled wanly. He muttered something about hoping that I was feeling better then returned to his paper, ignoring my presence.

I perused one of the Picasso's and turned my back to him. 'You drugged me. I believe.' It was a statement more than a question.

He looked up from his print. Shrugged his shoulders in affirmation and returned to his reading.

'I take it that you don't really want me to ask you any more questions?'

'Candy will answer your questions. I am too tired. I am being polite, waiting up for you. I should be in bed by now.'

What! He sounded as if I had just arrived, much later than expected. 'Maybe if you hadn't drugged me it would all be over by now and I would be on my way home.'

'You can't get home. It's snowing outside and you don't have chains in your car boot.'

'You checked?' I asked, trying to sound infuriated.

'Of course. You are a guest in this house and it's my obligation to look after you.'

A sudden glow caught my eye. I looked at the marble mantel to see the skull puffing on a lit cigar. 'Whose skull is that?'

Arbour grinned. 'It's my father. He likes to have a cigar before bed. I only allow him one a day. He sucks on it all day but we only light it for him at night.'

'You are kidding me,' I said.

A flash of annoyance crossed Arbour's features. 'Of course not. If we let him have a cigar whenever he wants one, he might get cancer.'

I crossed to the ivory coffee table and examined the Dali bronze. A beautiful piece of eclectic art. I lifted it to get a closer look at the detail. As I did so, the woman entered the room carrying a tray of food and drinks. I dropped the bronze, but caught it again just before it hit the table. My mouth opened and my jaw went slack. I couldn't breathe. I was looking at the woman who had accompanied Joshua Arbour to three Cannes Film Festivals. She had shiny black hair and elfin features but was tall and lithe. She looked to be around twenty-six. She was always twenty-six.

'I frightened you?' she asked.

I shook my head and clamped my mouth shut. I bit the back of my upper lip to drive some sense into myself. I stared like an adolescent boy seeing his first female nude. I was lost somewhere in space. I had gone to sleep and been transported into another dimension.

I bit my lip again. It had no effect on the washing machine tumble of my emotions. I couldn't focus on what I was seeing.

She placed the tray on the coffee table and smiled at me. 'You look as if you've seen a ghost. Am I that scary?'

'No...no. You're the woman who was at Cannes with Arbour. I saw the photographs. You haven't aged in twenty years. You're always the same. You can't...you must be. Oh shit!'

The words tripped over one another. I felt like an incoherent babbler.

I was afforded another benign smile. 'I have been to Cannes many times with Joshua. We are usually there around the time of the film festival. It allows Joshua to catch up with old friends, now that he has retired.'

I slumped into a chair. I held my head, squashed between pressing palms. 'You don't understand. I saw photographs of you. You haven't aged in over twenty years.'

She smiled again. 'We've done that bit.'

I was getting another headache. This one had no need for chemical stimulants. This was stress. I shook my head to ward of demons.

She poured coffee into a cup and proffered it toward me. 'Drink this. It will make you feel better. And, no, it isn't drugged.'

I sipped on the coffee and sat back. I closed my eyes and read a chapter from the little book of calm. I would keep quiet and see what developed.

'Why don't you tell me why you are here?' she said. 'I know that you told Joshua, but he has been asleep for a few hours now and I don't want to wake him. Maybe I can help.'

I glanced across at Arbour, he was sound asleep. 'Who are you?'

'That part's simple. I'm Candy Alloway. I'm the companion of Joshua Arbour. Please begin.'

I reiterated the tale that I had told Arbour earlier. This time I included the visit to Nice. I felt that this woman knew it anyway. I finished then held my palms open to show that I had concluded my story.

'I see. You are looking for Jacqueline du Pre. You don't know how to find her but you think that asking questions about Emily Washburn might solve the problem for you.'

'In a nutshell.'

'Are you a detective?'

'I'm a maths teacher.'

'A man who applies logic. Helpful, but uses the wrong side of the brain. You need to use more of your artistic side.'

'You think so.'

'I know so. You seem to be missing the inconsistency of what you are saying about Billy Squires and what you think of me.'

'Inconsistency?'

'Of course. On one hand you say that Billy Squires can't see Jacqueline du Pre on film. I guess that you think that there is some form of vampire non-reflection thing going on. Yet, you know that Jacqueline du Pre exists. Emelio Pim told you that he saw her. On the other hand, you think that I am a woman who hasn't aged for twenty years but you can see me. Surely, if Jacqueline du Pre can't be seen, I can't be seen?'

I was on the fast train to oblivion. I knew nothing and was getting nowhere. 'Can you help?' I asked.

'No…a little advice maybe. You were sent here because Marabou believed that Joshua might help you. There is a time when he would have, but that time has passed. All he wants to do now is wake up and go to sleep without pain. Nothing else matters to him. That is too bad for you, but maybe a little advice would not be too remiss.'

'What do I do?'

'If you want to find anything out, you need to be involved with Mortimer's movie. There are people who want people to see it. They are interested in what happened to Mortimer and his movie. The movie hasn't been released in the main markets yet and, the way it's going it may never see the light of day except in a few art house theatres. It may develop some cult status but it deserves more than that.

I had heard a similar sentiment before. 'Why do I need to do this?'

'You're dealing with movie people and movie fans. Everything about your request for help reeks of the film world. If you know nothing of that world, how do expect to get volunteers to help you?'

'I'm just looking for someone.'

'We're all looking for someone, but you're looking for someone by proxy. You want to find the woman who was with Peter Mortimer and yet you ask questions about Emily Washburn. You're mixing fantasy with reality. You need to concentrate on what you really want. Once you know what you want you will be able to see.'

'What I want is to find out what happened to Peter Mortimer,' I said, as I saw the end of the skull's cigar flare.

'You are on a journey. You just need to catch the right train.'

Arbour stirred. Candy spoke to him and he opened his eyes. Candy went to where the vodka bottle rested and poured a good measure into a glass. She gave it to Arbour then whispered something in his ear. Arbour nodded in affirmation.

'He'll tell you a story,' Candy said

Arbour sat upright in his chair, took a gulp of vodka and looked directly at me. 'You see, everyone wants to find Emily Washburn. Everyone, that is, who has had previous dealings with her and has made mistakes. The simplest digression from the path, that she sets, puts you on the outer. Mentioning her puts everyone on the outer. You can't find Emily Washburn even if she exists. She may find you, but you will never find her. You need to put yourself into a space where she can talk to you if she's interested.'

I shook my head. Nothing was sinking in. 'You're saying that she both exists and doesn't exist. Is that right?'

Arbour poured more vodka into his glass. 'I'll tell you the story as I heard it. Then you might understand.' He stood from his chair and joined me on the lounge. 'When the Cannes film festival started in 1939 it was a very small event indeed. Over the years, of course, it has grown to become what it is today. The first rumours of a woman named Emily Washburn started in around 1950. From what I hear, she was a woman who believed that true beauty lives beneath the outer surface that we display to the world. She was a woman who could see that physical beauty means nothing if the inner self is corroded and vain. However, she also saw that physical beauty allowed for much leeway when the character of a person was being assessed. In her own way, she decided to even the scales a little and give people who are not endowed with beauty a fighting chance to succeed. In order to do this, she decided that she would supply beauty to any man who was nominated for an award at Cannes and who was unable to avail himself of a beautiful companion. I understand that she provided beautiful women to act as escorts during the fifties, but then it ceased.'

I waited for Arbour to continue, but he took a sip of his vodka and stood. 'I must get to bed now. I am already asleep.' He turned from me and walked from the room.

I was perplexed. He had told me nothing that would get my mental juices flowing. It was a fifty year old story that appeared to have no conclusion. 'Was that supposed to help?' I asked Candy.

'It did. Think of who and what you already know.'

My mind returned to the photograph at the top of the stairs. 'How well did Joshua know Peter Mortimer?' I asked, expecting a negative reply.

Candy didn't miss a beat. 'They knew each other for about four years. Peter was here five times if I recall.'

'How did they meet?'

'I think that Peter rang one day, asking for advice on his career. Joshua agreed to help and they seemed to hit it off. Why do you ask?'

'I saw a photo at the top of the stairs.'

'It's small and black and white.'

'Yes, I know.'

'You miss less than I thought. I've booked you into a hotel in Castres. It's only about twenty minutes drive, in these conditions. The snow's light, so you won't have much trouble with the roads.'

I stared overtly at Candy. She didn't seem to mind the scrutiny. An image formed in my mind but the colours were wrong. 'You dye your hair,' I said.

'Of course.'

I nodded and headed for the front door. Candy intercepted me and handed me my car keys. 'Drop by anytime.'

I walked into the snow, then stopped. I turned around to find Candy leaning on the door. 'What will happen to you when Joshua dies?' I asked.

She smiled, knowingly. 'The same thing that is happening to Marabou Worthington-Peters.'

'Good luck.' I called, as the snow began to settle on my nose.

L.A. Law

MARABOU'S second e-mail had me winging my way across the Atlantic with the intention of gate crashing a Hollywood celebrity party in Los Angeles. This time the party of interest wasn't in the background of a photo but on the front page of celebrity magazines. I booked into my hotel in the early morning to wait for an event that would not take place until the evening. This fitted well with other plans, so I found myself standing in the entry foyer of the Edward R Roybal Federal Building in L.A wondering how I would get to Drug Enforcement Agency offices on the seventeenth floor.

I had never seen so much security in a public space. But then I guess they needed something. There's a thirty two foot sculpture outside and someone has filled it with huge bullet holes. I looked around for someone wearing a flak jacket with DEA emblazoned across the back but couldn't find anyone. Maybe they only wear those in the movies. I could see that I would have difficulty in getting access to the seventeenth floor so tried asking for Special Agent Aliput at reception.

A bearded secretary typed into his computer and shook his head, 'Special Agent Aliput has no appointment listed for you this morning sir.'

'Yeah, I know. I just dropped by hoping to see her.'

'She doesn't take social calls.'

'Ahhh, yes, she told me that. This isn't really a social call. I worked with her on the Billy Squires' case in Australia. I'm in town for two days and thought I'd drop by.'

The man showed a mild interest. 'You're on the force then sir?'

'Yes, Special Eucalypts and Branches. We make sure that there's no extra vegetation grown along the Murray River.'

'Extra vegetation, I like that. It's funny the code words you agents use.'

'We like it.'

'Murray River you say.'

'Yes.'

'My brother does the same job on the Mississippi.'

'We're almost kin then.'

'Yeah…I guess we've got to stick together. I'll tell Agent Aliput that you're down here.'

'Scott Mawson.'

'Good sir.'

I looked at my watch. Midday. I was hungry, despite the gourmet plastic served up on the flight from Fiumicino to L.A.X. I had been rooted to the spot for half an hour. Maybe I should have called ahead. Maybe she wouldn't remember me. If she did remember, maybe she wouldn't want to see me. Either way, I hoped that I wasn't wasting my time.

I had sought help from Kendra Mortimer but she was unable to peel back any of the red tape associated with the New South Wales criminal justice system. She had hit a brick wall and been unable to find any loose mortar. This was a longshot, but I needed help and Aliput was the only person that I thought could lead me to Billy Squires.

'Sir,' it was the bearded secretary. 'Special Agent Aliput has just said that she will be right with you.'

At least she remembered. Now the ball was in my court to play. I wondered how she would react. She appeared through the lift door, talking to a rangy man with a slight stoop. I heard her say that he should proceed to the meeting and that she would only be a couple of minutes. Obviously seeing me wouldn't change any schedule that she had. I caught her eyes, only to realise that her expression was as unwelcoming as that of an Australian immigration official. This visit would be very short indeed.

'Mr Mawson of the vegetation squad,' she said.

'Special Agent,' I replied.

'Is there something I can do for you?'

Straight to the point. An insipid greeting would not have been remiss. 'I thought that there may have been, but I don't think so now.'

'I'm sorry, but I'm very busy right now and you don't have an appointment. All I can give you is a couple of minutes.'

'I want to see Billy Squires and that will take more than a couple of minutes of your time.'

Her face took on the quizzical gaze of the uninformed. 'What makes you think that I can help you with that? As far as I know, Squires is in Australia.' She looked at her watch. Time was almost up.

'Maybe some other time,' I said, realising that I had made a mistake. I gave her a slight nod of the head and began to head for the front door.

I was outside the building, looking for a cab when I heard hurried footsteps behind me. I turned to see Special Agent Aliput about twenty feet away. She hesitated as if uncertainty was dominating her actions. 'I really am busy, where are you staying?' she called.

'The Marriott Downtown.' I pointed my arm like a gun dog controller. 'A few blocks that way, I think.'

'I'll see you there at three...but I can only give you half an hour. Be in the foyer.'

With that, she turned on her flat heels and returned to the building. Three o'clock it would be then. Plenty of time to shove over sweetened food down my throat.

***

Special Agent Aliput entered the hotel lobby at precisely three. I had expected her to be alone but stooped and rangy was on her right and a squat appendage in a dark navy blue uniform, complete with badge and gun, was on her left. She made eye contact with me and the trio headed in my direction. I wondered what crime I had committed. I caught a cab so it couldn't be J-walking. I had no drugs in my possession. I hadn't robbed a bank. I wasn't carrying a gun. I hadn't polluted the atmosphere. It was certainly possible that my language wasn't hip enough and also possible that I had once criticised the acting ability of the state's ex-Governor. Essentially, I had no idea why Ms Aliput considered that she needed an escort.

'Shall we talk in your room, Mr Mawson?' she asked, without even the whimsical pretence of a greeting.

'Only if you promise not to enter me in the Rodney King look alike competition.'

'That's not funny and it wasn't us,' Rangy said.

'Neither was Fatty Arbuckle and I don't give a shit,' I replied.

'An expert in L.A. history are we?' Rangy spat.

I felt that it wasn't time to back down. That would come later. 'No, just an avid reader of comic books.'

'That's enough. You two,' Aliput said to her kindergarten class.

We entered a spare lift and I told Rangy the floor number. He pressed the floor button. The lift door remained open. He looked at me. I shrugged and handed him my room card. I caught the slightest glimpse of either a grimace or a smile creasing Aliput's lips. We rode the lift in silence, overwhelmed by uniform's deodorant. I held my breath until we reached the filtered air of the corridor on my floor.

Uniform waited outside of the door to my room while the agents led me inside. Aliput took in the view whilst rangy went through my things and checked out the bathroom. When he finished, he shook his head, horizontally, as an indication to Aliput that he had finished.

'Would you care to sit? ' Aliput asked.

'Why not, It's my room.' I sat on the side of the bed, then swung my legs up. I leant against the headboard. 'Don't trust yourself to be alone with me, huh?' I asked Aliput.

'We'll ask the questions,' Rangy said.

Aliput sat on a chair, beside the bed. 'How did you find me?'

'What?'

'You heard, asswipe. Answer the question,' Rangy spat.

'For fuck's sake, I didn't know she was missing.'

Aliput spoke. 'I was undercover, in Australia, and I didn't tell you where I was from. How did you track me down to here?'

I was beginning to feel myself bristle. This was silly at best, bizarre at worst. 'Your accent, of course. I knew your name at Silverton and when I arrived here, I rang your headquarters and asked where you were stationed. In Australia you were on a drug bust. In the movies that usually means DEA. Your office wouldn't tell, so I just rang again and asked for you. I was told that you were due back at around eleven. There's nothing sinister to it.'

'And what do you want with an indicted felon?' Rangy asked

I looked at Aliput. 'If he's talking about Billy Squires, there's something that I need to ask him.'

'And what's that? The location of his stash,' Rangy laughed at his own comment

I turned to him. 'You watch too many movies. You really need to play your bad cop role a little better. After all, it's only a thin blue line and you don't want to get we public off side. Besides, you spit when you speak and it's quite unpleasant.'

'Is that a threat?'

I looked at Aliput again. 'Is this really necessary. I just want to talk to Squires about Peter Mortimer's movie.'

Aliput said nothing but cocked her right eyebrow. I continued 'Squires had an injunction placed on the movie to stop its release by Mario Pitelli. I want to talk to Billy about getting the injunction lifted. The movie has the shelf life of processed cheese and soon it will be too late to give it any release at all. It's probably too late already. To do what I want to do, I have been told to follow the movie. If it isn't released, there is nothing to follow.'

'What's he on about?' Rangy inserted.

Aliput ignored him. 'And how do you think I can help?'

Aliput's scowl was slowly being replaced by a mischievous grin that I had seen at Silverton. Something was calming the waters. I kept rolling. 'My client is drawing a blank in Australia. She tried Billy's lawyer but he can't contact Billy through the usual channels. He keeps crashing into a paperwork wall that usually doesn't exist. He thinks that Billy isn't in the country. I think that he's over here and, if that's the case, you will know where he is.'

Rangy stood over me, looking down as if at dog shit. 'You entered this country without luggage. Is your stay expected to be very short?'

'After meeting you, it isn't short enough.'

'Why no luggage?' he asked

There was pressure building on my fuse. 'Listen, pal, have you any idea just how much trouble it is to bring luggage into this country. You even make people use locks that your authorities can open. That's enough to give a dope importer a hard on. It allows anyone to tamper with luggage. Then again, I guess that you have no problems with drug trafficking in this country.'

'Leave it,' Aliput said, her voice tinged with malice. She looked at me again. 'You came all this way to find out if Billy Squires is here in L.A?'

I smirked, 'Of course not. I'm here to gatecrash a party. I thought I'd kill two birds with one stone.'

'Who's party?' Aliput asked.

'Julia Dendrobium's.'

Aliput smiled, 'You know Julia?'

'No...but you sound as if you do.'

'Yes. She's a friend of my mother. Mum and dad are going to the party tonight. I'm surprised you have an invitation. They're scarce.'

'As I said, I'm a gatecrasher.'

Aliput smiled and her eyes shone with an inner light. 'I thought you were joking. Why come all this way to crash a party. What if you don't get in?'

'I have been trying for weeks to get an appointment with her. Nothing ever eventuates. I read about the party and decided to give it a go. That and Billy Squires brought me here.'

'You believe this shit?' Rangy asked.

Aliput smiled at him. 'Sorry Joe. Unfortunately I do believe it. It's okay. Could you give me a couple of minutes with Mr Mawson.'

Rangy snarled one last time, like a schoolboy being saved from a bully. He said nothing but left the room.

Aliput waited for him to close the door. 'You had us worried.'

'I don't see why. It's just yank paranoia. You think every bastard is out to get you. You'll all look for the real reasons one day. It will be a revelation to you.'

'Philosophy 101?'

'No…common sense…sixth grade. Can you help me get to Billy Squires?'

Aliput shook her head. 'Sorry. But if you want to tell me what you want…and reasoning that may be useful…I'll see what I can do for you.'

I tried something lateral. 'What's your name? I can't keep thinking of you as Special Agent Aliput.'

'It's not Marilyn.'

'You didn't even blink.'

'I know.'

'Well…what is it?'

'It's Amelia….Amelia Marilyn.'

'Second name after your mother?'

'Yes. But how do you know.'

I smiled at her. 'I have a head full of useless knowledge.'

'I think that people may need to be wary of you. You could be dangerous.'

I had no idea what she meant, but *she* thought that I was keeping track with *her* knowledge. 'Maybe we can have a coffee downstairs and I'll tell you what I need from Billy Squires,' I said.

'I'll let my boys off their leashes.' She said as she nodded in Rangy's direction.

When we were riding the lift down, I noticed that she was beginning to smirk. 'What's so funny?' I asked.

'You're going to gatecrash the Dendrobium party. I don't believe it. You'll never get past the front gate.'

'Maybe I'll luck out.'

'But why?'

'I had an e-mail telling me that it would be worth my while.'

'E-mail from who?'

'Someone who makes me feel as if I'm a dog on a leash. Someone that I hope will lead me to Jacqueline du Pre.'

California Orchid

THE polite guard, who had a head like an unexploded cannon shell and shoulders to match, arched his eyebrows as I told him what I wanted. 'You're not on the guest list, sir,' he read from an electronic clipboard that was secured to his wrist by a gold chain.

'I know,' I said. 'I tried to tell you, I'm not here for the party. I'm an investigator and would like a word with Miss Julia Dendrobium.'

'Sir, we're having a party to celebrate Miss Dendrobium's birthday. I doubt that she will want to be interviewed by anyone.'

'Can you please check with her?'

The guard flashed a smarmy smile, 'Yes sir. If you insist. Do you have a card?'

'What?'

'A business card. Do you have one, with your details on it?'

'No. I'm not looking for work. I just want to speak with Julia Dendrobium.'

The guard walked away. I was surprised that he turned his back to me and picked up a wall phone, within his small guardhouse. He punched several buttons and then spoke. As he did so, I watched as a steady stream of people filed through the gates. Some held invitations in their hand; others used the darkness as cover. In either case, it was none of my business so I just waited for the guard to finish on the phone.

He finally hung up and was shaking his head again as he turned toward me. His face seemed to wear a pall of gloom that suggested that he had just heard that the world had ended. 'As I suspected sir, Miss Dendrobium is unavailable for an interview this evening. However, I am told that if you wish to leave us a photograph of yourself, you will be assessed.'

Assessed. I didn't understand. 'What do you mean?' I asked.

'Sir, Miss Dendrobium can sense things about people from their photographs. If she likes the look of your photograph, you may be allowed to make contact with her private secretary.'

'Does that mean if she has a photo of me I can see her?'

'Not at all, sir. It simply means that you discuss an appointment with her secretary. It has no guarantee.'

I had never heard of such a thing but thought that I would play along. After all, it was in my best interest to speak to Julia Dendrobium. I asked the obvious question. 'Does the photo need to be any particular size....you know, will a passport size photograph do or does it need to be closer to a wall hanging?'

'I don't think that you are taking this seriously, sir. I will now terminate this conversation. Please do not call again.' With that, the guard ignored me and returned to his task of checking valid invitations.

I waited and leaned against the guard house wall. Carload after carload of the Hollywood A League pulled up to the gate and held a quick discussion with the guard. He diligently ticked off each name and gave the person a smile. I couldn't remember seeing anyone so polite and so dedicated to the task at hand. It was always *yes sir, yes madam, yes miss, welcome sir, I hope you enjoy yourself miss*. The only thing that stopped me from giving the man ten out of ten was that every time he leaned into a car to study the faces of the occupants, one of a line of people that hid along the unlit outer perimeter wall would slip into the property unnoticed.

As I held up the stonework trying to decide what to do next, I noticed that one of the shadowlanders moved too quickly and the guard spied the elegantly dressed woman with his peripheral vision. He stood and called out to her. 'Stop!'

The woman stopped like a fawn in headlights. She slinked into the shadows of the huge entry gate and waited while the guard walked around the front of a red Ferrari. 'Just where do you think you are going, young lady?' the guard called to the woman.

'I dropped my shoe,' the woman said.

The guard looked astounded. 'Where?'

'Just over there,' she said, as she pointed to a dark patch of ground inside the gate.

'Get it then,' the guard said. 'But come straight back out. I'm watching you and don't forget it.'

The woman walked to the dark patch and started to look closely at the ground. The man in the Ferrari honked his horn and the sound of a raging bull fractured the ionosphere. I had never heard such a racket from such a small device.

The guard turned toward the car. 'Sorry sir,' he said. 'I'll be with you in a minute. I have to look after this lady first, sir. She's lost her shoe.'

The Ferrari driver looked at me and shook his head. 'My godfather. You just can't get good help these days. That man's an idiot.'

'Looks smart in the uniform though,' I said.

'I bet he's glad he has elastic sided boots,' the man said.

I smiled at his patronising joke. It seemed the thing to do. After all, he was driving a Ferrari and had an invitation to an A list party. I, on the other hand, drove a small rental and had no invitation. I figured that he could be as patronising as he liked. I looked at the guard and noticed that he was about to stand. Apparently, the shoe had been found. It was useless to hang around all night, so I decided to leave. Just as I moved from the wall, the guy in the Ferrari spoke to me.

'You waiting for someone?' he asked.

'Yeah, Bill Murray. He was supposed to meet me here with my invitation, but I arrived a little late. I guess that I missed him.'

'You know Bill, huh. Maybe he's already inside. Jump in and I drive you up to the house.'

I couldn't believe what was happening. I'd used one of the oldest lines on record and Ferrari man had bought it. And he thought that the guard had problems. 'Sure, thanks.' I said as I rushed around the car and jumped into the passenger seat. I was just buckling my seatbelt when the guard returned to his station.

'Invitation, please sir,' he said to the driver.

'We've already done that,' the driver replied.

'Oh yes, sir. On your way then. Use the carpark at the rear of the house. Just follow the signs.'

'Derek Hardman, News anchor for CAFUTV.' The driver introduced himself, as we accelerated along a concrete drive through an avenue of huge chestnut trees, toward a parking area.

'Scott Mawson, SE and B, from Florence, Italy,' I replied.

'Nice to meet you Scott. That's something in programming is it?'

'Yeah, just one of the backroom boys. Don't get out much'

We arrived at the grassed carpark to be guided into a parking space by a sprightly young woman wearing a tiny black and white striped bikini over knee length leather boots. Her long blond hair bounced slightly as she walked and when she bent at the waist, to remove a location marker from in front of the car, I heard Hardman gasp so loudly I thought he would faint. I thanked him for the lift and alighted from the car onto soft grass underfoot. Another black and white bikini pointed us toward an illuminated area that was still five minutes walk from where we had parked.

'You need to be early to get a good parking spot at Julia's bashes. I always seem to be too late. We'll have to get our liquid supply replenished as soon as we hit the bar.' Hardman said.

'I'm parched,' I said. 'It must have been waiting in amongst all those car fumes at the gate.'

'Yeah, I know. That's why I always drive a convertible,' Hardman replied.

We rounded a blue spruce that was set back from a coloured gravel and cobblestone pathway that ran from the parking area to the house. I stopped. I had to blink twice to ensure that what I was seeing was real. The mansion appeared as a two-storey glass elliptical tube that was cantilevered in space from a steep slope that formed a backdrop to the building. There were areas of shade and light throughout the building and I could see people milling on two separate levels. I had an image of hundreds of people inside a glass bottle. There appeared to be a windowed band of polished concrete around the centre of the building but that just seemed to highlight the wonder of the rest of the structure.

'Neat, huh?' Derek said. 'By the look on your face I take it you haven't been here before.'

'No.' I stuttered. 'What holds it up?'

'Columns of course. They are highly polished and you can't see them with the lighting set out as it is. You can see them in the daylight. The place isn't half as spectacular then.'

'It's all glass.' I wondered

'Glass, polished concrete and marble. It cost Joe Dendrobium a fortune. It's what Julia wanted and what Julia got.'

'I guess that there's a lot of sunlight and heat in the house.'

'I've been here during the day. There's a lot of light but the heat is moderated. It's a very well controlled climate within the house.'

I wasn't surprised. I walked with Derek toward the house and could see the huge columns once we were close to them. We entered a glassed in foyer and stepped through the open portal into the midst of the party. There seemed to be people mixing everywhere. Some seemed to be looking at me, as if trying to figure out who I was. It was a mutual feeling. At the gate it was going to be easy, but now I was inside and would have to mingle with people whom I didn't know and talk about an industry of which I had no knowledge. I was beginning to feel that gatecrashing might not have been the best thing to do. It wasn't the fear of getting caught though, it was getting caught out as an interloper who had no idea what was going on and who knew no one. I figured that I would have to shadow Hardman but then noticed that he had disappeared into the maelstrom of humanity that fought for each oxygen filled millimetre of space within the room.

I made my way to the bar and took a tall fluted glass of Moët and Chandon from a petite young woman in a mauve and white version of the same bikini that had helped Hardman park his car. I stood at a railing and watched the people at the rear of the house, who were mingling around a fluorescent blue swimming pool. I couldn't believe that I was looking down on so many beautiful smiles that enhanced so many sets of perfectly white and sculptured teeth. I couldn't decide whether it was genes, luck or money. I decided that it was probably a combination. I closed my mouth to sip the champagne. The people around the pool opened theirs to smile at one another.

I noticed Hardman by the pool. He had discarded his green sports coat with its golfing logo and was talking animatedly to a mid-thirties wasp, whose lips were too capacious for her face. My guess was that she really wanted to be Afro-American.

I was still smiling at my own inane joke when I heard the sound of a siren in the background. It began softly but seemed to increase in volume as it wafted through the house. Then it stopped and there was silence. Even the jazz band, at the far end of the pool, and the four piece classical ensemble, in the entertaining room, had stopped playing. It was as if everyone was waiting for something to happen before they continued their conversations.

This is Brereton Fox, the chief of security speaking. I'm sorry to bother our celebrated friends but it appears that we have more people at the party than invited guests. I have determined that the surplus number is nine. This does not include the thirteen reporters and photographers that have been removed from the gardens by the Rottweilers. Would all those people who do not have a silver on platinum invitation please leave the party. Please note that this does include those who believe that they should have received and invitation but didn't. We will give these people fifteen minutes to leave. Thank you for your time.

The noise of the crowd resumed as if it hadn't been interrupted. How could they count? How did they know that there were nine interlopers? Who were the others? Why did the metallic voice through the speakers seem to be chuckling when he mentioned the reporters? Were they let in deliberately? I couldn't supply the answers to any of the questions but knew that I had been caught out. I looked around and felt that every pair of eyes within the confines of the balcony was piercing my soul. There seemed to be a silent urging, which I felt might turn into a raging screaming of *out, out, out.* It would be like fifties unionism again. I stood for a moment, defiant, sipping my champagne with mouth pursed. I knew that it wouldn't last and the clock was ticking.

Then I noticed something odd. Derek Hardman had retrieved his green jacket and was heading for the carpark. I replayed the guard's movements in my head and realised that he had *not* checked Hardman's invitation. The woman with the shoe trick had either been a ruse or a case of perfect timing. I shrugged. It didn't really matter to me. Hardman was one down; there were eight to go. I finished the bubbly and began the humiliatingly long walk down the eleven glass and chrome steps between the upper level and entry level. I felt that I was being jostled and that the bumps were more hardened than when I had pushed my way up the same staircase.

Suddenly, I felt something pushed into my hand. I looked down to see that it was a card. It was the same size and shape as a credit card and was silver on platinum. I looked at it closely. The copperplate wording started "Miss Julia Dendrobium requests the pleasure of your company at her thirty third birthday party to be held..." I looked around quickly, but saw no one who looked like they could have palmed me the card. I was mystified but I was now at the party with an invitation. Champagne to celebrate; this time hardened to any feelings of being watched. I had exchanged the champagne flute for a beer mug when I heard the siren again. This time it was an evenly pitched mid volume drone. The conversations continued.

'What's that?' I asked the winner of the 1988 Barbie doll look alike competition, who stood beside me at the outer edge of a group that included two Oscar nominees.

She looked at me, askance. I felt as if I had just walked along a Parisian street and forgotten to clean the soles of my shoes. I twigged. I lifted the invitation from my shirt pocket and watched her frown change to a dayglow smile.

'You're new at these things, obviously.' It was more of a statement than a question.

'Yes. I'm Julia's new SE and B man from Italy.'

The woman looked me up and down. 'You don't look Italian.'

'I don't speak Italian either. I just live there…south of Firenze.' I hoped that one Italian sounding word would set her mind at ease.

'That siren's for the all clear. The riffraff have left.'

I was intrigued. 'How do they know?'

'They scan the invitations, of course. Some electronic device in the ceiling. I don't know. It happens everywhere these days,' the woman said, then turned back to her group.

Maybe the guard wasn't supposed to tie his shoelaces. I began to mingle, keeping my mouth closed and staying only at the edge of the various groups who gathered around those with names of distinction. There were actors, producers, directors, rehabilitated rock stars and has-beens who still remembered that they used to be someone important; each holding court and wowing his or her audience. It appeared that the rest were just the flakes of humanity who occasionally peeled from the edge of one group or another. What I didn't see was any sign of Julia Dendrobium or her illustrious husband Joseph. I was beginning to wonder if they were here at all but guessed that they had to be. After all it was Julia's birthday party.

Just as I was beginning to worry a trumpeted fanfare rang out and rattled the three champagnes and as many beers that now impacted on my thoughts. I waited for the accompanying announcement. I wasn't disappointed.

Ladies and Gentlemen. Please gather at the southern end of the pool and our illustrious hostess will cut her birthday cake. The voice had the melodious tones of a circus ringmaster.

Southern end? I had no idea really, but I followed the throng making their way to the outer pool deck. I soon realised that the southern end was the one closest to the house. Between the house and pool was an expansive, multi-coloured marble tiled deck. It was accessed by two sets of stairs and a lift. I figured that Julia would emerge from the lift.

The crowd jostled into position and I was pushed forward until I was just to one side of the golden lift doors. When the crowd settled I was able to stand upright, instead of supporting myself to stop the crushing sensation of being pushed through a wall.

A path had been cleared from the lift to a podium ready for a gigantic, sumptuous birthday cake that was now trying to push its way in from the back of the crowd. Even from my position I could hear the pastry chef cursing the myriad people who were taking the glory from his latest mind blowing creation. Then the crowd gave an imitation of the Red Sea and the chef and his cake arrived, right on schedule. I couldn't see all of it, but the upper half was a vertically layered edible stack of delicious looking white chocolate. Pink and mauve candied flowers clung to the side of the cake for dear life and atop the two storey marvel was a single white orchid of a variety that I instantly recognised.

Applause rang out to celebrate the pâtissier's work and a recently reconfigured matinee idol, standing on the far edge of the crowd, took a small bow. I decided that I didn't want to be at the front so asked an elderly woman of rotund proportion if she would care to change places. The gesture made her day. We then waited for the moment to arrive. It was almost exciting.

The lift doors opened and my heart collapsed. I had seen Julia Dendrobium on the big screen but the real thing placed everything else in the shadows. I don't know what I expected, but I guess that I had prepared myself to set my eyes on beauty that showed the unrefined semblance of a woman before the PhotoShop marvels and makeup artists have worked their miracles and forever modified the original. This image would be enhanced by makeup and jewellery and a dress that would transport the assembled audience into raptures. What I saw, instead, was beauty that transcended thought. There was no make-up other than a touch of pale pink lipstick and a light dusting of blush on her cheeks. The dress was a simple white knee length sheath that was set off by a simple mauve and pale green necklace. Her blond hair reflected the light as it bounced gently on her shoulders as she walked toward the podium in steps that were measured and refined. Here was the essence of beauty.

Beside Julia, and guiding her as she walked, was a man who looked to be in his late fifties. He was broad shouldered and broader stomached. His face was narrow and his eyes beady and watchful. His nose was capable of inhaling a surfeit of oxygen and his lips were thin to the point of being almost non-existent. This had to be the enigmatic Joseph Dendrobium. His image fitted.

I noticed that Joe wore the casual slacks and open necked shirt that was de rigueur for the party. This meant that Julia was the only person at the party who didn't look like she was having a bad shirt day. Maybe she would change after the official ceremony. I hoped so. I stepped into the lift and pushed the button marked 3. The lift doors closed and I felt as if I was being lifted on a cushion of air.

The lift doors opened and I found myself in what looked like the entry foyer to an executive suite. The room's floorplan was the same elliptical shape as the building itself, with a white marble floor and a single glass and marble column dominating its centre. There was a glass case in the centre of the column. Two doors, that were set into the far curved wall, were in the same pleasant mauve and green tones as the necklace that currently adorned Julia's neck.

I walked to the centre column and looked at the glass case. Inside the case stood a single white orchid nestled into a tubular glass flute. The flower had rounded petals and a mauve centre. At the rear of the flower, the mauve interfused with pale green. The flower was singularly exquisite.

I moved to one of the doors and found it locked. I tried the handle on the other and heard the slight clunk of its lock mechanism as the handle moved. I opened the door and stared into Julia Dendrobium's inner sanctum. The room was as understated as its occupant. The same whites, mauves and greens that I had come to expect adorned the space in subtle tones. The bed was a simple queen size with curved flowing lines. The dressing table was a fixture that was set into a wall and adorned with a tabletop to ceiling mirror. Then I saw my reflection in the night mirrored curve of the outer wall. There was something that didn't fit in the scene. *Me.* I had no right to be at the party and now I was in the hostess' bedroom.

I stepped from the bedroom just as the lift moved into place on Level 3. I stood behind the display column and waited. Hopefully she would be alone. The lift door opened and Julia stepped lightly onto the marble floor. Her high heels clinked. She looked at me and blinked once. She looked again and smiled.

'I assume that you are admiring the beauty of the flower,' she said, her voice soft and smooth, with a slight French accent.

'Yes,' I said. 'I hope you don't mind.'

'Why would I mind? It's on display.'

'I thought that I may be intruding,' I said.

Julia smiled and my heart melted. 'You've been intruding all evening, Mr Mawson.'

I was bewildered. Julia Dendrobium had just said my name. I watched as she walked to the viewing case and looked at the orchid. She pressed on the column, just below the glass case, and a find spray of mist began to float from the ceiling of the case to the petals of the flower. 'I take it that you know my orchid.'

'I think so, but I'm still tracking its origin.'

'Very wise. One must learn everything about the things that one seeks.'

'I try.'

'This is the *Dendrobium bigibbum*. But you already know that,' Julia said as she nodded toward the flower. 'It prefers a controlled environment in order to exist. We try to keep it away from its natural predators.'

'Do you think I'm a predator?' I asked.

'No. But what you are looking for is not what you will find. But soon you will believe and then you will see.'

I was intrigued. 'How do you know this? How do you even know my name?'

Julia walked from the column to her bedroom door. She opened the door and motioned me to follow.

'I have to get changed for the party,' she said. 'Why don't you tell me why you are here while I change. Sit on the bed if you like.'

I sat on the bed and watched while Julia touched a wall and part of it slid back. It revealed a dressing room complete with racks of clothing, a shoe stand and a dressing table similar to the one in the bedroom. She removed her white sheath dress and stood at a rack wearing only her mauve lingerie and white high heels. She glanced at me over her shoulder. 'To your taste?' she asked.

I didn't want to blink and miss anything. 'Perfect.' I answered.

'Not too small in the bum for you?'

I smiled.

Julia removed a pale green blouse and a pair of white slacks from a rack and placed them on a stand beside the dressing table. 'I had trouble getting you in. I thought that you might get cold feet and leave,' she said. She then removed her bra and displayed perfectly proportioned breasts of exactly the same size. 'When John rang me from the guardhouse I told him to turn a blind eye... so that you could sneak in. But you just stood leaning against my wall. I had to get Derek Hardman to drive by and pick you up. Then my fool of a security chief decided to do an invitation scan so I had to have one of my friends slip a card into your hand. You've taken quite an effort.' She slipped on the slacks and then the blouse, without replacing the bra. She replaced the high heels with scuffs and walked back into the bedroom. 'I guess, after all that effort, that I should ask you what you expect to gain from our meeting. Let's go, we can talk as we walk.'

I sat on the bed, praying for erectile dysfunction. I needed a little time. 'I'm trying to track down Emily Washburn. I need to find her.'

Julia smiled. It was warm and showed her perfectly moulded, sparkling white teeth. 'I understood that you are looking for Jacqueline du Pre.'

'I am...but if I can find Emily Washburn I feel that my search will become much shorter in duration.'

'Then it will be a very long search. Emily only exists in the mind of believers.'

'You are proof that she exists ... and Marabou and Candy and Quenna and Cali Darlington.'

Julia's smile was benign. 'You have been given knowledge. You are now an expert in a variety of flowers and you wonder why or how you attained such knowledge. However this knowledge is not for the reason that you think. It is for enlightenment pertaining to your true purpose. It will help you understand when the time comes.'

Julie walked from the room and waved for me to follow.

Biting the inside of my bottom lip, until the pain was unbearable, worked on my libido. I stood and followed Julia from the room.

Outside the bedroom, there was something wrong. The entry foyer wasn't clear. A very fine mist floated within the confines of the room. It seemed to be settling on me. Julia didn't seem to notice and pressed for the lift. She turned as the lift door opened. I tried to follow but the distance seemed to have changed from just a few steps to a mile. I called to Julia but she didn't seem to hear. I grabbed hold of the column and slid down its length. The floor surrounded me and took me into its cocoon. I couldn't breathe. It was getting dark. I screamed 'Why, Julia!'

Child of the Tulip

THERE are times, when making love, that seismic shocks trammel the world and feelings are so intense that you wonder if you will ever survive. There are other times when you drift into a languid garden of absolute serenity and feel as if you want to relive the moment until the end of eternity. Sometimes, you simply fuck for all you are worth and hope that your efforts will be rewarded by a return bout. Then there are the times when your lover's eyes become the words from a song and *have a mist like the smoke of a distant fire.* Some lovers would see this as indicating that their partner was thinking of another, but I was dreaming of Amelia Aliput and simply pleased to be imagining sex. I moved forward and our lips met, tongues entwined and she gripped me with her thighs, urging me on. I had never experienced such a thrilling sensation. I kissed her lips, wanting to devour her. She drove her lips into mine, clashing teeth and scoring my top lip. It stung a little but dreams do that sometimes. Fingernails clawed at my back, scraping and urging. I closed my eyes and wanted the dream to last forever.

California sunlight played on my eyelids as slumber gave way to a new dawn. A buzzing sprang from deep in my psyche. It was soft and low, like the drone of a single bee but, somehow, sweet and soothing. I listened but it was not a sound that I recognised. The buzzing stopped.

Silence, except for fan blown air passing through the room. I tried to remember where I was but my erotic dream interfered; surreal in concept. I was pleased that it was not one of those cyclic nightmares that take you on a disjointed journey then returns to the beginning so that it can restart the process or the restrained feeling that always leaves you wrapped in blankets like a Russian doll. This was the other type; the dream that makes you wonder if there is a reality of semiconscious thought that confuses when it abruptly terminates.

I lay still and listened to the air conditioning, waiting for another sound that would help me identify whether or not I was in some form of imminent danger. I pushed the dream aside and tried to recall the events of the night. I could remember nothing after sliding down a length of a column and seeing Julia Dendrobium disappear into a lift. From then until now ... whenever now might be ... was lost in the shadows of darkness. Thoughts rushed through my mind like liquid through a sieve; none staying long enough to take hold. I couldn't grip events; I couldn't comprehend what was going on. Julia Dendrobium had organised for me to remain at her party uninvited and she had not been perturbed when she found me in her bedroom and yet she had enveloped me in a drug-laden mist. I assumed that event to be the precursor to what was happening to me now. But what was happening? In my minds eyes I could see myself on a comfortable bed in an air-conditioned room.

I decided to roll over, feigning sleep but flashing my eyes open to gain a glimpse of my surroundings. I counted to three then, moaning slightly, rolled onto my side. When I flicked open my eyes there was nothing but the carved timber of a bed-head. I remained in my new position and waited. Nothing stirred. I noticed something else. Subtle, with a hint of afterthought and the erotic scent of spent passion. I sniffed at the sheet and inhaled the fragrance. It was definitely the afterscent of sex. That must be it; the reason for my dream. I had been dumped on someone's shagging bed. I didn't know whether to be pleased or annoyed.

The buzzing returned; subtle and distant, like a sound emanating from another room and muffled by walls. Then I felt the sound on my leg. I began to sweat and pump adrenaline. It was fight or flight time. I decided that there was some inevitability in what would happen so it was better to face the demons than pretend to sleep. I counted to three again, coiled myself like a spring and sat up quickly, ready to pounce on whoever was with me in the room.

I looked around, startled. I was in my bed, in my room, in my hotel. I leapt from the bed and scampered around the room, looking into the bathroom and along the small anteroom. I opened the door and perused the corridor. Everything was in order. I returned to the bed and slumped down, mentally exhausted. Nothing made sense. Every thought required a response but there was nothing forthcoming. How did I get back to my room? Who was fucking in my bed? What created the buzzing sensation? I was full of answerless questions. I stood and walked around the room, slowly, with eyes peering into every nook and cranny: a thorough examination. There was nothing amiss, everything was in its place; even my clothes were strewn over the occasional lounge with the disregard that only I can muster. I closed my eyes in an attempt to remember how I had returned to the room. Nothing would come except the blackness of an unclear thought.

I remembered the buzzing on my leg. Maybe one of the questions had an answer, after all. I pulled the blankets and sheets from the bed with a swift, jerking motion. A small metallic object flew into the air and then bounced on the floor like a matt silver egg. I looked at it in wonder. I knew what it was, immediately. I leaned down and picked up the cell phone. It wasn't mine and I had no idea as to whom it belonged. It was one of the small compacts that require the fingers of a ten-year-old and the manual dexterity of a safebreaker to operate. I flipped the top and saw that it was switched on.

There was a message received icon on the screen. I pressed OPTIONS and followed the instructions. I waited impatiently as the digital operator went through her motions. Then the message: *Your package is leaving LAX at 1:00pm. QANTAS flight 8.* The message had no meaning. I looked at my watch. 9:15am. I dropped the phone onto the bed and headed for the shower. I would settle my mind under running water.

Once the water purled in the shower, it took less than a second to realise that my mind would not be settling. I flinched and arched my back as thousands of water droplets pounded my back like stinging nettles. I stepped from the stall, twisted my neck like an actor from an exorcist film and glanced at the bathroom mirror. A soggy creature with heat heightened scratches across his back stared at me with the dropped jaw of disbelief. I agreed with his sentiments as I pulled my skin tight. There were eight scratches, two of them on heightened welt ridges. I stood still, water puddling on the floor at my feet. This was worse than the dream. If the sex was real, then why couldn't I remember? My snippet was that of a manic with a remote control who channel surfs and sees nothing of value until he comes to something that is ending and makes him wonder about what he has missed. The window into my mind was as wide as a bow slit in an ancient castle but there was no beginning and no end, just a flicker in the movie of time. I stepped back into the shower and turned up the pressure. I would either remember or drown. I expected a short life span.

***

I was packing when I remembered the message on the phone. *Your package is leaving LAX at 1:00pm.* It had to have meaning. Suddenly, it did. Billy Squires leaving L.A. at 1:00pm. It had to be a message from someone to Amelia Aliput. The phone had to belong to Amelia. I looked at my watch. 10:25am. I needed to be elsewhere.

At 10:45 I was in a cab on my way to the airport, willing the mobile gridlock to take another route. At 11:45 I was within sight of the airport wondering how the cellphone could come to be wrapped up in the disorder of my bed. At midday I was rushing toward the *Departures* notice board, looking for QF8. I found it and rushed toward the exit gate.

Then it struck, like a Gyro Gearloose brainwave. The departure lounge was on the other side of customs. I had no boarding pass and no chance of getting any further. I stood like an automaton, staring at the customs gates and feeling as smart as a sheep who had just flunked an intelligence test. I began to think of what I could do.

Thoughts came and went, none sticking long enough to take hold on a psyche that was in the early stages of panic. That was it…panic. I could panic. That would fill in some time. I looked at my watch. 12:09. Fifty one minutes until the flight departed. What if I did get inside, somehow. What then? It was certain that Billy Squires would not be having a last minute coffee in a flightside lounge. They would get him to the plane through the *staff only* system and he would be on the plane whilst I waited at the boarding gate hoping for a glimpse. I thought back to my rush from the hotel and slid it into my mental page marked *flights of futility*.

As I lumbered toward a coffee outlet, with the enthusiasm of a French nobleman at a guillotine party, I realised that it was not only the trip from the hotel but the entire sojourn that had been futile. I had not made contact with Billy Squires and, whilst successful in crashing the Dendrobium party, had achieved as much as a water gatherer with a bottomless bucket. I glanced again at my watch and smiled, as I realised that I only had another six and a half hours until my flight back to Florence. What to do? Fill in the time back in LA or drown my sorrows in the club lounge. I opted for the latter.

***

I was sitting at a round table, wondering why I could only buy coffee in one of a variety of bucket sizes, when I felt a familiar buzz on my leg. I slipped the phone from my pocket and pressed the green phone icon. 'This is a found phone. If you tell me who it belongs to, I'll return it to the owner,' I said.

'Amelia, is that you?' said a feminine voice that I didn't recognise.

'No…but I found her phone.'

'Ohhh,' said the voice.

'Yes. I'm trying to find the owner…so that I can return it.'

The line went dead.

I shrugged and placed the phone on the table as an overweight girl placed a muffin of similar proportion on my table. I thanked the girl and thought of the amount of sugar that would be hidden amongst the blueberries. I wondered if restaurants of this type should be fitted with scales at the checkouts. Maybe one could check their weight before placing an order.

I broke off a small piece muffin and washed it down with sickly rich coffee. I would be hyperactive for hours. I revisited my watch. I had filled in all of twenty minutes. Only another three hours and I could check in for my flight.

The phone rang again, 1:02pm. This time I just made the connection, hoping that the person on the other end would speak. I could hear that the line was open but there was no sound other than background hum.

'You're paying for the call.' I said finally.

'Try Uncle Sam.'

'Nah … he only calls iPhones. This one's foreign rubbish.'

'It fits my pocket.'

'It won't if you don't come and get it.'

I told her where I was, expecting to find that she would be unsuspecting of my presence at the airport. She wasn't. She uttered something about it being anticipated and that she had rung her phone to leave me a message. I was miffed at my own predictability and verged on telling her where to go, but that would get me nowhere so I waited and took another shot of sugar.

When she walked into the café, she looked every part the hardened DEA agent; blonde with shades and resplendent in denim jeans with a black tee shirt and gun holster. The jeans were tucked into bovver boots. The badge, pinned to a clip on her belt buckle, mimicked the DEA patch on her tee shirt. The look so matched the stereotype in my imagination that I looked around for a movie crew. She sat opposite and flicked her blond hair from her forehead then lifted her ubiquitous sunglasses and rested them atop her silky tresses. I offered to get her a coffee but she looked at mine and declined.

'Did Billy get away safely?' I asked, skipping any re-introduction.

'He's never been here,' she said.

'If we played hypotheticals and I asked whether or not Billy got away safely…how would you answer?'

'Hypothetically he's on his way home. It was a waste of time really.'

'His or yours?'

Amelia shook her head. 'Both…I guess.'

'How so?'

'Billy Squires always claimed that his stash was for personal use. He's always been a dope head and always struggled to find enough bucks to feed his habit. He told us that when he came into money he bought enough to never run out again. He may have had enough to keep a moderate sized town high but we never did prove that he was dealing the stuff.'

'And why did I get the cryptic phone message?' I asked. 'I take it that I was never going to see Billy.'

She picked a lump from my muffin, sniffed it and returned it to my plate. 'It's a wonder you're not fat.'

'I always try to blend with locals. I was beginning to feel anorexic, here.'

'You're not anorexic.'

'No...but I feel as if a soggy bun has been pushed into my head and exploded...or was that a lobotomy. Maybe you can help me. What happened last night?'

Amelia smirked. 'You don't remember?'

'Humour me. Assume that I remember nothing,' I said. It was close to the truth.

A look of genuine concern flashed across Amelia's face and rested on her eyes. 'I could say that you know how to make a woman feel bad but you seem to be asking a real question. Are you saying that you really don't remember?'

'About thirty seconds sometime in the wee hours. Apart from that...nothing.'

'Then you don't remember calling me and taking me to dinner at your hotel?'

'I can't have eaten. I was starving when I woke up.'

She smiled and our eyes locked. 'Or going back to your room?'

'Or crashing the Dendrobium party and being hit with some sort of drug,' I added.

She leaned back on the chair in a way that would give a body language expert a wet dream. 'You couldn't get in. That was why you called me. You were lucky that I had nothing better to do.'

'You could have woken me for the sex. I missed my performance,' I said.

Amelia shrugged, ignored what I said and changed the subject. 'Billy did what you wanted.'

I missed the segue but rode with the flow, my comment apparently unheard. 'And that was?'

'He called his lawyers in Sydney and left instructions that you would be calling and they were to do whatever you asked. He even seemed keen to help you out. I don't know why, but he didn't even seem to have any angst toward me...and I put him in the mess that he's now in.'

'He may not care anymore,' I offered.

Amelia pulled another chunk from my muffin. This time she slipped some into her mouth. 'You're probably right,' she said around a mouthful of crumbs. 'He said something about liking being buggered and was looking forward to more when he gets back to prison in Sydney. I really don't understand that though. I thought you Australians used buggered to mean tired. Maybe he doesn't sleep well on planes.'

'He was probably being literal,' I said, acknowledging that the main difference between our two countries is that they are separated by a common language. 'You say that all I have to do is tell Billy's lawyers what I want and they will do it?'

'That's what he said. *Whatever you want.*'

I thought of Joshua Arbour. He had said that I needed to get involved in Peter Mortimer's film. Now there was a chance but I had no idea what Arbour had meant. If I was right, any connection with the Mortimer film would do no more than get me a film to watch. It would not be nominated for Cannes again and would get me no closer to Jacqueline du Pre. However, I was pleased that Amelia had followed through.

'Couldn't you have gotten me five minutes with Billy?' I asked.

'He wasn't here. He was arrested in Australia and there's been no extradition request. If anyone finds out there may be hell to pay.'

I had no idea why she told me that. I stored the information. 'Just put it down as rendition. You lot are past masters at that.'

'Someone's got to run the planet.' Aliput changed position and leaned her elbows on the table. She rested her chin on her thumbs. 'You really piss me off, you know. I tried to talk a couple of colleagues into giving you five with Billy. I knew they'd be worried about being caught out and I didn't want to put it to them by phone so I rushed over here to try to do a deal that has nothing to do with me but may help you...and all I get are smartass remarks.'

'Smartarse. The word has an "r". I don't like to be called things in a foreign language.'

She scanned me with her eyes. 'I thought you would be pleased.'

'I am. I just wish that I wasn't being pissed around so much.'

'Who's pissing you around?'

'You are...last night. What happened?'

'I can't help it if you can't remember,' Amelia said.

I stood from the table and grabbed hold of my carry bag. 'I guess it's time for me to go.'

Amelia stood and joined me on my side of the table. 'You've got a few hours before you can check in. Why don't we go for a drink somewhere?'

'You'll tell me what happened?' I asked, pointedly.

'No.'

'Then there's nothing more to discuss. I'll see you around...Special Agent Aliput.' I pulled at my carry bag and started to wheel it across the terminal building. I turned to see that Amelia was still standing at the table. I realised that I still had her phone in my pocket so I pulled it out and waved to her, to get her attention. She looked in my direction. I waved the phone at her and then placed it on top of the cabinet that I was passing.

Mortimer's Film

FEBRUARY in Ashford and the once green vista of Tudor laneways was now covered in winter's white mantle. Whilst the frosted landscape glistened in the morning sun with a sheen that might tempt poets, the slush and overused gravel surface had my rental car sliding like a banana through a child's fist. When I spotted the gate that led to the Pitelli offices, I braked before pulling onto an icy verge and tearing the handbrake cable from its moorings. The car slid to a stop against a stone wall, then stalled. *Close enough,* I thought as I eased myself for my warm cocoon into the bitterness of the English winter. This was my first taste of it and it, somehow, lacked the panorama of the views from my Italian apartment. Maybe it was the fact that this view was from a narrow laneway in a suburban backwater and I was standing up to my boot tops in an icy mud cocktail.

I wondered if my reception would be as chilly as the temperature. Surely not, I thought. Then I recalled my previous visit and shuddered with enthusiasm. I pulled the hood of my parka around my ears, walked the few yards to the gate and saw that it was locked. I wondered how anyone could run a business, especially in winter, where guests have to climb over a gate to enter. There was no answer written on the wind, so I climbed onto the first gate panel and swung my leg over the top. Without

warning, something disengaged and the gate began to
open. I hooked my leg over the top rail and hung on for
dear life. The gate jerked to a stop. I glared toward the
office; someone had to have set me up. I threw my leg
back over the rail, only to feel the slow seeping of a
dampness of the crotch that looks so becoming on a man.
I looked at the length of my parka and thanked the
designers of calf length coats.

I took a peek into the garage and then headed for the
office. Behind me, the gate closed without visible assistance. I entered the doorway to the outer office. There was
no one to be seen, but then I heard a polite cough behind
me.

'You must be Mr Mawson.' It was a polite voice with an
accent that hinted at a layman's idea of a boarding school
education.

I turned to see a petite brunette whose standout feature
was a gold chain running from her left ear to a ring that
pierced her right nostril. She was so short that her head
looked like it had been mounted on a wooden plinth as she
stood behind her reception counter. I looked down at her
as I approached. 'Yes. You're expecting me, I believe.'

'Mr McWhirter is expecting you.'

'My appointment is with Mario Pitelli,' I said, hoping
my voice reflected the warmth of the outside temperature.

The woman looked up at me with dewy eyes and
smiled. 'Mr Pitelli has been delayed in Prague. Mr
McWhirter will look after you.'

'Look here…um.'

'Thursday!' she said.

'Yes, I know it's Thursday. This is the day for my appointment.'

'You don't understand. I'm Thursday. I thought you were trying to remember my name.'

'We haven't even been introduced,' I said. 'How could I know your name?'

'I assumed that Tuesday would have informed you that I worked on Thursday's and Friday's...seeing that your appointment is for Thursday.'

I was being bombarded with useless information again. 'So you weren't telling me that it's Thursday?'

'No...My name is Thursday. Thursday Fryday.'

'I assume that it matches the days that you work.' I quipped.

'Of course. I timeshare with Tuesday. Tuesday is Monday through Wednesday, I'm Thursday and Friday.'

My wet crotch was beginning to freeze and I felt my voice rising an octave. 'I understand,' I said. 'But what about Mario Pitelli? His car's in the garage.'

'He has a hire car. Mr Pitelli has been delayed in Prague. He rang about half an hour ago and told me to show you through to Mr McWhirter when you arrived. He's on his way from the airport now.'

'McWhirter!'

'No, Mr Pitelli. Mr McWhirter is in his office. I'll take you through.'

Thursday's head disappeared and then she appeared at the end of the reception counter. I realised that she must have been standing on a box for me to see her at all. She walked ahead of me and I had visions of her using a ladder to climb onto a toilet. She stopped at a door at the corridor's end and knocked. Without waiting for some sound from within, she twisted the door handle and ushered me into McWhirter's office.

McWhirter stood and proffered his hand as I entered. He had the pleasant expression of a bereaved mortician and was resplendent in a black suit with a neon blue shirt and yellow tie. He offered me a seat as I shook his hand. He dismissed Thursday with a flamboyant flick of his wrist.

'Pleased to meet you Mr Mawson…. Mungo McWhirter…my friends call me George.'

'Scott Mawson,' I replied, wondering whether to call him Mungo or George. 'Thank you for seeing me.'

'But you're not here to see me. Mario will be along presently.'

'So I believe,' I said.

McWhirter pushed a button on his desk and one office wall whirred softly and displayed a palm-fringed beach somewhere in paradise. 'I'm a little cold,' he said. 'The office will heat up soon.'

'A little warmth won't hurt,' I said, wondering if my tackle would ever thaw.

'Got caught on the gate, huh?'

And I thought that no one had seen. 'Yes.'

'Happens a lot. All you have to do is lean on the gate, directly above the lock, and it opens automatically.'

'It didn't last time I was here,' I offered.

'We didn't know you then.'

'And you do now?'

'No…but now you have something *for* us. Last time you wanted something *from* us. There is a world of difference.'

'But I do want something from you.'

'Yes, but this time it's different. Now it's part of the quid pro quo. Things will work out…unless you want something that we don't sell.'

I was wondering what to say, when the office door opened and Mario Pitelli strode into the office. I immediately noted that his slicked black hair and long sideburns had been replaced by a number two clipper cut and he now sported a two-day growth. His eyes sparkled as he shook my hand with the vigour of an erstwhile comrade and threw an arm around my shoulder. 'He's come good George. Mr Mawson, 'ere, has done us a great favour. He's got the Mortimer distribution rights for us,' Pitelli said.

McWhirter smiled and then began a long, slow laugh. Pitelli remained poker faced for a moment but then joined McWhirter in his fit of mirth.

I felt like the nerdy school kid who is the butt of a misunderstood joke. The two men were, obviously, finding something funny in my actions. I had no idea what was going down. 'There's something funny in what I've done?' I asked Pitelli, a modicum of rancour tingeing my voice

'I'm sorry, Mr Mawson,' Pitelli said. 'But your Mr Squires' injunction only covered Australia and the other ignominious conglomerate of countries in your area of this enlightened planet. We did a deal, ages ago, to distribute elsewhere. We're only dealing with the dregs of distribution now. But I'm sure your SBS television people will be appreciative of your efforts. After all, the film's destined to become a cult classic.'

I slumped into McWhirter's spare chair, defeated. I thought I had something of value that I could trade for information on Emily Washburn and Jacqueline du Pre. I had contacted Billy Squires' lawyers and they had, for an exchange of information, sent me a copy of their removal of the injunction that impeded the distribution of Mortimer's movie. In reality I had nothing more useful than a soggy crotch. *Fuck,* I said out loud, to no one in particular. I looked at both men and saw a reflection of sympathy from behind bold eyes. However, the looks didn't disguise the smirks on two enlivened faces. I nodded my head up and down in abject ruin. I felt as strong as a rusty roof in a cyclone. I had nowhere to go and two men were enjoying seeing my squirming body on the rack. 'Who did you deal with?' I asked.

'Your client, I believe. Peter Mortimer's sister.'

Kendra Mortimer! But why? I racked my brain for a moment. Of course. The Mortimer's would get nothing if the movie failed to deliver. No, it couldn't be. Making sensible decisions wasn't part of the Mortimer psyche. My mind was in free-fall again, trying to gather permutations and deliver some sense. Nothing would come.

'I've wasted my time then,' I said.

Pirelli pushed the button McWhirter's desk and the wall scene changed to an arctic iceberg breaking away from its sea cliff. 'It's too hot in here,' he said.

McWhirter nodded. 'Sorry, Mario. I wasn't thinking'

Pitelli scanned McWhirter, dismissing any concern. 'You've done well, Mr Mawson. I didn't ask you for any favours but you used initiative. You deserve some reward. What can I do for you?'

Maybe my luck wasn't out after all. 'I'm still trying to find Jacqueline du Pre. I still need answers from you.'

'I thought that we agreed that I couldn't help you...last time we met?'

'We didn't agree,' I said; with as much as defiance as I could muster.

Pitelli leaned against McWhirter's desk. 'We should have. I can't help you with that.'

I looked across at McWhirter. 'Is this one of those things that you don't sell?'

McWhirter shook his head. 'There's nothing to sell. We don't know this du Pre woman. As far as we're concerned, she doesn't exist.'

'She exists all right. She's been seen. She was seen with Mortimer at the time that he died.'

Veils descended over both men's faces as they looked at each other. I had hit a nerve somewhere. I had information that I wasn't supposed to have. The knowledge made me tremble; the look in McWhirter's eyes had turned from bland to malicious. I was looking at a man of muscle; I hadn't realised it before. I had thought of everyone in the Pitelli organisation as being part of a menagerie of bizarre fools. I hadn't thought enough about what they all did for a living. I was on thin ice with a heavy backpack. It was time for caution.

Pitelli stared at me, his bright eyes taking on the sheen of the driven. 'If you know that she exists, why are you still asking us what we know of her?'

I saw no reason to lie.

'I was told to get involved with Mortimer's film. Getting it released for exhibition was the only way that I could think of. I have no other path.'

'And who told you to get involved? The same person who told you that they saw du Pre?

'No. Different people,' I said. I hesitated a moment, gathering my failing wits. 'No one knows anything of substance but someone is trying to help me. If you don't want to help ...fine...I'll leave you alone and look elsewhere.'

'What if your client wants you to stop looking?'

I wondered what they were on about. What influence could they have over Kendra Mortimer? 'I'd stop looking....for her.'

'You have some parallel interest?' McWhirter asked.

I shrugged my shoulders. 'Just self-interest. I'm a man who likes to know what's going on.'

'But you have no idea what's going on, Mr Mawson. If you did, you wouldn't be wasting your time with us. Look, why don't I pay you for ya effort and you can piss orf. Just stop lookin' for Emily...like a good boy,' Pitelli said.

I remembered the terms *postal* and *undertaker* from *Lock Stock and Two Smoking Barrels* and envisioned myself being diced and posted across the universe or being buried alive, breathing through a tube until I starved to death. I decided to remain defiant. 'Okay' I said, with head bowed sheepishly.

'Show Mr Mawson out will you George,' Pitelli said

'Wait here a minute.' McWhirter said as we passed by Bethany's room. He knocked and entered. I waited outside and leaned against the corridor wall. Soon, I could hear moaning from inside the room. Had McWhirter stopped off to shag Bethany? I listened at the door and heard the sound of orgasmic moaning. The door opened and McWhirter gave me the look that he reserved for perverts only. I could still hear the moaning from inside.

'She still at it then?' I asked McWhirter.

'Still at what?' he asked.

'Bethany...masturbating!'

McWhirter shook his head. 'No...she's moved on.'

'To where?' I asked.

'She's turned from BDSM to religion. She's found god.'

'That him with her now? I asked.

McWhirter laughed. 'Of course not...she's watching a homemade porn movie. Her local priest's in it.'

'Why did you go in?' I asked, changing subject.

'To get her to countersign your cheque. I have it here,' he said, brandishing a cheque. 'All you have to do now is sign the contract and we're set.'

I was lost, a familiar feeling. 'What contract is this exactly?' I asked.

'We can't give you money without a contract. That would be illegal. Thursday will run you through it.'

From somewhere behind the reception desk, an outstretched arm handed me a sheaf of papers. I sat on a chair by the window and read through the contract. I was to be paid £200,000 for the sale of my yellow Ferrari to Pitelli Enterprises...Registered Automobile Traders. 'I don't have a Ferrari,' I said to Thursday, somewhere behind the desk.

'Of course you do,' McWhirter said. It's in our garage at the moment. I saw you park it there on your way in.'

I remembered a yellow Ferrari but had paid no real attention to it. 'Did I really?'

'Of course. Your papers are in the glove box,' McWhirter said

'I assume that you have a buyer for it?'

'Of course. We were lucky to find someone with a car that one of our customers wanted. Very lucky indeed.'

The look in McWhirter's eyes led me to see the source of the luck.

'Off the record,' I said. 'Do you do many contracts like this?'

McWhirter replied. 'You know, I write dozens of contracts a year that are legally binding for products that don't exist. It's a way of life here. For example, if you want to buy a car, I could sell you a painting with provenance. If you can drive that painting away and have fun on the highways and byways, we have cemented a good deal. If you want to be free to travel the world at leisure, you could sell us a car. That would also be a good deal.'

'I'm glad that I had the car, then,' I said.

'So am I,' McWhirter replied

I took the cheque from McWhirter and left the building. I was almost to the gate when McWhirter caught up with me. 'Maybe there is something that you can do for me...a favour, perhaps.'

'A favour?'

'Yes...I need someone to deliver a vehicle for me.'

I was incensed. This was a bridge too far. 'Do I look like a delivery boy?'

McWhirter smiled. 'No, but I thought that delivering the Mortimer film to a contact in southern France may have been of interest to you...and you get to drive a new Mercedes Viano 3.5, especially decked out for a very special client.'

The Mortimer film...delivered to southern France. The Mortimer film. I had to get close to the film. Was this the chance? Was this what Candy Alloway meant? 'Where do I pick it up?' I asked.

'It's in the garage...beside your Ferrari. It's left-hand drive, so be careful here in England. You're booked on this afternoon's Calais ferry with Sea France. The only downside is that you can't deliver it for week. Its new owner won't be home until then.'

'Is it okay if I take it to where I live near Florence. I can park it there for a few days and deliver it when the client is home.'

'That's fine by me. Leave your rental. Thursday will return it for you.'

An American Blossom in Europe

THE steep and windy road leading from the village to my apartment was covered in the breath of some arctic ice pack and I had no chains for the Merc. I tried to decide whether I was fortunate to have a month off from teaching in Duclair or unfortunate that I was not elsewhere.

Duclair is never like this. It hardly ever snows there and the roads are usually clear. Mostly, I don't even consider the difference, but sometimes I wish that this part of Italy was just a red dot on a tourist map. My problem being that my journeys precluded me from ordering in a new load of wood for the fireplace. Subsequently, I found myself surrounded by blue smoke as the open fireplace in my apartment stuttered and disgorged its contents into the room, filling it with a cutable haze. I coughed and held a handkerchief to my face as I raked at the ashes and willed the newly cut olive trees to burn instead of smoulder. I had forgotten just how cold my apartment is in winter.

I needed something to warm me and was looking for a tot of rum when the phone rang. I let it transfer to message bank. I was too annoyed with myself to conduct a polite conversation with anyone. I was surprised to hear an American twang rain down on my little space from a satellite somewhere in geostationery orbit. The voice was hard, with a venomous edge best left to arachnids and words tumbled forth in a tirade that began to strip the paint from the walls. It was unabated and undisguised abuse and all directed at me. The words bode me ill will and there was even a mention that castration with a blunt knife would be too good for me.

I could say that I was surprised at the malice hurtling through the sound waves of the universe but I wasn't. I guessed that I had expected that telling Billy Squires' lawyer that Billy had been on a trip to the United States would have caused some chagrin, somewhere along the line, that would lead to my being identified as the source of the information. I had even read about the political fallout from the rendition on the net.

I was a little put out, however, that Amelia Aliput was threatening violence that would make a horror film eligible for a G rating, by comparison. I smiled at the thought of my relative safety and continued to choke on smoke. I poked at the smouldering logs and saw that a couple of them were starting to show signs of life. They were glowing orange and small yellow flames began to lick their sides. Eventually the room would clear.

I found my rum and took a swig directly from the bottle. I then poured a full measure into a converted jam jar. The fire began to dance as I swallowed some warmth. I was beginning to feel at ease when I heard what seemed to be a knock on my door. Impossible! There was no one about; all of the apartments were empty. I heard the sound again. Weak and rapid, like the incessant pounding of an eagle with a broken wing. I walked across to my door and opened it.

My mind froze as I stared at the apparition outside of my door. My time was up. Amelia Aliput stood on my doorstep, pounding her shoulders with gloved hands and looking like a snowman. Her face was flushed pink with cold and her eyebrows were encrusted with icicles.

'Outa the way, you fuck,' she screamed, as she pushed past me and rushed to the fire.

I noticed that, like me, the fire was in fear of its life. It began to roar and orange red flames licked at the insides of the chimney. Its behaviour had improved markedly. Amelia was facing it. I could see that she was covered in a snowy mantle and was shaking her head furiously from side to side.

'I'm fucking freezing,' she screamed into the flames.

I had a choice between laughing at her and doing something. For some subconscious reason I chose the latter. I rushed to my bedroom and pulled the duvet from my bed. I rushed back to wrap the blanket around Amelia's shoulders. She pulled it close, shivering. She started to shake and jump up and down on the spot, dripping water onto my tiles. 'I'm fucking freezing,' she screamed.

'Get your clothes off,' I ordered. 'They're wet. You'll never warm up with them on.'

She just stood there, so I pulled the duvet away and pointed at her dripping clothes. 'Get them off...now,' I commanded.

Her fingers fumbled at jacket buttons; no grip. I reached forward and started to undo them for her. She slapped my face. I staggered backward and stumbled over my lounge. Flames roared with laughter. Amelia stood on the spot, ripping at her sodden jacket. It wouldn't slide from her shoulders.

'You've got to let me help,' I said. 'Otherwise you'll freeze.'

I heard words expelled through chattering teeth. I couldn't comprehend. She spoke again. There was something like *touch me and I'll fucking kill you.*

I shrugged my shoulders and walked to my kitchen. I lifted the rum bottle and poured a measure into my glass. I toasted Amelia's health before I tipped the glass to my lips.

Filling the glass again I returned to find Amelia shaking like a leaf in a gale. I rushed to her and put the glass to her lips. She opened her mouth and gulped at the warm liquid. She coughed and spluttered as she realised the potency of what she was drinking. She retched and vomited the rum onto the tiles.

Standing behind her I undid the last button on her jacket and ripped it from her shoulders. I worked on the belt of her soggy jeans and undid it. I worked the zipper, dropping to my knees and peeling the jeans down her legs. Her boots were in the way, so I pushed her backward onto the lounge and unzipped her boots. I saw that they were summer weight with narrow heels. *In Italy, in winter. Madness.* The boots came off with a quick pull. I returned to the jeans and pulled them from her legs. I glanced up in time to avoid another slap. I pulled at her legs and dropped her onto her back on the lounge.

'Take your top off, while I get you a towel,' I told her. Rushing from the room I grabbed a towel and returned just as Amelia was undoing the last button on her blouse.

Blouse and jacket. Lightweight jeans and light boots. Anger from another season. I threw her the towel and returned to the bathroom to fire up the shower. I turned the tap and waited for hot water to bounce from my outstretched fingers. I mixed in some cold. I returned to the lounge room to find myself looking at a beautiful woman, holding a duvet in front of her and warming her arse in front of my now raging fire.

'Shower's ready for you,' I said.

Amelia nodded her head toward me and rushed past. I replaced her in front of the fire and rubbed my hands together. I was surprised at how cold they felt. *Bloody women*, I thought.

There was no bag outside of my door. Surely she had some luggage. I picked up the discarded clothing and carried it to my clothes dryer. A cellphone was in the jacket pocket. The jeans and jacket would shrink in the dryer, but there was no choice. The boots would be written off. I was wondering about the repercussions when I noticed that the shower had stopped running. 'There's a warm dressing gown in my wardrobe,' I called through the door.

I heard a grunt from the other side. The mood hadn't lightened.

I cooked up some scrambled eggs and poured a tin of beans into a saucepan. There was little choice for something quick. Amelia would need instant gratification for her hunger. I felt eyes piercing the back of my neck as I cooked. There was no sound but I knew she was there. Then I saw her distorted reflection in the round curve of the saucepan. I smiled at the image. 'You eat eggs?' I called over my shoulder.

'Where're my clothes?'

'In the dryer in the laundry.'

'Fuck...you can't dry them like that...they'll shrink.'

'Only way,' I said.

She raced up the corridor, toward the sound of tumbling. She flung open the door and retrieved the soggy mass from the rotating bowl. She held up the clothes and winced, audibly. 'They're fucking ruined. You idiot,' she screamed down the hall.

'They've only been in a couple of minutes. Some idiot walked through the snow in them. Don't blame me for that flight of fancy.'

'You idiot...you put my boots in the dryer!'

'They were wet,' I said.

I waited for a terse riposte, but silence filled the house like an unsatisfied audience. Then the fire crackled and blue smoke resumed its reign. I tipped my remaining dry kindling into the dwindling flames. If this didn't work I would have to spend the night in bed, under a duvet and over an electric blanket. *The warmest place in the house.* What would I do with Amelia? *Shit.* There were no blankets for the bed in the spare room. This was no place for company. I hadn't been expecting any and Amelia, in her current mood, wasn't welcome.

'You're not very good at fires,' Amelia said.

This was the second time that I hadn't heard her approach. 'The wood's cheap. It just doesn't burn...but the olives are good.'

'What has that to do with anything?'

I ignored the question and rifled through my woodbin, trying to find something that wasn't as green as a new apprentice. If only I'd stored the wood for a year like I had been told. But that would take forethought and that wasn't my forte. I preferred to flick a switch and watch the radiator bars glow or feel the warmth of circulated air. Next year I would do better. Maybe I would remember to store wood. I doubted it. 'Why are you here?' I found myself asking.

The reply took no thought. 'To kill you.'

'Before or after we eat?'

'It can wait.'

'Good…make yourself useful. Behind that small door at the end of the kitchen is my wine collection. Grab a bottle will you.'

'Red or white?' Amelia asked.

'Chianti or Chianti. Either sort will do.'

We ate over-fried eggs and refried beans washed down with a rough red - a delicacy in any three-hat restaurant – eaten in silence under a blanket of undisguised malevolence. 'Why are you here?' I asked, trying to break the silence.

'I told you already,' she said.

'What'd you do…just get the shits then get on a plane and fly here…without thought for the weather here.'

'It's hot in California.'

'It ain't here. It's winter. You know…snow and shit.'

'You have no idea how much you piss me off,' Amelia said, as she spat beans onto my shirt.

I wiped orange gunge from my shirtfront. 'You vote Republican don't you?' I said.

Amelia shook her head and furrowed her brow. 'What brought that into the conversation.'

I began to laugh at the absurdity of the situation. 'You just invaded Italy without any forethought. I assumed it to be the Republican in you.'

'I don't know what you think is so funny. A man who's about to die has no reason to laugh.'

The fire roared behind me, then spat a shower of sparks onto the floor. 'And how do you accomplish your goal. I see no gun…bare handed perhaps…or a black handled kitchen knife. That might do it…but if you want that approach you'll have to get mine sharpened. They wouldn't penetrate skin without a gorilla pushing on the handle...and you're no gorilla.'

Amelia dabbed at the corner of her mouth with a napkin and rose from the table. She crossed to the fireplace and began to stack more olive branches onto the fire. She placed them carefully in a neat pile. Then she pulled the white sheet from my sofa, displaying its cracked leather, and hung it in front of the fireplace. The fire began to burn orange/red and a slow roar built to a crescendo. 'It needs to draw...anyone knows that,' she said. She held the sheet in place until flames flicked on its fire side. She pulled it away with deft stroke of a matador. 'Easy really.'

'Not just a pretty face then,' I said.

'Just keep the wood up to it while I find which of your clothes will fit me.'

'Packing would have been handy,' I said.

***

Three out of three. I was both impressed and more than a little concerned. She was there again, in the doorway that leads to the rear of the apartment. I continued washing up and watched her inverted reflection in the concave base of the stirring spoon that hung under my saucepan rack. I turned. My blue jeans and white cotton shirt had never looked so good but the ugg boots were incongruous in the image. 'You found something then?'

'I'm warm now.' She looked at the fireplace. 'Fire's going well.'

'The deft touch of a hit-woman,' I said.

'You have a scotch?' she asked.

I open the door to the cupboard above the bench and pulled out a bottle of Edradour. 'Nectar of the gods.'

'You want one?' she asked.

'If I'm about to die, I might as well have one last tipple.'

She poured scotch into two tumblers and passed one to me. 'I should kill you, you know. I'm indefinitely suspended from work...pending the results of an inquiry.'

'Maybe you shouldn't have transported Billy to America.'

'Maybe you shouldn't have blabbed. I gave you what you wanted and you just shat on me.'

'Your expression?'

'No...not really. Squires used it all the time. I just picked it up. Why did you do it?'

'Do what?'

'Tell Squires' lawyers that he was in California.'

'They suspected anyway. I saw no reason not to confirm their suspicions. Besides....ah, you're right. It's none of my business. Though I had no idea that you would get dragged into it.'

'It took all of five minutes to find out who had leaked. I was suspended two days ago.'

'Took them more than five minutes.'

'They needed undeniable proof. It took time.'

'What a novel idea. Who said that justice is blind. Where to now...after the murder.'

Amelia laughed. 'I'll get off. Justifiable homicide. No one would convict me. I'll show them what you did to my boots. An all woman jury will understand.'

Two scotches later the mood had mellowed. We sat watching television, where an Italian football star was being interviewed by a pair of breasts, and soaking up the warmth from the fire. Amelia was in wonder as the camera moved from one breast to the other. 'Is it like this all the time?' she asked.

'No...sometimes they show the interviewer's face...but not often. Mostly it's just tits.'

'Doesn't anyone complain?'

'I don't know if they are far enough out on the right wing here. But nothing has changed since I've been here.'

'It's disgusting,' Amelia said

'Says the woman who flashed in Silverton,' I added.

'That wasn't on TV.'

'No...you're right. Just in a street.'

'The bottle's nearly empty.' Amelia said, pointing to the near empty scotch bottle on the sink.

'I have more...don't worry,' I said.

'I'm not.'

'Are you going to tell me why you came here?' I asked.

Amelia blinked rapidly, as if caught off guard. She stood from her seat and went to the firewood bucket. 'This is nearly empty.'

'Yeah...and that's all there is. The stuff stacked outside will be sodden by this. Why did you come?'

'To find you, of course.'

'Why?' I asked.

Amelia emptied the remaining contents of the firewood bucket onto the flames. 'I want you to tell me about my mother.'

I had no idea what she was talking about. 'I don't know your mother. What do you mean?'

'At Squires' camp, you called me Marilyn. You expected that that was my name. It's my mother's name. How did you know?'

'I still have no idea what you're on about,' I said.

'You knew my mother's name and she knew you. She had me pick you up from the Dendrobium party. She knew to call me and she knew that I would know you. I just want to know what's going on. How do people, who supposedly haven't met, know about one another?'

'Coincidence. Happens all the time.'

Amelia walked to the kitchen and poured the remainder of the scotch into her glass. 'You're on a quest and you say that things are coincidence. I don't think so.'

'Okay,' I said. 'What do you want to know about your mother?'

'Why her history starts when she met my father. There are no records that she existed before then and I want to know why.'

Thoughts of Willie

I have always been intrigued by how people can sometimes tell, first thing in the morning, whether or not they will have a good day. Normally, in my experience, the day requires development and the chance to turn sour, but sometimes the day just gets better as it marches through time. This would be one of those days. I knew that it would be, as soon as I opened my left eye and gazed at Amelia Aliput's fine curves disappearing into the bathroom. My memory reeled and jigged with the delight of an adolescent schoolboy. I rolled over and became instantly absorbed in the residual fragrance of Amelia's body. Intoxicating, with no hint of regret; a beautiful perfume. I breathed in deeply as I hugged her pillow. This time it wasn't a dream. This time I had been awake throughout the entire thrilling episode. I felt like a man who had visited Rome and was prepared to die.

You may wonder, dear reader, why I was in such high spirits and how I had managed to end up making love to a woman who had travelled to Italy with a view to precipitating my demise. I could tell you that it was as a result of my charm and wit but, alas, that would be to mislead you. The truth is that it was as the result of a mathematical equation and the water from the peat bogs around the Edradour distillery. The maths equation was easy. *Two bodies into one bed won't go...unless the wood fire has fizzled and the electric blanket on the bed had been thoughtfully switched on earlier in the evening.* The nectar is one that one has to experience to understand. Anyway, the evening turned into a clash of sexual wills between one who kept themselves in superb athletic condition by indulging in an exhausting physical fitness regime and a maths teacher. After thirty seconds of unabated lust I followed Billy Connolly's lead and did a lap of honour around the bedroom.

You might also be wondering if I was able to explain, to Amelia, the story of how her mother came to be without a past. Again, if I said that I gave her an adequate explanation, I would be fibbing. You see, I had no idea. This disappointed Amelia, no end, and would have cooled her ardour, had it not been for the fact that she was half pissed and wanting to indulge in a degree of horizontal dancing.

'I have nothing to wear. My clothes are still wet,' Amelia called from the bathroom.

'You should have left them in the dryer. They would have been dry by now.'

'And ruined,' she added.

'Maybe the boots.'

She appeared from the bathroom, wrapped in the duvet and ugg boots, and deflated any early morning lasciviousness that I may have been imagining. She walked to the bedroom windows and flung them open.

I felt the chill of age wash over me like an arctic gale. 'Shut the fucking window,' I screamed.

'It's brisk,' she said, leaving the windows open.

'No it isn't. it's freezing.'

She ignored my comment. 'Which car is yours?' she asked, as she stared through the window.

'The BMW.'

'Who owns the Mercedes van?'

'Long story. I have to deliver it to someone.'

'When?'

'Why do you ask?'

'No reason really...except that someone is trying to shove a coat hanger down the driver's side window. Looks like an under instructed car thief...very amateur. They would be thrown out of the thieves union at home.'

I leapt from my bed and raced to the window. I looked out to see a head of slicked back black and blond streaked hair crouched over the car door. He seemed to be being egged on by a vertically challenged woman. 'What are you doing there, Mr Jones?' I yelled from my window.

A head flashed around and a chain rattled against a cheek. Thursday Fryday craned her neck to peek up at me. 'We're here to collect the van,' she said.

'Under whose authority?' I yelled.

'Mr Pitelli...he says that McWhirter shouldn't have asked you to do the delivery.'

'Get away from the van, Jones.' I called down. 'Come to my door and we'll sort this out.'

'What's going on?' Amelia asked.

'Just when I was expounding my certainty of a good day, shit happens. Wait here.'

There was a loud knock on my door. Jones and Fryday had had no time to encircle the building.

'Someone's at the door,' Amelia said.

'Can you get it? I'll throw some clothes on.'

Amelia was back in seconds. 'There an Asian woman at the door. Beautiful...to say the least.'

'Did you let her in?'

'Some of us have manners.'

Amelia was right. There was a beautiful Asian woman standing in my entry doorway. The morning sun was behind her and surrounded her with a golden aura. She wore a lightweight purple coat over a bright yellow blouse and skirt. She seemed immune to the cold that crushed the room with icy claws.

'Mr Mawson...I am Taishono Homari. I am pleased to meet you,' she said, performing a small deferential bow.

'Of the Moutan family?' I enquired, remembering Quenna Knight.

'Yes.'

'I'm pleased to meet you, Ms Homari. To what do I owe the honour?' I said.

Jones came into view. His weight hadn't increased. Fryday was beside him. I observed that she could give him head without bending. They were both puffing with exertion.

'Mr Pitelli has made a mistake. McWhirter gave you the incorrect car to deliver.'

'He could have phoned,' I said.

'Mr Pitelli did not want to disturb you,' Taishono replied.

'So he sent his armed forces, instead?'

Taishono smiled softly. 'Some do not understand, Mr Mawson. They do not know the correct way to undertake commerce.'

'Do I take it that I will be paid not to deliver the van?'

'You are an astute man, Mr Mawson.' Taishono said.

I didn't hear what she said. My feet were beginning to adhere to the floor tiles. I looked down to realise that I had no shoes on. I needed my ugg boots. They were already occupied. I began to shiver as I let Jones and Fryday in.

'Look...I need to light the fire, it's bloody freezing in here,' I said to a woman who was wearing lightweight clothes yet giving no sign of feeling the cold.

'Do you have the keys, Mr Mawson?' Taishono asked.

I needed time to think. I couldn't afford to lose the van. Timing would be everything, from here on in. 'I wish that I could say yes, but, alas, no. I put the keys in safe keeping...in case of tall thin thieves.'

'You don't have them? Jones asked.

'I have them,...but not here. They're down the road.'

'Where?' Jones asked.

Taishono looked me in the eyes then spoke softly. 'Go down the hill. Turn right and walk along the track. Once you get to an electricity substation turn right and walk on a hundred metres. Look over the embankment and you will see the remains of a garden. There is a fountain, shaped like a snail. The keys are behind the fountain. Jones and Fryday...go now.'

Taishono smiled at me after both Jones and Fryday disappeared from view as fast as greyhounds on the scent. 'Your thoughts do not become you, Mr Mawson.'

I slumped onto my sofa. I was distraught. Taishono Homari read my thoughts. She could see a picture of my thoughts about the keys. How could it be? I was so close to resolving my mystery but was now faced with an unexpected twist....and was about to lose the van. 'Do you mind if I finish dressing?'

Taishono nodded. 'Of course. They will be some time...no?'

'They will be some time,' I said.

I had the wafture of a used mattress in suburban broth-el. I needed a shower but there was no time. I dressed quickly, crossed to my window and looked out. The coast was clear.

I climbed out of the window, shimmied down the drainpipe and crossed to my car. I opened the boot and rummaged through the boxes that sat there like unwanted garbage. It had to be there. It had never been taken out of its wrapping. One of those detective things that you should keep handy...just in case. But where had I put it? I tipped over the last box. Nothing. I remembered. My wardrobe drawer, bottom left.

I looked up to find Amelia looking down at me, her brow furrowed, one eyebrow lifted.

'Wardrobe...bottom left draw...brown box. Get it and throw it down to me.'

Amelia nodded and disappeared from view. She returned a minute later with a shoe box.

'No...smaller!'

'There's no other box there,' she whispered

I thought again. I tried to gain a mental picture. I thought of Taishono's capability. 'Try the top right drawer.'

Amelia disappeared again. She returned with a small brown box. I nodded and had her throw it down to me. I ripped the box apart and withdrew its contents. It was in my hands. I leaned under the Viano and set the magnet onto the van's frame. It felt secure. Good. I threw the rest of the equipment into the boot of the BMW.

I tried the downpipe. My hands froze at the touch. It had been easy descending. I blew hot air onto my hands. It made no difference. My hands froze onto the pipe. I looked up. Amelia looked worried. She had good reason. 'Distract them in the kitchen. I'll walk around.'

I picked up an armful of wood from my neighbour's stash and walked to my front door. I twisted the door handle and pushed with my shoulder. I walked in and dropped the wood into my wood bucket. 'I'll light a fire,' I said to no one in particular.

Taishono sat on the sofa, reading something in Chinese script. She didn't seem to notice me.

I had a sudden thought of mayhem. 'Is McWhirter okay?' I asked.

Taishono raised her eyes and looked at me. 'I do not know any McWhirter. I only know the two that are with me now.'

***

Jones waved the keys like a successful pirate at the end of a treasure hunt. Thursday had the pale mien of a disabled mountaineer at the end of a long day. Taishono Homari looked disinterested.

'We shall go now, Mr Mawson,' Taishono said. 'May I have your car keys?'

'You have them,' I said.

'Your BMW...both sets and the spare...thank you.'

***

'What now?' Amelia asked, as she watched the van disappear down the hill.

'We follow them. I have a tracking device on the van.'

'How do we follow them?'

'In my car.'

'They took all the keys you idiot.'

'Don't you have a spare set of spare keys? I lose too many not to be covered. All we have to do is find them. Lucky I can't remember where they are.'

Ten minutes later I held them in my hand. 'Let's go. We'll stay just out of sight of them.'

'Where are we headed?'

I shrugged. I had no real idea. 'I was told to the take the van to a place near Grasse in southern France. The address is in the van.'

'Good work...detective!' Amelia laughed.

'My guess is they'll head toward Nice via Genoa. Let's go.'

'What do we follow? The van or the Lancia that they arrived in.'

'I have no idea,' I said. 'I guess that the van's more important. It's what I was supposed to deliver.'

I threw a pile of clothes onto the back seat of my BMW. No suitcase or luggage bag, just a pile of clothes from a wardrobe. Amelia turned up a few seconds later with underwear, socks and shoes.

'I thought you might need these,' she said as she climbed into the car.

'Thanks...I wasn't thinking.'

'Not unusual for you. Let's go.'

I pulled out of the small carpark at the rear of my apartment and nosed the car into the steep decline that leads to the village below the escarpment. I braked and thumped my fist into the steering wheel.

'What is it now?' Amelia asked.

'I'll never get down this fucking hill without chains.'

'But you watched that tall thin guy put chains onto the van. Didn't you think then?'

'Yes and no,' I said. 'Yes I watched him…no I didn't consider doing it myself.'

Amelia laughed out loud. I found the sound both melodious and annoying. It reminded me of everything about her; the juxtaposition of opposites.

She was still laughing an hour later as we snaked our way past the city of Lucca and headed toward Genoa. This time it was caused by her staring at the dead face of my tracking device. The batteries were not only flat, they had corroded in their case. My device was useless.

'We could try new batteries. Get a set somewhere. I can clean up the corrosion. Things might still work,' Amelia said between bursts of schoolgirl giggling.

'No…I think that we need to catch them. We'll have to keep a visual surveillance.'

Amelia laughed again. 'We don't even know if they're heading this way. You just assume that they're heading for Grass.'

'Grasse' I corrected, invoking my best French accent.

'Okay…Grasse. Well…are they on this road?'

I was defeated. I was following a van that may not have been on the same stretch of road and expecting to detect its whereabouts with a defective scanning device. 'Fuck,' I screamed.

'Maybe you could pull into the right lane and take the next off ramp.' Amelia said.

'Why?' I asked.

'Because that's what the van and the Lancia are doing. They're about two hundred yards ahead of us…in front of the blue truck.'

I could have kissed her, but I settled on a nod of gratitude.

***

Piazza Guiseppe Verdi is a tree lined street that lies two streets from the La Spezia waterfront. It was easy to remain in the background and watch three people alight from two vehicles outside of *L'Albergo Economico*. I wondered what they were doing until I remembered that Jones and Fryday were English and the two and a half hour drive from my place to La Spezia was a full day's travel for them. This would be it for the night. We would continue the journey to wherever in the morning. I looked across at Amelia, who wore a smirk of unknown origin. 'We'll need to book in somewhere.'

'Incisive,' she said, the smirk remaining in place.

'Then we have to find a way to keep an eye on the vehicles without being seen ourselves.'

'Maybe our backup team,' Amelia offered.

'We'll take turns.'

'You'll take turns. This has nothing to do with me.'

It was my turn to develop a smirk. I looked across at Amelia, noticing that she was still wearing my clothes. I looked her up and down. 'Maybe you should go shopping. You look like you need some clothes.'

'I do. No money though.'

'I noticed,' I said.

'You'll have to lend me your credit card.'

'Maybe you can get yours back. You can use my mobile,' I said.

Amelia sat back into her seat and flicked hair from her forehead. She smiled softly and dimples appeared in her cheeks. She adjusted the collar on my shirt and fiddled with the top button. 'Who shall I ring?'

'I don't know. I guess that same person who's holding onto your passport and other belongings. Someone in the carabinieri I would guess. Maybe the same person who dropped you off near my place so that you could pretend that you had braved the cold. I was impressed. Could be the same person who attached the replacement antenna to the top of the van. Good job that. I hardly spotted it myself. In fact, if I hadn't noticed that the original one had a cracked top cap I wouldn't have seen it at all.'

'I underestimate you.'

'No you don't. You're too smart for that. You just think that I'm into something illegal and you want to find out what. You're basing your assumptions on the Billy Squires' position. You think that I have something to do with him but you're making the wrong links. My guess is that you tie me into Squires' drug running. Then you find out that I want to talk to some underworld character in England and I leave England in a van. QED...your ideas are vindicated. I figure that you think that the van is full of drugs.' I hesitated, waiting for a response. None came. 'The van isn't full of drugs. I thought that it may have been, myself, so I had it checked out before I left England. It's just a vehicle that has specially been fitted out for a particular purchaser. It was probably stolen and modified but I'm not concerned with that. I'm only concerned with who it is to be delivered to and what's in one of the van's storage cupboards.'

'And what's that?' Amelia asked.

'Copies of Peter Mortimer's movie....what else am I dealing with?'

High Fashion

AMELIA Aliput looked good in black. She had the aura of
the rogue female agent in spy movies, dressed in a black
roll neck jumper, black slacks and black runners. As I
watched her, I could imagine her flowing blond hair curled
up under a hood and her face painted with camouflage.
Maybe that would come later but, for now, she was sitting
opposite in the dimly lit restaurant of the L'Albergo
Difettoso, supping on a preservative free local red and
staring blankly at the remnants of local shellfish that
perched like broken limbs on a flowered plate. I could see
that she was trying to project a look of calm that belied her
inner turmoil but her features displayed a mood that
matched the blackness of her clothing. She had been that
way for hours. She was pissed off, big time.

One might think that it would be something relatively
important that had turned her controlled aggressive
temperament into something that verged on a maniacal
desire to kill, but the entire mood shift had been brought
on by two words. Two simple Italian words that began
with a blank stare at the person uttering them but soon
turned to rage as she realised their meaning.

Amelia was looking to buy an Italian dress. Not any
dress, but one that she could show off in when she
returned to downtown LA and her friends. Her *Italian
fashion purchase*, she called it.

The search started well. The afternoon drifted along like a small cloud in a light breeze. I was happy. I had even elicited, from Amelia, a guarantee that the Viano would be allowed to complete its journey to wherever, without interference from either the Italian or French authorities. Albeit subject to an after midnight visit to a locked garage to be stripped down and rebuilt before morning. And, she had agreed to share a room, at her chosen hotel, in return for my taking her shopping.

I had agreed unreservedly, but I should have known better. I should have given up the chance of more sex instead of saying that I would accompany her on a shopping expedition. I should not have acted as translator.

It was my fault that she was sitting across from me with a snarl that would make a rabid dog appear as friendly as child's Labrador. *It was all my fault.* In some ways it was déjà vu. The journey reeked of my meandering in Cannes, walking from dress shop to boutique to negozio di moda along wide streets and narrow lanes of La Spezia.

Then she saw it, in the window of *Gatto Nero*. I should have realised that the name had similar connotations to a boutique in Cannes but didn't think. I just meandered like a goose and gave lame comments about a dress in the window. It was slender and chic and had the colour of golden flames in the midday sun. Amelia loved it at first sight and all I had to do was translate for the purchase. We walked into the shop and were attended to with much haste and Italian charm, by a diminutive woman wearing a white snow cone. As she spoke, she flicked black hair into staccato ripples with the swipe of her head.

It was only when Amelia pointed to the dress of her desires that the woman adopted the brooding demeanour of a hunted squirrel. She shook her head and uttered the words *molto grande*. I was stunned as I realised that translation was akin to a death sentence.

'What is it? Amelia asked, feeling the dress's fabric against her right cheek.

'The dress in unavailable,' I lied. 'The woman says that they only had a few sample sizes. This is the only one left.'

Amelia pointed to a rack that held, at least, ten of the sample dress. 'Really.'

'Maybe I misunderstood,' I said. 'I'll ask her again.'

I spoke to the woman in my less than adequate Italian and received the same comment. This time, however, it was accompanied by the woman cutting a curved figure in the air, using both hands and arms to emphasise her point.

I caught the look in Amelia's eyes. She understood the gesture. 'What's she saying? What does molto grande mean?' Amelia snarled.

'Ummm,' I hesitated.

'Molto…multi…grande…grand. Multi grand. Is she saying that I'm fat?'

'I'm sorry, but by Italian dress sizes, you are too big for her range,' I said, instantly regretting my utterance.

Amelia laughed. 'I'm no bigger that the tits that appear on the box every night. I've seen them. Nothing else, just big tits. They don't even pretend to have anything else.'

I shrugged my shoulders. 'That's how it is, here. Small sizes in the boutiques. Maybe we can look for another dress in one of the department stores. There'll be one around here somewhere.'

'Maybe we can look for a tent outlet,' Amelia screamed.

I apologised to the shopkeeper for the outburst and followed Amelia along the street and back toward the hotel. I figured that our accommodation would be subject to adjustment.

'Are you going to get over it?' I asked, as I looked at her scornful scowl.

'Not soon.'

'You didn't enjoy your food. You just woofed it down. You usually pick.'

'Shut the fuck up,' she said.

I did, momentarily. Then decided against it. 'You still on for the van theft?'

'Look asshole. The van holds illegal contraband. We'll search the van and then arrest all of the associated people...including you.' Amelia hissed, through clenched teeth.

'Guilty already, huh? I told you that there is nothing in the van that's of interest. You're barking up the wrong tree again. Though...I guess *you* don't need any proof to assert guilt.

'We'll see.'

'Ahaaa. It is still on then,' I commented. I stood from the table. 'I'll get the bill. I guess I'll see you in the morning.'

'You look after yours...I'll pay for myself.'

***

I looked at my watch. 1:00am. I was parked in my car around one hundred metres from where the Viano was parked. It was in shadow on a moonless night. Heavy cloud cover threatened early morning rain. At least it wouldn't be snow. I lifted binoculars to me eyes and focused on the van. No movement so far. I moved the binoculars to the left. There was something stirring. A black silhouette approached the van from directly across the road. The ominous image moved to the driver's side door and peered in through the window. An arm waved in the gesture of an ancient cavalry leader bidding his troops to move forward. Two more figures appeared beside the van. I recognised a rear end; shapely and fit. International co-operation at its best; I, mentally, toasted the Italo-American alliance. I dropped my head below my car's dashboard as I noticed a head turning; a head wearing night-vision goggles. I counted to ten and lifted my head again. The van was open. They were clambering aboard. A moment later, I heard the engine roar.

I followed at a distance, my headlights off and keeping at maximum visual distance. I travelled past the marina and headed toward the industrial area to the south of the city. The van moved slowly then stopped outside a French vehicle dealership. I had expected German, to match the van, or Italian. French was a surprise. I pulled to the kerb and switched off my engine. A huge roller door opened, at the front of the dealership, and I could see the inside of a workshop bathed in metal halide. There seemed to be, at least, eight men waiting inside the workshop. The door descended as soon as the van rolled in.

I looked at my speedometer. Four kilometres from the hotel; twenty minutes walk. There was plenty of time. They would take ages to strip down and rebuild the van. I restarted the car and returned it to the hotel. I travelled via the street adjoining *L'Albergo Economico* and found no sign that anyone had realised that the van had been moved. Maybe Amelia and her associates would get away with their actions, unsuspected.

Three quarters of an hour later I stood on the corner across the road from the auto dealership. The only sign that it was occupied was light leakage around the edges of the roller door. I crossed the road and stood beside the wall, adjacent to the door. I could hear the dynamic discord of enterprise. Metal clanking on a concrete floor. The grunt of exertion. The blue language of amateur mechanics. I walked to the side of the building. A window; high on the wall. A chance to become a casual observer to what was happening inside. I looked around for a climbing aid. Nothing available. Mentally, I measured the distance to the window. Less than a good lay-up. I crouched...then leapt. My fingers gripped the windowsill and held. I hung like a wet towel on a clothesline, recovering breath and relaxing muscles. I took a deep breath and lifted myself to the window line. I peered in at an industrial shower room. *Shit!* I exclaimed.

I lowered myself again. I felt something on my left leg. Something solid, prodding softly. I looked down at Amelia Aliput. She wore the hidden grin of the satisfied. She was prodding me with a piece of exhaust pipe.

'You're lucky I can vouch for you,.' she said. 'Luigi wanted to shoot you on sight.'

'Do I put my hands above my head?' I asked.

Amelia shook her head. 'No. You walk back to your hotel and leave us to our business.'

I noticed a black shadow at the corner of the building. 'And if I don't?'

'It would be a shame.'

'How come?'

'I'm sure that you don't really want to know. Just leave will you.....please. It's better for me if you do.'

Something twigged. I had a feeling that I knew the answer before I could think of the question. Amelia was far too casual and the shadow hadn't moved. 'I take it that van will be back in its place by morning.'

'We've replaced the tracking device. You can sleep in.'

'Find anything interesting?'

'You already know what's in the van. Of course it's interesting…but it isn't illegal.'

I began to walk along the street beside the dealership. Amelia walked beside me. I stopped at the street corner. 'I guess this is it, then.'

'For now. I have to get back home. But I need to know about my mother so I'll be back to haunt you.'

'When?' I asked.

'Mum gave me two tickets to this year's Cannes. Very privileged tickets. Every session that I wish to attend. I thought that you might like to accompany me.'

I leaned forward and kissed Amelia on both cheeks. 'We'll see,' I said.

She kissed me on the lips and hugged me close. 'We'll see,' she said, as she moved away. Then she added. 'Leave your car door unlocked. We'll fit a tracker for you. Yours is fucked.'

The Garden of Emily Washburn

SITTING upon its hilltop, like so many other French provincial towns, Grasse looked grey and drab and gave no inkling of the vapours of exotic lust that are produced within its myriad factories. It was mid afternoon and a light mist covered distant hilltops and blanketed the countryside in melancholy winter. I pulled to the side of the Penetrante Grasse-Cannes looking closely at the image on my satnav screen and then to the golf course that nestles between the Penetrante and Route de Cannes.

The van had stopped on rue Chemin des Plaines on the far side of the golf course. It had been a four hour drive from La Spezia with two comfort stops for the English and a petrol stop for the Viano. The Lancia and Pitelli's cronies had pulled off the motorway toward Nice Airport and Taishono Homari had driven on alone. I had followed her, keeping at least half a kilometre between us, all the way from Nice.

I pulled back into the line of traffic and sought the next off ramp. Within minutes, the tracker's beep became a steady whirr and its light pulsed like a miniature beacon as I parked outside of a pair of enormous wooden gates that were set into a three metre high rustic stone wall that dominated the streetscape for two hundred metres. There was a tingling on the back of my neck that I didn't recognise. Was I nearing the end of my journey?

I jumped from the car and peered through one of two vertical slits in the gate's panelling. The van was parked under the canopy of an immense chestnut tree beside a turreted wall that seemed intent on spearing the low hanging clouds. I stood back to look for some kind of gate latch. There was nothing visible. I pushed at the gate but it stood firm. I needed an entrance. I scurried along the stone wall to its end, looking for either an entry point or somewhere that I could see over the parapet. When I reached the end, there was another wall section, perpendicular to that along the street-scape and at the same height. I went on until I reached the next corner. From there, I could see a portal cut into the rear wall of the property. I reached the portal to find a beaten oak door. The oak was gnarled, weathered and studded with copper nails. Like the main gate, there was no sign of a latch. I leaned against it with unrewarded hope. I stood back and looked up at the top of the wall; so near yet so far. I considered a mighty leap without faith for there was no discernible way in.

I had walked for six hundred metres and all I had found was more and more impenetrable wall. I felt as ineffectual as a paper umbrella and it was a long walk back to the car...either way.

Then I heard something drifting on the airwaves; the sound of music, as lilting as a Fogelberg family melody. I smiled at the thought that some Pied Piper might guide me. I walked back to the oak door and leaned against it. This time it moved. I pushed again and found myself staring into another epoch. To my left was a walled chateau, frozen in time like a childhood image. At each corner stood a round, turreted wall, topped by a conical spire covered in the patina of age. The building was completely surrounded by a moat with a single, lowered drawbridge. To my right, incongruous in its surroundings and resting against the outer wall like an afterthought from an architect's night on the tiles, was a small modern building. This building appeared gauche beside the third structure that was straight ahead, and which dominated its surroundings like the sublime brush stroke of a master artist. The building, the largest glasshouse I had ever seen, was immense yet it floated in space. I could sense its weight yet was dazzled by its lightness. Towering and rectangular with extensive glass panels that reflected the leaden clouds and engendered them with ominous proportion. Circular fluted columns bore witness to a bygone era and filigreed wrought iron lacework decorated its upper reaches as if painted by a delicate brush.

I was drawn to the building by an unseen guide and was soon standing at its frosted glass doors like an alien at a private party. I pushed the door and it swung open on noiseless hinges. Once inside, I gazed at row upon row of trestled flowerbeds, each effusing a wonderland of colours and hues. My eyes blinked as I walked toward the trestles in bright sunlight and I began to shake as I could see blue sky refracting through the glass panelled roof. Impossible; the sun shone within the building. I walked on, toward the centre of the building, stopping occasionally to read the neat stencilled signage painted on the side of each flowerbed. Each sign denoted family, genus and specific epithet. Someone had paid laborious attention to detail. I noticed that the signs were in English, which surprised me.

I walked on, spending time at each flowerbed and reading the signs and noticing something that seemed bizarre within the botanical environment of the glasshouse. Instead of almost infinite variety, there was but one example of each genus. There were orchids, cobra lilies, dahlias, daffodils, tulips, peonies and many others. My temples pulsed as I realised that I knew each flower's epithet before reading the nametags. I had met some of the flowers. I had spoken to them. Several had helped me on my journey. I looked at dahlias and thought of *Alloway Candy* at the Chateau de Trouffe and skulls smoking cigars. I read *Cobra Lily Darlingtonia* and remembered flashes of Lycra on a stairwell. Next came the beautiful orchid, *Dendrobium bigibbum*. A daffodil with a flash of French elegance bore the name *Marabou 4 w-p*, a lily flowered tulip named *Marilyn Tulipa* displayed in the sunlight and deep purple peonies brought Taishono Homari of the Moutan family to mind.

I moved on, realising that I hadn't seen the flower that I coveted most. I looked around for splashes of white, walking quickly along the rows of trestles. The walk turned to a slow jog and then to a run as my heart rate climbed. I ran across rows and along columns like a marker in a snakes and ladder game. I saw flashes of white but they were never what I sought.

I found myself at the diagonally opposite corner of the building to where I had started. *Nothing!* I leaned forward and placed my hands on my knees as I gulped for air in the broiling sun. *Sun!* It was raining outside. I breathed deeply and stood upright, perusing the scene before me. A panoply of flowers just prior the peak of bloom.

As I stared toward the far end of the greenhouse I realised that mist descending like a screen, discrepant to the brightness of the sun. I thought of Julia Dendrobium. I looked at the far end of the building and could see the open door through which I had entered. The door was fading in the fog's filtering glow. I held my hand over my mouth and nose and began to run. Half way along the runway I stubbed my right foot on an outstretched garden hose and stumbled. I ran on, willing the door to stay open; longing for its open portal.

I rushed through it and burst into pouring rain. I stopped and looked back at the green house, motionless, feeling as soggy as a wet sponge and wondering what I had just achieved. I realised that I was being pounded by large droplets of French skywater. Then I heard music again; the Pied Piper was back. I listened closely, searching for direction. The music became louder as it flooded my ears with the wondrous sound of the third movement of Elgar's cello concerto. I was close but lacked direction. I looked across at the lawns to the Chateau. The drawbridge had been raised. I closed my eyes and concentrated on direction, turning slowly until the sound had centred. The sound emanated from the incompatible building that leaned against the outer wall. It was concrete slab with curved glass windows and copper downpipes under the rustic ochre of a bronzed roof.

I hurried to its doorway and dripped excess water onto a rubberised doormat. The door opened automatically. I stepped into a small foyer that led to a single stainless steel door with a porthole at viewing height. I looked through it and froze. In the centre of what appeared to be a laboratory was a single table. Atop the table was a cluster of charming, elegant semi-double, milk-white blooms that were open to show their rich wine-coloured centres. Several dozen Jacqueline du Pre roses were in full bloom. I opened the door to be immediately assailed by a wonderful musk perfume that flooded my senses with cardinal intoxication and rendered me oblivious to anything except the beauty of the rose that blossomed before me. I couldn't avert my eyes from its beauty.

'Ohhh'

I heard the gasp behind me. I turned toward the door and my mouth took on a clown-like gape. Perfection stood before me. The woman's blond hair was parted in the centre and curled around a lightly tanned face. Bright greyish eyes shone from above high cheekbones. She possessed the perfume of the roses. Peter Mortimer's description had not been exaggerated.

'I'm sorry,' the woman said. 'I thought that I was alone here.'

I could feel my heart pounding and my mouth was dry. 'Jacqueline du Pre?' I asked, around the bulk of my tongue.

'Of course,' the woman said. 'You know your roses, I see.'

I gulped for air.

The woman smiled. 'Something wrong?' she asked.

'No! I meant, are you Jacqueline du Pre?'

'You are impertinent, Mr Mawson.'

I spun toward the new voice behind me. The doorway, through which I had entered, was surrounded by an immense pear shaped blancmange wearing a flowered tent. She was as wide as she was high and seemed to increase in girth as her body descended toward the white marble of the floor tiles. Many chins rested on her enormous chest and a cigarette appeared to be glued to the fleshiness of her bottom lip. Pince-nez glasses rested at the end of a bulbous nose and a pig trotter hand encircled the delicate

stem of a champagne flute. I recognised the face. I had
seen it in a photograph at Chateau de Trouffe. It had been
of no consequence then but now I knew that I was looking
directly at Emily Washburn. 'Impertinent! How?' I asked,
stumbling for something to say.

'In this case…as in brazen. You steal onto private
property and make yourself at home wandering through
the greenhouse and into this very private laboratory.'

'I guess that I should have called ahead and made an
appointment,' I said, lamely.

'You did. I have been expecting you. For a while there
we were afraid that we might lose you.'

'Lose me?'

'Yes. To the French or Italian authorities. Drug running
maybe, or van theft.'

'Not my style.'

'Then what is your style, Mr Mawson?'

I was stumped. I had no idea. 'I'm just a seeker of
knowledge Madame Washburn. I take it that I am talking
to Emily Washburn.'

'Would you be disappointed if you weren't?'

'Indubitably so. After all it has taken some considerable
effort to get me here.'

'Then you aren't disappointed.'

'Thank you.'

'Perhaps you shouldn't thank me just yet. Seeking
knowledge can be a dangerous pastime. Do you ever
consider that aspect of what you are doing?'

I walked to the roses and inhaled their perfume. I was
almost at the end of my journey. I could sense it. I looked
around to get another glimpse of the beautiful woman but
she had disappeared.

'I haven't considered myself in any danger.'

'I meant danger to others. Have you ever considered the impact of the outcome of your investigation...should you find whom you seek?'

She was right, of course. 'No.'

'Then maybe you should. Come with me, Mr Mawson.'

Emily turned and waddled through the door and out of the laboratory. I followed closely behind and watched how, at each step, she tottered like a child's top before planting her foot firmly and moving on. We crossed the drawbridge and it rose as soon as we were on the chateau side of the moat. I looked back in desperation. I was entering the unknown. We reached the immense entry doors and the portcullis clanked and rose on ancient chains as the doors opened automatically. I followed Emily through the gate and into a gravel courtyard, which lead to another doorway and into a vaulted room that smelt of moss and age. On the walls were medieval tapestries depicting scenes of nobles in gardens and hordes of people carrying flower stems aloft in outreaching arms. Stained glass windows depicted flowers in bloom and on the vaulted ceiling. a mural of a single blood red rose appeared to smile on all who stood beneath. I looked across the room at a grand stone fireplace that bore the hallmarks of a thousand winters. Within its confines was a glass vase containing a *Tulipe noire*. Unlike deep plum coloured varieties, this tulip was the colour of ebony.

'Been reading Dumas?' I said to Emily, who was pressing buttons on the wall adjacent to the entry door.

Emily ignored my comment but smiled and touched a wilting petal. 'It is old and can no longer propagate. Soon it will die...but it has given much pleasure and more than a measure of prestige. It was central to the establishment of our reputation.'

She pressed another button and projected images began to appear on unadorned sections of the walls of the room. Images of men. Some old; others not so old. I watched the images focus and looked at them intently. I didn't recognise most of the men but some faces were familiar. I wondered how many were from the backrooms of the entertainment industry. Some certainly were not.

'Do you recognise any of these men?' Emily asked.

I glanced at Lovett, Polanski, Davis, Windsor... all recognisable in many circles. 'Some.' I replied

'Then you should look closer. Without exception, all of the men that you see represented on the wall have contributed a significant amount to society within their chosen professions.'

I had no idea where the lecture was leading. 'I don't see what that has to do with me.'

'And that is the problem. You see...if you are successful in your quest, we will be unable to assist men like those who are shown here. We will cease to serve a useful purpose.'

I was beginning to feel a deep and abiding anger rising from some hidden cavern within. No one ever seemed to understand. 'You seem to be like others that I have met along the way. You don't seem to understand that the total breadth and depth of my search is to find out what happened to Peter Mortimer. That's it all I want. Anything else is superfluous.'

Emily let out a deep sigh, as if losing patience with a delinquent child. 'You are right...of course. But you are stumbling into something that you don't need to know. If you continue, you may learn what happened to Peter Mortimer and we simply can't allow that to happen.'

I looked Emily straight in her slits of eyes. 'I am not stumbling. I am being guided...by one of your own. Marabou Worthing-Peters sets my direction by e-mail and I follow like a lemming...but I'm sure that you know that already.'

Emily smiled through a smattering of gold teeth. 'Of course. Marabou and I decided to give you a glimpse of what is possible. So that you will have seen with your own eyes what your knowledge will destroy.'

'I don't see how.'

'Mr Mawson, once you have your information, you will report to your client. For us, that will be the beginning of the end. There are those who will pry. The word will spread concerning our location. People will know that I exist and seek my favour. I cannot work like that.'

'What damage could that do?'

'I can tell you that there was a time when it didn't matter. From our inception until the late nineteen seventies the greenhouse was surrounded by beautiful gardens that were visited by the public. The chateau and moat were here but the moat was devoid of water. Then, in the early eighties there was an incident. At that time, there were those who believed that they could buy their way onto my list of customers. People began to believe that money was the only thing that mattered. One man, who had achieved nothing but enormous wealth, became so disgruntled that he sought to enter the greenhouse under the cover of darkness and spray the flowerbeds with a weed killer. It did much damage and forced us to build the outer wall and let it be known that the gardens were closed.'

As I listened, the words '*herbicidal maniac*' came to mind but they were too trite. 'And you don't want that to happen again.'

'Of course not.' Emily said. She turned her head as she heard a door open. Taishono Homari entered the room carrying a silver tray with two strategically placed champagne flutes resting on a lace doily. She bowed to the waist as she stood in front of Emily. The champagne didn't even ripple. I turned away and returned my gaze to the single black tulip. I tried to make my mind go blank but the effort made me ponder the connection between flowers and beautiful women. I had met some of Emily Washburn's creations. Taishono smiled benignly as she proffered her tray. She bowed slightly, then turned and left the room. There were no words spoken between Taishono and Emily yet I knew that they had communicated.

Emily spoke as soon as the door closed behind Taishono.

'I am surprised, Mr Mawson. You seem to believe that I, somehow, conjure up beautiful women from nowhere. Is it that you think that I am a shaman who has the power to create such an illusion and that I simply separate women from some supernatural vortex. Or is it that you believe that I am a sorceress who conceives of potions and my women are creations from the land of darkness? Maybe you think that I am a magus with the power to create life? Alas, Mr Mawson, you are mistaken. I am a simple gardener.'

'Your women are flowers. The same range of flowers that grow in your garden.'

Emily continued. 'You think that I have the power to turn flowers into women? Surely, that is science fiction.

With cloning it may one day occur, but I will be but a distant memory by then.' She paused for a moment, as if trying to recall the lines of some written script. 'Let me ask you something. Have you ever considered how close some women are to flowers?'

'No.' I replied.

'You should think on it. Do flowers and women not share beauty? Is there not perfection in some and flaws in others? If you are close to a flower, do you not smell its texture? Do you not do that with a lover? Do flowers and women not blossom in Spring? Do they not hibernate in winter? Do they not wilt and die?'

'Mr Mawson, flowers and women are both part of life's cycle. They both exist for a moment in time and then return to the earth. I have no more power to create women than you do. I have no secret knowledge or gift. I am but a poor woman who tries to help those who do not meet the modern world's criteria for existence. You see, if you are not beautiful in this world, you have nothing of value to offer. Intellect once mattered as an individual entity but now it must be accompanied by more than a modicum of beauty. I try to help the less fortunate and allow them to show the rest of the world that they do have something to offer. The company of a beautiful woman makes others think that the man has something that others can't perceive.'

'Anyone with money can hire a beautiful escort. That happens all the time,' I said.

'But nothing goes beyond. With my ladies, there is a chance for more...much more. Do you not consider Joshua Arbour, Joseph Dendrobium or Claude Worthington-Peters to be men of good fortune?'

I pondered the question but there was no answer. The three men mentioned were proof that there was an opportunity to go beyond the escort stage, but all three had both fame and money. Could they not have attracted beautiful women anyway? There are always gold diggers and enormously cleavaged models on the make for an easy fortune. 'I guess so. But I'm not convinced.'

'Then I need to convince you. Have you wondered why you were able to arrive at this destination? After all, it could easily have been prevented.'

Memories of Chateau de Trouffe and the city of angels swam through my mind. 'You mean by drugging me...and maybe getting rid of me.'

'Not at all. They were simply ploys to maintain interest in your journey. I admit that our initial reaction to the quest that Quenna Knight had started you on was to have some fun with you for a while then derail you. But then Amelia Aliput entered the scene and her mother thought that it might be best if you were to continue your journey.'

I had an inkling that I knew the answer but asked the question anyway. 'To what end?'

Emily's smile was benign. 'To the same end as your search for what happened to Peter Mortimer.'

'You mean that I shouldn't track the history of Marilyn Aliput.'

'You are astute man Mr Mawson.'

'Then convince me,' I said.

Emily moved her head in a nodding motion and the jelly of her chins wobbled in unison. She turned from me and walked from the room. I followed along a columned corridor until we arrived at doorway with a viewing window in its oak-panelled door. She bid that I look inside.

I stepped to the window and viewed a classroom. At the front, holding a laser pointer with its red dot etching a thin line in the centre of a vivid white-throated red bloom of rhododendron, was Vicki Reine, the American kick ass actor of numerable chick flicks. I couldn't hear what she was saying but her audience appeared spellbound. From where I stood, I could see the backs of at least twelve women, but I was certain that there were more inside.

'All of my women need to know the heart of their flower. They need to interpret its essential life force. They are from the best stock in Europe.'

I stared into the room for a long time, realising that I had indeed been on a flight of fancy. It was now dawning on me that Emily Washburn was a collector and purveyor of women. I had hoped that it would end up as being far more exotic. I felt as flat as a used tyre on a scrap heap. There was no story to tell. Maybe Peter Mortimer had just stepped onto the road at the wrong time. Nothing explained the absence of Jacqueline du Pre from the television footage but I expected that I would never garner an explanation for that. 'Thank you for that.' I said to Emily. 'A picture painting more than words.'

'I see that you are disappointed,' Emily said.

'But you aren't.... I can't see a story here...so you have no danger from me.'

'Marilyn will be pleased. I'll show you out.'

'One moment, if you don't mind.' I walked to the black tulip and touched it lightly on a petal. 'Quenna said to tell you that she will be fine.' I felt the petal vibrate.

I followed Emily along the corridor until we reached the entry. The portcullis and drawbridge moved to allow me to pass. Emily pointed me toward the main entry gate.

'Your car is just outside. It's quicker for you than the rear entrance...besides, you can look in on one of your own. Behind the door at the right of the entry portal, there's a hydroponics room. We're perfecting a strand of the *Strangea linearis* waratah. It's been around for a while now but we need to reset it a little. It's called the Kate....'

I held up my hand to stop her. I didn't want to know. 'One last question. What will happen to Candy Alloway when Joshua dies...or Marilyn Aliput when her husband dies?'

Emily smiled and shook her head. 'Small question, large import.'

'Maybe I'm trying to find out what happened to Jacqueline du Pre.'

'That's easy. She is here. You saw her...but she won't talk about your Mr Mortimer. It upsets her too much.'

'Candy Alloway?...hypothetically.'

Emily's eyes darted from side to side, as she pushed a few strands of wispy hair from her forehead. 'Alloway is eternal. She will regenerate. She does so every year. Joshua wanted it that way. It isn't for anyone else to decide.'

'And Marilyn?'

'She has a child. She ages with her husband.'

'Marabou doesn't have children.'

'No...but she has choices. She decided not to regenerate. She is old...like me...she will live out her life in comfort.'

'Jacqueline du Pre isn't old. From what I saw she is young and beautiful. I assume that I may see her again.'

Emily peered over the lenses of her glasses. 'You are persistent, if nothing else. She may be glimpsed again but not for a while. She has a flaw.'

'I didn't notice.'

'I would be surprised if you did. You see, she is too susceptible to black spot.'

'But that can affect most roses.'

'Yes.'

Black spot was important. There had to be a reason for Emily to divulge the information. Something had happened between Mortimer and Jacqueline that involved a fungal disease. My mind boggled. Surely the beauty didn't have sex with the beast.

'Nothing like that but he *was* responsible,' Emily said, smiling.

'I wish you people would stop that.'

'Soon this will all be a fading memory.'

'Retribution?'

'Not at all, but Joshua told you that one can't break the rules. Mortimer broke the rules.'

'And paid with his life.'

Emily shook her head. 'We would simply have cleared his mind. He would not have remembered his time with Jacqueline. Those who don't believe can't see.'

'Fate stepped in at the wrong moment.'

'Unlucky for him. For you, however, your fate still awaits you. Amelia does have a flaw however. She cannot have children.'

I closed the gate behind me, walked the few paces and dropped into the driver's seat of my car. I pushed the start button and listened to the roar of the engine. The car pointed to the east. It raised a question. Should I return to Italy for the rest of the week and then drive up to Duclair over the weekend or should I go straight through France. It had been cold when I left Italy, so I hit the Penetrante

Grasse-Cannes and headed toward Cannes. As I accelerated down the road I saw the walls of the castle fading behind me. Not in the sense that they drifted into the distance but in the sense that the scene changed until all that was left were rolling hills and frost on the grass. It seemed that Emily Washburn didn't exist after all.

***

It was just after sixteen hundred when I entered the Boulevard de la Croisette. I pulled off the road in front of the small park through which stood the *Palais des Festivals et des Congres* building. In the late afternoon it looked forlorn and desolate, despite myriad of suits with briefcases descending its uncarpeted staircase. Like most buildings, it needed the glitz of a festival to enliven its character. I pulled up a chair from under the tarpaulin covering the Cannes Carousel and sat with my arms resting on the back of the moulded plastic marvel. I began to wonder what I was doing there. It wasn't necessary to go to Cannes. It was out of my way in fact. Maybe it was the realisation that the adventure that had superimposed itself on my past nine months had finally ended and this was a means of saying goodbye. Maybe it was that I would soon return to the mundane world of teaching bright young things with a thirst for the knowledge of any other subject. Maybe it was that I hadn't thought of asking Emily Washburn why it was that all of the males who were married to her women had adopted names or anagrams of the names that represented flowers. I stood from the chair and pushed it back under the tarpaulin. It was time for a stroll along the promenade. It would be brisk with a southerly blustering

over imported sand and sand-blasting flagpoles along the
way. I decided against it and leaned against the balustrade,
looking across to the cylinder of the lighthouse. I could
hear Dan Fogelberg's *Ever On* drifting on the wind. I
slipped into its melancholy. The Carlton was just along the
road. I tossed a mental coin and it fell face up. The prices
wouldn't be too bad off season.

I was opening my car door when I heard something
behind me.

'Your vehicle sir?'

I recognised the voice and spun around. 'No it's stolen.
Would you like a lift?'

'Yes…to the Carlton. I'm booked in there.'

'One should never do that by oneself. You need company to stay there.'

'I've been expecting some.'

I looked across the car bonnet at Amelia Aliput and
smiled. 'Get in.'

'Did you get what you wanted?' Amelia asked as we
cruised along the avenue.

'More or less. Probably less. Why are you here?'

'I've taken leave between now and the festival. It
seemed such a waste of time to fly home and then return
in a couple of months. I thought that I might do the grand
tour or Europe.'

'I'm off to northern France. Place called Duclair. You
can use that for a base for a few days if you like.'

'Only if you tell me about my mother.'

I contemplated for a moment, then decided that I could
never tell. 'Okay…you want the truth or a lie.

Amelia smiled and the world was at peace. 'I'll settle for
whichever you wish to divulge.'

'In that case, all that I can tell you is that your mother has no history because once upon a time she was a flower that was grown in the garden of Emily Washburn. She was a protected and well nurtured tulip and she was given to your father when he was nominated for an award at the Cannes film festival. They fell in love and married.'

Amelia laughed out loud and the sparkle of her eyes sent daggers through my heart. 'You expect me to believe that?'

'I do. Why shouldn't you.'

As we drove, I realised that I had unfinished business. I had nothing to tell Kendra Mortimer and I had no idea what happened to her half-brother.

Later that night, as Amelia slept the sleep of the innocent I fired up my computer and looked at the file containing Peter Mortimer's walk along the red carpet. He was no longer alone. One day I would show the file to Amelia.

The Beginning

ON the fourteenth of May at precisely seventeen hundred hours, Peter Mortimer found himself kissing Emily Washburn's hand in the plush surroundings of La Merde Riches Hotel's cocktail lounge. He leaned forward for the kiss, comprehending Emily's size and having a vision of an obese warthog which, of course, he immediately dismissed as a politically incorrect thought

'Please sit down,' Emily said as she gestured to the small space still available at one end of the lounge. She summoned a passing waiter, ordered a bottle of Bollinger and readjusted her bulk on the plush crimson fabric of the lounge.

As they waited for the champagne, Emily concentrated on the handful of cashews that she had removed from a bowl. She sat in silence, with only her jaws moving and teeth sawing like a chipping machine, until the waiter reappeared with the bottle and two fresh glasses.

'Whilst I am pleased that you have finally been nominated for an award Peter, I must remind you that what you want is very expensive,' she said, as she cast her eyes over his tousled hair and crushed linen suit. 'And I know you are not, as yet, a man of means. Frankly I thought that you would settle for something on the second tier.'

'Don't let appearances fool you Ms Washburn,' Mortimer replied, as he scratched at the stubble on his chin. 'I missed a connecting flight in Thailand. If I'd arrived as expected, I wouldn't be at the end of the list.'

'You would have to have been here for two weeks and your type is never that organised.' Emily rasped around a cigarette that rested on her bottom lip as if adhered with glue. 'If you were, I'd be unemployed and poor and wouldn't need to spend a fortune on invitations. So let's not kid ourselves.'

Mortimer's mind struggled for a retort but he decided that he had no strength of position and shrugged his shoulders in a gesture of submission. 'Do you still have a woman available?' he asked.

'Of course, I have one who will adorn your arm with such beauty that the world will envy your good fortune.'

Mortimer thought for a moment. 'If she's that good, why is she still obtainable?'

'She is a rose,' Emily quipped.

Mortimer didn't understand, but he decided not to make a fool of himself by asking for an explanation. 'The most beautiful of flowers...when can I meet her?'

Emily fumbled with one of the many gold bracelets that adorned her left arm, moving a jewelled plate aside to reveal a watch face. She pondered the dial for several seconds as if waiting for inspiration. 'As soon as we have cemented the deal.'

'I assume that it is simply a matter of money. I *can* pay.'

Emily's smile chilled the air. 'My ladies are not for sale, Mr Mortimer,' Washburn said, reverting from the friendly Peter to his more formal name. 'They are from the finest stock in Europe. They allow men like you to be seen with rare beauty. They are not a commodity and money is not the driving force here. It is merely the means to an end.

The thing that allows you to escort one of my ladies is a strict adherence to the rules. Do you understand?'

Mortimer nodded, his mouth suddenly dry. 'There was nothing in the invitation concerning any rules.'

'I can assure you that they are, in the fine print that is written along the edge of the invitation. However, as you do not seem to have read them, I will reiterate for you. The main rule is exceedingly simple to understand, even for you. You are to be seen only in public with the lady and you do not attempt to spend time alone with her in intimate surroundings or kiss her. If you agree, you will be able to have a beautiful woman on your arm at all of the right functions and nightclubs. You will be the envy of your peers.'

Mortimer sipped on his champagne but his mouth remained parched. He sat silently and nodded like a fool.

'I take it that you agree?' Emily asked.

'Yes.'

'A desperate man Mr Mortimer. To have beauty so close, yet so far. One other thing…also on the invitation…is that you must provide the lady with all of the clothing that she wears to the functions. She will, of course, keep what you purchase for her.'

Mortimer pondered for a moment, a melting platinum credit card conjuring a searing image in his mind, then offered his hand to seal the agreement.

'I trust that you will look much better when you meet the young lady. I am unimpressed by your lack of thought and consideration for appearance. After all, we do not want people to see beauty and the beast.'

Two hours later, Peter Mortimer brushed an imaginary spec of dust from the breast pocket of his jacket as he reviewed his reflection in a mirrored shopfront near the Galerie de Cannes. Certainly he looked better; he was now clean and resplendent in a navy blue woollen jacket with grey cotton slacks and a sky blue cotton shirt. He would have preferred to wear navy or grey shoes, to complete the ensemble, but those he would have had to purchase and he foresaw a requirement for every inch of credit on his much misused slither of plastic.

He had no intention of being dilatory so, as he pushed at the door to gain entry to the gallery, he checked the faux Rolex on his wrist and prayed that it hadn't stopped. He didn't know where to look or for whom he searched. All he had was a name, the name of the art gallery on Rue d'Antibes and the appointed time.

As he searched, he noticed that every room of the gallery seemed to be populated by women in yellow floral dresses who stood in high-heeled shoes and gently touched fingers to uplifted chins whilst providing salacious utterances of *Umm*. They mingled with matrons in grey tents and flat shoes who led bored men by unseen leashes from masterpiece to trash without ever considering the difference. The men knew where the real art was hidden; their eyes never roved above the horizontal and spent most time amongst the cleavage in yellow dresses.

He was lost until he arrived at the gallery displaying the floral artworks of Alain Géneau. The only woman inside, now looking in Mortimer's direction, was part of a rare breed that carries beauty with casual ease. It was hard to imagine that the vision in his eyes was ever less than perfect. The woman's blond hair was parted in the centre and curled around a lightly tanned face to further soften a smoothly rounded jawline. Bright greyish eyes shone from above high and only slightly made-up cheekbones. As she turned to stand, he noticed how smallish breasts pushed at her mauve blouse, making petite conical peaks. His eyes were taking in the lower regions when she spoke.

'Mr Mortimer?' she asked.

'Miss du Pre, I presume,' Mortimer replied, as his eyes drifted back to her face.

'You may call me Jacqueline, or Jacque, if you prefer.'

'Peter.'

'Peter, I'm pleased to meet you,' Jacqueline said, in a voice with the timbre of melted honey. 'I trust that you aren't disappointed.' She stood and twirled with the finesse of a ballerina.

'I'm in love,' Mortimer uttered, grinning broadly.

'And so quickly.' Jacqueline's eyes lit the room with their brilliance. 'Shall we go?'

'Where are we going?'

'I thought that we might get to know one another. Maybe a stroll through the gallery or along the promenade.'

Jacqueline linked arms with Mortimer as they left the gallery. He didn't know where they were going so simply kept pace with the sensuous movement of her hips as she strolled. Immediately he felt that everyone they passed on the street was looking at them.

He was pleased that they were the same height and that she didn't tower over him. For some reason he had imagined the woman would have the elevation of a supermodel, and his lack of platform soles would make obvious that they weren't really a couple, but this woman was his height in the three inch silver spikes that adorned the heels of her shoes.

As they strolled along the promenade, between the skaters, hawkers and vague tourists who were seeing the city through miniature camera screens, they made small talk that drifted from topic to topic. Sometimes it concentrated on Mortimer's reasons for being in town and his desire to have his film distributed. Often it drifted to the film itself and its surprise nomination for the awards, or the gold embossed invitation and its flight of fantasy. After a time, Jacqueline walked two paces ahead and turned around, taking both of Mortimer's hands in hers and walking backwards with consummate ease.

'What is our plan for this evening?' she asked. 'Where are you taking me?'

Mortimer gave the impression that he thought about the answer, but the events were already set.

'Well...tonight will initially be a little boring for you. There's a sales meeting with a film distributor. It's very important to our film. It will only take an hour or so, then I thought that we might go clubbing. Tomorrow night is the awards ceremony and, hopefully, we'll be invited to one or two parties.'

The smile on Jacqueline's face possessed the wonderment of a child in a candy store. 'Then I will need two dresses and some new lingerie. Will you like to choose for me?'

Mortimer's brain was subjected to a minor loss of blood as his control centre stirred. 'I would be delighted.'

La Mode is the most exclusive boutique in Cannes, so Mortimer shuddered as he ushered Jacqueline through its gleaming marble portal. He was only mildly surprised when the head saleswoman left her toadying post, beside a living advertisement for the porcelain of botox, and greeted

Jacqueline with warmth and affection. He was more surprised when four dresses were brought from an ante-room, and draped over the back of a plush cream satin sofa, for Jacqueline to admire. He expected that she would not want clothing from a rack, but it appeared that this moment had been planned in advance.

He caught a smile on Jacqueline's face that intrigued him. Such perfection. He joined his thumbs and index fingers, held them at arms length and looked through the aperture, capturing her image as if through a lens framing her face. She smiled when she noticed his gesture and, in turn, held each dress to her body before feeling its texture against her cheek.

'Which would you like me to try on?' she asked as she held the last to her body.

Mortimer was lost. He had no predilection for women's fashion. He only knew what he liked and didn't like. 'The turquoise silky one, I think. The sheath with the spilt down the left side. You will look beautiful in that.'

'Any other?' she gestured to the remaining dresses.

'Tomorrow night I want you to be the sexiest woman on earth. I have something in mind, but I can't see it here at the moment. We need something really stunning. Something to make every head turn. Something that is exceptionally special.'

'For special, should I read revealing?' Jacqueline said, as her perfect white teeth appeared, between the sensual bow of her lips, in a broad smile.

'Not too revealing. Just enough. Maybe we can leave it for now and go shopping tomorrow morning?'

'That's fine. I shall try this on,' she said, pointing to the turquoise silk fabric that lay strewn across the lounge.

Exquisite was the only word that came to mind when Jacqueline paraded the dress that clung to her like a second skin, emphasising her slender curves and long legs.

Mortimer was enthralled.

'I think that he likes it, mademoiselle,' said the saleswoman, in pseudo conspiratorial tones, within Mortimer's hearing.

'If that grin means anything, I think that he does,' Jacqueline quipped.

Mortimer was mesmerised by the sight and said nothing. He didn't want to replace his dropped jaw with anything. This was visual heaven. This was a filmmaker's dream.

'Would mademoiselle like to look at some lingerie?' the saleswoman asked.

'Is that alright Peter?' Jacqueline asked.

Mortimer sat on his chair, his head nodding like a backseat dog.

***

Jacqueline's breasts were firm, she had a narrow waist and long slender legs but her well-formed rear drove Mortimer insane as she bent forward to adjust her breasts into the half cups of a bra. He still couldn't believe that she had stripped in his presence as soon as they entered the lingerie fitting rooms. Jacqueline turned slowly and let him admire her lithe form in the pale blue silk underwear. It was obvious that he approved. She knew the effect that her type of figure had on most men and was pleased that Mortimer wasn't immune. 'Is there another set that you would like me to try?' she whispered.

Mortimer sat down quickly and crossed his legs. He viewed the assortment of lingerie that had been provided and pointed to a pink set. 'I like those,' he spluttered.

'You have eye for style, sir,' said the saleswoman, whose presence Mortimer had totally forgotten. He assumed that the smirk on her face was due to his obvious discomfort.

'Yes, we'll take the blue that she's wearing, the pink and the silver grey, thank you. Is that okay, Jacque?'

'You're a wonderful man,' Jacqueline replied.

Mortimer waited until Jacqueline was in the change room and then stood. He walked to the serving counter and waited for the saleswoman. 'How much is all that?' he asked as he handed over his credit card.

'If one needs to ask, one cannot afford to shop here,' Came the clichéd reply. With that, the woman swiped the card and returned it to Mortimer. He waited for a receipt but none was forthcoming. 'The receipt will be in the bag when the clothes are delivered to the mademoiselle, sir. There is no need for you to worry.'

'You mean that we aren't taking delivery now?'

'Of course not, sir. The mademoiselle will not want to roam the streets carrying a shopping bag, despite the jeneseque' of its logo. No, sir. We deliver.'

Mortimer considered the ways that he might turn the woman into an incendiary device but the thought was suspended by Jacqueline emerging from the dressing room and taking his arm.

'Where to now?' she asked and they stepped back into the bright sunlight.

Mortimer had no idea. He was taking it minute by minute but was pleased that she didn't suggest another shopping venue. 'I guess I need to prepare for tonight's negotiations with Mario Pittelli of Merjak Film Distribution. I'm warned that he's a pretty smooth operator.'

'To study hall then.'

***

The room was dark. There were three small LED lights over the conference table but these had been dimmed so that the faces of the negotiators looked like morphed figures in a puppet gallery. Mortimer realised that he was out of his depth. He was both outnumbered and outgunned by the film distributor's representatives. They numbered five and were all introduced by name, without function, so Mortimer had no idea about the role of each participant. However, in the past fifty minutes they had all spoken. Jones, in the crimson shirt and green suede jacket, had talked financing. Jerome Balltacks, with the glass eye, had eulogised on the need for a follow-up film. Bethany ran through legal matters. McWhirter, in the black Armani suit with the pink shirt and pink polka dot tie, looked like an overdressed hill climb leader from a cycling race and spoke solemnly on the topic of merchandising as if the film's only purpose was to create a merchandising opportunity. But then, he considered everything to be an opportunity.

Mortimer's side of the table was represented by himself, his business partner Billy Squires and Jacqueline du Pre. He was intimidated by the mismatch and was distraught to think that Jacqueline would witness the impoverishment of his negotiating power.

After an hour it was obvious that negotiating with Mario Pittelli was an error. Merjak wanted to distribute his film but Mortimer felt that he'd only break even if he accepted the offer. Unfortunately, as a first time director, the majors weren't clamouring for his product, so it was a case of giving in for now with a hope to being in a better position next time.

'Well Mr Mortimer, do we 'ave a deal?' Pitelli asked. 'We've been at it now fa too long and we're beginning to repeat ourselves,' he said, as he held out his hand as an offer to finalise the deal with Mortimer.

'There is no deal,' stated Jacqueline, to everyone's dismay. 'You're still well short of any figure that we will accept.'

The gulp from Billy Squires was audible. Even in the semi darkness Jacqueline could see his throat bulge. Mortimer seemed calmer but that was because a hand was grasping his knee with considerable force.

'Just where do you fit in to this, Miss...du Pre wasn't it,' Pitelli asked, as he looked directly into the eyes of the beautiful woman sitting opposite. Even in the subdued light of the room he had noticed her. There was even a moment when he had considered ramping up the lighting so that he could focus on her beauty. He found himself enthralled by her style: the way that her hair swept back to a bob that highlighted the swan like curve of her neck: the sensual way that her lips moved when she spoke. But he had guessed that she was Mortimer's toy and not part of his negotiating team.

'I'm Mr Mortimer's financial adviser,' Jacqueline lied. 'I let him know when he has a deal that he can live with.'

Billy Squires' temperature rose as molten lava made its way to the exit fissure. He couldn't believe that Mortimer's tart was speaking, let alone getting involved. He wanted to shut her up before she made fools of them, but then she stared at him and he saw steel that he hadn't thought possible.

'This is as good a deal as he'll get from anyone,' quipped Pitelli, as he smirked toward his supporters and acknowledged their inane giggles.

'Mr Pittelli, Mr Mortimer will win the prize tomorrow evening for his category. Then the majors will want to distribute it and you'll be left in the cold. The only way for you to procure the distribution rights is to do a deal tonight but, alas, that doesn't look as if it will happen.'

'There's no guarantee that Mortimer's film will win,' Pitelli scoffed.

'That risk is yours Mr Pitelli but if you didn't think that it could win you wouldn't be here, would you?' Jacqueline retorted, as she rose from her chair. She gestured for Squires and Mortimer to follow her. 'We'll give you ten minutes to revise your offer or we walk. We'll wait outside.'

Mortimer bit his lower lip to diffuse his anger but his face carried the crimson hue of elevated blood pressure. When he confronted Jacqueline, he spoke in a low monotone. 'How dare you do that? I was on the verge of a deal. You just cost me distribution of my film.'

Jacqueline smiled at the two men and gestured for them both to sit, ignoring Mortimer's tirade. 'You were about to be ripped off, Peter. Just give it a couple of minutes. If I'm wrong, you get your money back'

Mortimer's voice rose an anger octave. 'If you're wrong I have no deal. What you cost me is inconsequential.'

'I won't be wrong, trust me. It's just a matter of time,' Jacqueline said, smiling.

Time dragged on. Each minute took an hour. Mortimer and Squires viewed their watches every ten seconds. Jacqueline rested patiently on a sofa, reading an antiquated gardening magazine that she had found on the side table.

Mortimer imitated a countdown from ten to zero. 'Time's up. Thank you very much Jacque,' he snarled, as he started to walk down the stairs.

'No!' exclaimed Squires as he followed Mortimer downstairs. He grabbed hold of Mortimer's arm and tried to drag him back. 'We can't just leave. We almost had a deal.'

'There *is* no deal, Billy. Tell him, my learned friend.' Mortimer spat the words toward Jacqueline.

Jacqueline rose from her sofa just as the door to the office opened. She gestured for Mortimer and Squires to keep walking.

'Oh, Mr Mortimer,' came a voice from above.

Mortimer turned to see Bethany leaning over the railing. 'Mr Pittelli would like to see you again.'

Mortimer looked up at Jacqueline, who was still at the top of the stairs. She smiled back at him before she spoke. 'Tell Mr Pittelli that Mr Mortimer would be pleased to speak with him. This time, however, it's one on one. No need for surplus armies.'

***

Two bottles of champagne were upended in a silver ice bucket. A third stood on the table, a strawberry jammed into its neck. A fourth was being upended into Squire's mouth. Jacqueline saw that Mortimer had changed over the previous three hours. Gone was the nervous businessman on a mission. Now, he sat with glazed eyes and reiterated his final conversation with Pittelli for the umpteenth time. He was the epitome of dishevelled disregard with his shirtfront open halfway down his chest and jacket askew. His hair was a tousled mess on his head and he kept raking it to clear his mind. He failed, in that regard, as he was in both a drunken stupor and besotted with Jacqueline's company. He couldn't believe his luck. The most beautiful girl that he'd ever seen sat beside him. He had just organised a contract that would distribute his film and he was in the most exclusive nightclub in the city, at an invitation-only party for the glitterati.

'We should get you home,' Jacqueline said.

'I need another drink,' Mortimer replied, waving his arm at a passing waiter.

'No you don't. You need to get back to your hotel, so you can sleep this one off and prepare for your big night tomorrow.'

'Will you come back to the hotel with me?'

'Of course,' Jacqueline said, as she rose from her seat and gestured to the waiter that they were finished.

Outside the nightclub, Mortimer shook his head in horror as flashbulbs exploded in front of his eyes. Black stars filled the void and he squinted to regain composure. Jacqueline placed her arm around him and her eyes sparkled in the moonlight. She allowed the photographers to get as many shots as they wanted, always posing so that Mortimer could be acknowledged as a lucky man. Being drunk and dishevelled wasn't a problem; it was who you were with that set tongues wagging. A few minutes later, they had traversed a city block and run the gauntlet of the early morning traffic, with cars driven by partygoers who were too drunk to walk.

The foyer of Mortimer's hotel was deserted. Even the security guard was missing. Low level lights provided an eerie glow that gave a gargoyle appearance to the sculpture that was the centrepiece of the foyer during the waking hours. A greenish glow marked the entrance to the lift lobby. Mortimer almost tripped over his feet as he fought the cobwebs of his mind. He could sense that Jacqueline was helping him along but was too far gone to absorb anything except the perfume of her soul; a natural fragrance that seemed to diminish the esters of man-made concoctions. He couldn't quite identify it. He was in no condition to try.

'Would you like some assistance, Madame?' came a bodiless voice from a dark recess.

'No, we're fine thank you. He's just been a little exuberant,' Jacqueline said.

The open steel cage made Jacqueline feel like a zoo animal as the lift screeched out a discordant tune between floors. Mortimer rested against the rustic iron of the lift's lacework oblivious to anything except Jacqueline, who was holding him upright. The lift reached the fourth floor at the speed of gridlock but finally it stopped and Jacqueline opened the inner and outer doors to free herself from the experience.

Mortimer raked the sides of his head furiously to dismiss the lethargy but he could sense failure as his mind refused to clear. He let Jacqueline assist him to his door and then fumbled for the key. 'I'm so sorry, I think that I drank too much,' he said, his words expelling around the bulk of his tongue.

'Don't worry about it. I'll be here at ten in the morning. We can have breakfast together.'

Through his fog, Mortimer heard what she said and smiled like a Cheshire cat. He then fell through the doorway and nose-dived toward his bed. He almost made it.

Jacqueline descended the dimly lit staircase and re-entered the foyer as Billy Squires arrived. Clinging to him, like a limpet, was a girl from the dark side of the street. Jacqueline decided that they looked like a well-matched couple.

***

The morning sun filtered through the cobwebs and dust of the hotel's skylight giving the corridor of the fourth floor the soft glow of suffused decay. The place had seemed bad enough the previous evening but the daylight made Jacqueline wonder how Mortimer had raised the money to afford her services. She rapped on the door to Mortimer's room and waited. She rapped again, then rested her ear against the timber frame and listened. The sound of silence issued forth. She looked at her watch and rapped with increased vigour. The agonising squeal of the lift rent the air and stopped at the floor. Mortimer rushed from the lift with his breath punctuating staccato interludes into an uneven melody. Perspiration beaded on his forehead but, unexpectedly, his eyes were clear.

A look of boyhood excitement shone through the sweat and a pained expression that gave Mortimer the appearance of a constipated greyhound. 'Thank god, you're still here. I was afraid that I might miss you.' Mortimer said between gasps for air. 'I've been out for my morning run and I found it.'

Jacqueline remained cool. 'What have you found?'

'The dress. One that will be just right for tonight. You'll look more fabulous than you usually do. It's perfect for you. Do you want to look?'

'I'd love to rush off with you, but breakfast would be nice.'

***

Mortimer couldn't settle. He fidgeted for the entire time that he and Jacqueline sat at one of the outside tables of the Coût Plus Dehors Brasserie. Whilst his agitation grew, Jacqueline sipped coffee and nibbled at croissants. She could see that something agitated him but she was in no hurry to satisfy her curiosity. She tried to calm him but he remained seated on the edge of his chair, his body hardly in contact with the cane seat. She was amused and a wide smile creased her cheeks.

Mortimer noticed. 'Okay, okay. We have the whole day, right?'

'Yes we do. More particularly though, is that shops don't open, today, until fourteen thirty.'

Mortimer's guffaw turned every head in the brasserie. His eyes sparkled and he slapped his thigh. 'Does anything faze you, Jacque?' he asked.

Jacqueline used a serviette to dab the sides of her mouth. 'The usual things. The difference between us is that I grew up here and know the local customs. You're a stranger.'

'How long have you worked for Mrs Washburn?' Mortimer asked the question from left field.

'I don't.'

'I don't understand,' Mortimer said, his curiosity spiked.

'Does the agent work for the writer or does a writer really work for the agent?'

Mortimer pondered the response. 'I guess that it varies…according to the business relationship.'

'Exactly.'

Mortimer had no idea what she meant, but said nothing.

They strolled along the promenade to watch the heads turn until Jacqueline decided to look at her watch. The witching hour was nigh. 'Shall we go and see this marvellous dress that you saw for me?'

Mortimer led the way but, after walking half a block, Jacqueline's blood turned to ice. She knew where they were going. The shops were closed when Mortimer first saw the dress, so it had to be on display. She steeled herself to disappoint him. She slowed her pace while she thought about her predicament. The dress would be black. She didn't wear black.

Mortimer subconsciously increased the grip pressure on her hand as they approached the boutique. His excitement grew. The most fabulous dress that he'd ever seen for the most beautiful woman that he'd ever known. A perfect combination; hand and glove. 'Voila,' he said as they stood in front of the display window. 'Isn't it beautiful?'

Jacqueline nodded agreement as her stomach turned. The black dress reposed on a mannequin as an eclectic gathering of styles that formed one perfect whole. The airiness of an Ancient Greek tunic, the texture of the finest Chinese silk and the understated elegance of Valentino combined in a creation that was bound to please even the most discerning admirer of the style. One of the mannequin's legs was exposed almost to the thigh; the other covered to the knee as the angled drape combined formality and freedom in an unusual paradigm. Jacqueline had not seen its like before. 'Oh, Peter,' she said, squeezing his hand. 'It's gorgeous.'

'Stand here, stand here.' Mortimer had Jacqueline stand in front of the window as he stepped back and framed her with his hands in the same manner as on the previous day. 'Perfection. And it must be your size.'

Before Jacqueline could speak, Mortimer grasped her hand and led her into the inner sanctum of La Bouton Noire Boutique.

Jacqueline hesitated. 'It probably isn't for sale. We'll need to look for something else,' she murmured to Mortimer, in conspiratorial tones.

Mortimer nodded to a saleswoman, whose flashing teeth reminded him of a shark preparing for lunch.

'May I be of assistance?' she asked as she approached.

'My friend thinks that dress may not be for sale.'

'Everything in the store is for sale, sir...except the saleswoman of course.' The woman giggled at her own joke.

Mortimer chuckled in sympathy. If pressed, she would probably be cheaper than the dress.

'May we try this one on?' Mortimer asked.

'It is an original sir.'

'I expected as much.'

The saleswoman was surprised that a man was doing all of the talking. She directed her gaze to Jacqueline. 'Madame doesn't like the dress?'

'Ohh...not at all, it's beautiful.' She looked at the nametag on the saleswoman's jacket. 'Janelle. It's just that black isn't a good colour for me.'

Mortimer chipped in. 'You have to be kidding. You'll look sublime.'

'It's not the way I look. It's just that black always brings such bad luck to those around me and I don't want that to happen.'

'How could you bring bad luck? Since I've known you I've had nothing but good luck. Even if that stops now, I won't regret a minute. I would have been ripped off on the film sale if it weren't for you.'

'I wasn't wearing black then.'

'Try it on. I'll take the risk,' Mortimer said seriously.

Janelle unpinned the dress from the mannequin and guided Jacqueline to the dressing room. She undressed slowly. She wore the pink lingerie that Mortimer had purchased the day before but the feel of it against her body was no longer enticing. Without pleasure she slipped the black dress over her head and let it glide into position. She looked closely at the mirror, looking for imperfections. There were none. If only it wasn't black, she thought. Maybe if she wore it sparingly. Yes, that was it. She could spill something on it at the awards ceremony and she could change for later engagements. She left the dressing room pleased with her decision.

The expelling of breath, by every person in the boutique who saw her, came as a shock. Women stopped mid sentence and overtly stared. Men stood with their mouths agape. Janelle clapped like a small child at a party. Jacqueline pirouetted and the bottom of the dress rose as if suspended on an air cushion. Her legs evoked involuntary gasping from the males. Mortimer's mouth wouldn't close. He had never seen such beauty. As Emily Washburn said, Jacqueline was a rose.

***

Mortimer felt like a kid who'd found a million-dollar note as he was delivered to the function in a stretch limousine. He glanced at Jacqueline and *eyes like fire in the night* came to mind. Her hair was swept to one side and her elongated neck reminded him of the fragile stem of a hand-blown glass. She appeared not to be wearing makeup yet she was flawless. He gripped her hand a little too hard and she winced.'

'Oops, sorry,' he said, sincerely.

'You seem a little excited.'

'This is the first time that I've ever been to one of these things as a nominee. Usually I have to scrounge for tickets from friends in the business.'

'After tonight you'll be a winner and never have to scrounge again.'

'If only it were true.'

'We'll soon find out,' she said, as she squeezed his hand with genuine affection.

The limousine pulled up outside of the festival hall and Mortimer saw the red carpet carving a path to the door. Thousands of people lined the footpath and flashguns created a resonant blur of bluish light. Reporters with microphones stood in ambush between them and the door. Mortimer loved it.

As they stepped from the comfort of their cocoon there was silence. Then, as at the boutique, an audible gasp emanated from the crowd, followed by the most tumultuous applause that Mortimer had ever heard. He knew that it wasn't for him but he didn't care. He was *with* the object of their devotion.

Microphones prodded their faces like gauze chicken legs, each carrying the breath of its holder. Inane questions were answered with smiles and spontaneous quips. Adrenaline coursed through Mortimer like a flood. He felt as if he'd died and gone to heaven. He longed for the feeling to last forever. He finally felt as if *Peter Mortimer had arrived.*

For the first time in his life, He was escorted to a seat at the front of the theatre. He noticed that even famous heads turned to overtly stare his companion. He couldn't believe that his luck held. He paused to let Jacqueline precede him to their seats, which placed her between him and Billy Squires. She stopped.

'This is your night, I'm just an appendage,' she said. 'You and Billy must share the moment, be it good or bad.' She couldn't believe what she'd uttered. Her job was to keep Mortimer flying, not open up possibilities of defeat. She looked at the black dress and cursed. 'When are you up?'

Mortimer opened his programme and ran his finger down the events list. 'We're not one of the big awards. We're on in the first half-hour. Why do you ask?'

'Nothing really...it's just that I'm not feeling well. Must be the excitement.'

'You'll be fine,' Mortimer said.

Jacqueline nodded affirmation. She sat back and cast her eyes over the gathered crowd. She saw no one that she knew personally yet many faces seemed familiar. She even felt closeness to some, but nothing tangible. She looked across at Mortimer who was in deep conversation with Squires. She would leave him for a short time in order not to spoil his chances of success. She wouldn't spoil his evening simply because she wore black. She would stay as long as possible but knew that what she dreaded wouldn't be long in coming. She waited.

When it hit her, it took the form of a slow creeping paralysis. Something that she had learned to dread, like prickly heat crawling up her legs to her torso and then her upper body. A flush that embodied the crushing of her spirit. She grabbed Mortimer's attention and silently indicated her problem. He nodded, with a look of deep concern on his face, as she left. Once outside the theatre she rushed along a corridor trying doorknobs as she went. They were all locked. She ran on, stumbling in her high heels, looking for respite. A toilet. No, that wouldn't do. She staggered on, trying each room. Then a lock moved and she rushed through the door. A small broom closet. She turned on the light and found herself staring at the tangled tresses of a mop head. This will have to do, she thought. She pulled the dress over her head and stood silently in her underwear, trying to regain composure. She knew that Mortimer wanted her near when the announcement was made but she also wanted him to win. She glanced at her watch. Timing would be everything. She took deep breaths and stood motionless willing herself to remain calm.

It was ten minutes before she pulled the dress back over her head but, at least, her skin tones had returned to normal. Mortimer and Squires didn't notice her resume her seat. They were both too focused. Mortimer leaned back on his seat as if relaxed and comfortable but his mind floated above it, his senses primed. A fixed smile bathed his face like a children's clown. He was ready to applaud the winner. He felt the television cameras of the world boring into him, robbing him of his soul yet giving affirmation of his success. He looked at Squires and had an urge to hold his hand so that they could live the moment together; to be as one, whether it be in success or failure. They waited as the nominees were read out. They knew the names and the quality of the work; theirs paled by comparison. They had to be kidding themselves. Panic struck and Mortimer fought an urge to wretch but kept his nonchalant smile in place.

'And the winner is…'

The air rushed from Mortimer as if he'd been punctured, his heart dropped and he sat heavily into his chair. His brain told him to applaud the winner but he couldn't move his arms. Billy was suddenly all over him, hugging him and yelling for him to stand up.

'We won, it's us Pete, it's us. We won the bloody thing.'

Mortimer's eyes bulged opened as if forced from his head by internal pressure. It registered. He heard his name in slow motion. He stood like an automaton, his mind in freefall, his body robotic. He placed his hands on either side of Jacqueline's head. She moved in close and hugged him.

'And you said that black would bring me bad luck. If this is it, then I want more,' Mortimer jibed, as he left her and moved, with Squires, toward the stage.

Jacqueline had never seen a man so happy. She waited until an usher escorted her to the winners' reception area and mingled with the growing crowd, drinking champagne and bathing in reflected glory. As each award recipient entered the room applause rang through the rafters. Mortimer and Squires bowed as they entered, as if winning had been a realistic expectation.

Mortimer handed Jacqueline the trinket as soon as he reached her side. 'We're expected to stay here for a while and then go off to the official reception. Is that okay?'

'Fine by me, except I'd like to get out of this dress. I spilt some champagne on it and it's a little uncomfortable. Maybe I can change and join you at the reception'

'You're kidding. You look fine. It's that luck thing again isn't it? You're my lucky charm, my talisman.'

The words *Well done, Peter, I knew you'd do it* floated on the air like characters written on the wind. There was no truth of course but Mortimer savoured the moment like a child with an ice cream. Everyone was his friend. Celebrities that he venerated now shook his hand with vigour, as if they were old friends. This was *it*. This was what all the work was for. Recognition by one's peers is the epitome of one's career. He dismissed the thoughts as pretentious, then turned on his heels as he was slapped on the back.

Jacqueline moved away and returned to the broom closet. The heat was back.

When she returned, Mortimer noticed that the glass trembled in her hand like a small seismic shuffle. Her knuckles were white with exertion and she fidgeted with the rim of the champagne filled glass. 'What is it?' he asked. Genuine concern creased his face.

'I just keep getting these hot flushes. They come and go but I'll be fine. You enjoy yourself.'

'You look great,' Mortimer said, overtly casting his eyes around Jacqueline's lithe form. 'You don't look flushed.'

'Comes and goes. Don't worry. Let's just have fun. After all, this is the last night.'

Billy Squires arrived. Jacqueline thought that the girl on his arm this time was a vast improvement on his last effort.

It seemed that winning opened previously closed doors. 'Hey, you two…we're off to a party at the Carlton. Coming?' Squires asked.

Jacqueline shrugged approval. Mortimer nodded.

They left the theatre through a rear door and down the stairs into a narrow alley with steam and smoke rising from ventilators set into the building walls. Refuse and other assorted comestible garbage belied the glittering entry on the other side of the building. Mortimer let Jacqueline walk just in front of him, admiring her rear view. The black dress flared slightly over her hips, giving her a seductive wiggle. He knew that he had to kiss her, despite the rules that he had agreed with Emily Washburn. He had to break the ice with her and see where things led. They walked along the beach side of Boulevard de la Croisette, with its palm tree lined median strip that ran to the edge of view in both directions, until they came to the crossing point that they wanted. Squires grabbed his girl's hand and headed out through the line of oncoming traffic. Mortimer hesitated, then took Jacqueline's hand and followed suit. Car horns blared and lights flashed as they skipped and jigged to the centre of the road. On the other side of the median strip things were worse, the traffic was non-stop as if traffic lights had no effect on the flow. Squires and the girl set off again between cars. The shrill sound of a whistling kettle horn blared as a car rushed by. Another car slammed on its brakes and buried its nose in the bitumen with a screech. They made it across, laughing at their death defying feat.

Mortimer waited, then decided to act. He turned Jacqueline toward him and placed his hands squarely on her shoulders. He kissed her.

There was no reaction from Jacqueline. His ebullience evaporated like water on hot concrete. Then he felt it; she'd bitten his lip. The sensation was strange. He didn't feel teeth; it was more like the sting. The same sensation was on both hands where he gripped her shoulders. He looked at his palms and saw blood spots forming from pinpoint specks. He couldn't comprehend. Perspiration formed on his forehead and ran from the back of his neck. He wobbled as he stared at Jacqueline, whose expression was passive, as if a veil had descended. Blood began to gush from his bottom lip and fingers like tiny fountains. He stepped backward, to get away. He didn't notice the van.

Jacqueline looked down at Mortimer's body as it bounced from under the van. Tears ran down her cheek. She shook her head from side to side, mumbling softly to herself. She pulled the sleek black dress over her head and walked to where Mortimer's crumpled body was strewn, like so much garbage, on the road. She dropped the dress to cover his unseeing eyes and walked away in her lingerie. She saw Emily Washburn at the corner, holding out a coat to cover her. Tears ran down Emily's face as she placed her arms around Jacqueline. She held her close and felt the trembling.

About The Author

Barry Dean is the fossilised remnant of a young boy born in 1949 in Lithgow. He has worked as a musician, electrician, construction inspector and engineer. When not writing he is an engineering consultant with a love of travel and old ruins. He lives at Lake Macquarie with his wife Theresa.

Thank you for reading
THE GARDEN OF EMILY WASHBURN.

We hope you enjoyed it.

If you would like to be kept informed of further
releases by Barry Dean, or other new books from Hague
Publishing, why not subscribe to our newsletter at:

www.HaguePublishing.com/subscribe.php

And if you loved the book and have a moment to
spare we would really appreciate a short review. Your
help in spreading the word is gratefully received.

Hague

Publishing

www.HaguePublishing.com

PO Box 451 Bassendean
Western Australia 6934